LISA DAWN

Hope and Love's Legacy

Contents

One

Amoura

England, 1590

I bent down to lift the sack of barley seeds as big as a sow when a sharp tug pinched at the back of my neck. The pink gem on my pendant swung into the sack as I leaned over, causing some stray seeds to spill onto the floor below. I wrapped my arms around the sack, securing it against myself to avoid losing more seeds. Carrying it out of the shed, I saw Father in the distance, hitching up the plow to till the soil. His blemished brown tunic matched his unkempt hair as he worked.

The scent of hay, oats, and manure rolled over the fields. Fresh morning dew filled the air, which tickled my skin as I prepared to help my father with the annual crop rotation.

I found him in the barley field, trying to hitch a new collar to my favorite draught horse, Jackson, a Suffolk Punch bred for us by Lord Thomas's stable hand. Each time Father lifted the collar toward him, Jackson dug his hooves into the soil and reared back. My father's skills with a hoe or scythe were unmatched, but the responsibility of tending to the animals usually fell to me.

My father threw his hands up into the air, revealing the brown stubble protruding from his chin. "By the saints! What ails him?"

I dropped the sack of barley seeds, sensing the horse's anguish. "I know not, but I can try to find out. Let me look upon him."

My hands grasped Jackson's damp chestnut-colored muzzle, giving him a gentle caress. He calmed under my touch.

"You have such a tender way with animals, Amoura," said Father. "They treat you like one of their own."

The corners of my lips curled into a warm smile as I gazed at Jackson's large, intelligent eyes. "Indeed, we are not so very different from one another."

Sweeping my arm past his head, I reached up to stroke his neck. When my fingers grazed over one spot in particular, my hand vibrated as Jackson's neck shuddered beneath it. A rough patch in his coat revealed a scratch swelling into a small lump on his neck. The rubbing from the collar likely irritated it. Jackson neighed and kicked the plow, forcing Father to jump back right before the large wooden wheel could crush his toes.

I shook my head. "He is hurt. We'll have to use a different horse."

Father grimaced. "He was the only horse available for the

crop rotation today. If he isn't able to work, the vegetables will not be ready in time for the fall harvest."

The village depended on us to feed their families, and a sinking feeling entered my chest at the thought of letting them down. A warm twinge radiated over my heart where Mama's pendant rested. In the nine years I held it close, I had yet to uncover its mysteries. Could this be the key to accessing her magic?

I pray you, Mama, lend me your strength.

Placing my hand over the injured spot, I thought about Jackson growing strong and healthy to harvest delicious food for our neighbors from the village to enjoy with their loving families. A twinge of power flowed from my pendant through my body, filling me with warmth, and entered Jackson's neck, where his wound faded back into his shiny brown fur coat. He gave me a grateful neigh. My shoulders grew heavy as weariness washed over me. I adjusted my posture to avoid causing my father undue worry.

I nuzzled Jackson's nose against mine. "Atta boy."

I nodded toward Father. "He'll stop fighting you now. Mama's magic healed him."

Father hitched the collar around Jackson's neck. I soothed Jackson by petting his soft mane as Father hooked him up to the plow.

"I know not whether I should be grateful or worried that you've inherited your mother's talents. She was hardly able to show her face anymore after the rumors of witchcraft began floating about."

Before Mama left us, a maid from Lord Thomas's manor had caught her using magic to speed up the growth of a legume patch to provide food for the villagers during the great drought. The maid accused Mama of witchcraft, but Lord Thomas brushed it off because of his kinship with Father and the excellent sales that he derived from our crops. Ever since then, Mama took great care to hide her magic from the public. Still, she only had their best interests at heart, just as I did.

"I know. I'll be careful."

Mama never hid her powers from us, nor did she explain whence they came. As I grew in years, more questions arose that I wished I could have asked her before she disappeared. Why did she leave? Where was Imperium? When did she learn to use magic? Could I learn to do so as well?

I ran my calloused fingers through Jackson's mane. "Do you ever wonder why she never came back?"

Father finished hitching up the plow. He cast his eyes down toward the unplowed earth, slumping his shoulders.

"She loved us very much. If she could come back, I think she would have. Something must have happened when she went back to that Imperium place."

I twirled a lock of brown hair around my finger. "If only I had some way to visit Imperium and learn what became of her."

"There is no use distracting yourself with all these fantasies when there's work to be done now. Go harvest some fresh wheat and head to the market to put your mind at ease."

My burdens would never ease until I learned the truth about Mama. Her memory held a permanent place in the pink gem over my heart. I harvested some fresh oats and grains and headed to the village marketplace to sell our goods. Even without Mama's help, Father was such a good farmer that we didn't take too much of a loss when she left. The only silver lining of her absence was the chance to grow closer to our small community now that we no longer needed to hide. When we received the occasional question about her whereabouts, we would tell people she was ill in bed. After enough time had passed, they stopped asking.

* * *

I enjoyed my walks to the market, taking in the fresh spring air. It made me feel like one with nature. The narrow dirt road spilled through the trees, leading to a row of stalls and tents lining the marketplace. My shoes crunched over the sharp pebbles in the road when I noticed a little girl playing with her poppet. The girl's mother purchased a fresh measure of wheat from my stall every Tuesday without fail. She tossed the poppet recklessly into the air when it landed in the path of an oncoming carriage. Caught up in her excitement, she ran to recover her precious toy directly in its path.

Without hesitating, I raced to her aid, reaching her just before the carriage made contact. Shielding her with my body, my pendant grew warm on my chest, enveloping us in a soft pink light, spooking the horses. They reared up and snorted, bringing the carriage to an abrupt halt. Its wooden wheels scraped the road, causing a cloud of dirt to puff up over our feet.

The driver climbed out to see what had happened. "That was a mighty stroke of fortune!" he exclaimed, helping us to our feet.

The girl's brown eyes widened as the light dissipated from my pendant. "You saved us!" she gasped.

The weariness of the spell pulled my mind somewhere far

away. I snapped my attention back to her. "Us?"

She presented her well-loved rag doll to me. It was made from coarse cloth with a sewn-on face, button eyes, and a light blue dress that was smudged with dirt stains and red yarn for hair. "This is Emily."

I decided to play along and gave my best curtsy. "Well met, Emily."

Her mother raced over and pulled her out of harm's way. "Anne! How many times have I told you not to play in the street?"

She was tall and prim with sleek black hair under a white linen coif. I followed them to the market stalls near the side of the road.

"I had to help Emily," insisted Anne.

"No, you did not. You are more important." She turned to me. "Amoura, you are a treasure, always lending a helping hand to the people of our village."

My eyes darted away in embarrassment. "It was nothing. I cannot simply stand by while people are in trouble."

She reached into her purse and handed me a coin. Father and I didn't have much, but I couldn't accept a reward for doing something that came naturally to me, especially when I had an unfair magical advantage.

"Pray, let me thank you. We've all fallen on hard times of late."

I raised my hand to her. "I'm sorry, but I cannot accept that."

"I insist."

I reached into my basket and handed her a potato, our newest trial crop from Spain, and a fresh measure of wheat. "I will only accept it as payment for these goods. Give Anne a good meal tonight."

She accepted the offering with a warm grin. "I will. Bless your kind heart."

I pulled out a sack of fresh legumes, apples, and wheat, arranging them with fair order at my usual table. The man on my left spread colorful pottery across the wooden table in front of him, while the woman on my right set up a delicious-looking display of muffins, biscuits, and crumb cakes. Sometimes, she let me sample her honey biscuits when it was not too crowded.

There was a commotion among the other vendors about the library that the Queen had funded for our village. I loved the idea of books about history and culture, though I still struggled to recognize the letters of the alphabet that Mama had shown me before she left.

"I wish I knew how to read," said a seamstress a few stalls down. "There will probably be lots of information on the latest fashions."

"I heard the library would have some of the newest recipe books from France. Imagine the fine pastries I could learn to bake with those!" added the baker.

The scent of blueberry muffins crept into my nostrils, filling me with both hunger and delight. "I'm sure anything you make will taste wonderful, Jane. Too bad we have to wait so long before the library opens."

"Can you read?" she asked me. "I'm still a novice."

I gave her a sympathetic smile. "Only a bit, but I'm eager to get more practice. I pray it opens soon."

"Have you heard?" asked the potter on the other side. "They ran ahead of schedule and are opening it to the public already. They say it's the biggest repository in the kingdom of knowledge from this world or the next."

His odd choice of words made me think of Mama and where she came from. If she refused to tell Father about Imperium, perhaps the answer rested within the pages of a book. Her magic reached out to me today, and I needed to find a way to reach back. The library seemed like the perfect place to start. I decided to suggest it to Father right after I finished selling our goods for the day.

Two

Spero

❧

California, Present Day

I t was another lonely day at the mansion, which had way too many rooms for just the two of us. The staff members were around somewhere, but they usually left us to our own devices. At least I could tell they were doing their jobs. The air in the hallway smelled of lemon cleaning fluid, and the black and white tiled floor shone with a fresh coat of polish. Who needed to go outside when I could get lost in my own house?

My phone buzzed in my pocket. I leaned against the wall and checked it. The decorative crown molding pressed into my back.

Shooting in Ireland got extended by another month. More

reshoots. You know the drill. Send my love to you and Mels. I'll be home soon.

"Is that from Mom?"

My little sister, Melanie, stood on her tiptoes trying to peek over at the message. I pulled my phone away before she could see it. At eight years old, she wasn't the world's fastest reader, but better safe than sorry. No matter what wing of the house I escaped to, she always managed to find me, not that I minded. At least there was always someone to talk to without having to worry about the paparazzi outside.

"Yeah, she said the movie's going great."

Melanie tried to grab my phone. "She's going to be away longer than we thought, isn't she?"

I held the phone up over her head. She jumped up to try to grab it, but it was no use for the little shrimp. "She says she'll be home soon."

She stuck out her bottom lip at me. "She always says that. So does Dad. But it seems like we always get stuck with Fran and Jeffrey."

"Hey, they're not so bad. They let you stay up late last Saturday."

She crossed her arms. "They're not Mom and Dad."

I personally didn't mind being stuck with our nanny and butler, but then again, I was too old to need a chaperone anymore. I had just graduated from private school and was trying to make the difficult decision between Harvard, Princeton, and Yale. My only regret about going off to university was leaving Mels all alone. Being the kids of two wealthy celebrities isn't all it's cracked up to be. Sure, we got everything we wanted except the one thing we really needed— our parents.

Their lack of presence in our lives probably accounted for my issues with authority. I got into trouble at school a few times for talking back to my teachers, but I rarely got detention since no one wanted to be held responsible for punishing the son of the CEO of Star Tech. Something about people in authority telling me what to do always rubbed me the wrong way. If my parents were able to find so much success by doing everything they wanted to, why couldn't I?

I browsed through some emails on my phone. There were several follow-ups to the college applications I sent out. Then an email popped in from an unknown sender. I almost marked it as spam until I noticed what the large attachment was. Someone had sent me a test version of a new video game to play, probably someone Dad had met at the business conference he was stuck at in New York. It wasn't too uncommon for Dad to send me free stuff from other companies. Having a dad who was CEO of a tech company had some great perks, like a personal home theater with every game console and streaming service known to man. The game seemed like just what I needed to cheer up my little sister.

"Hey Mels, Dad sent me access to an early release of Fantasy Quest VIII. Want to check it out?"

That did the trick. Her eyes perked up, and she leaped down the hallway like a little slinky. "Really? The last one we played was so cool! Start it up! Start it up!"

Her short blond curls bounced on her head as she bolted through the door to our home theater and made a beeline straight for the plush velvet sofa. I plopped down next to her and opened my favorite gaming app on our massive HD screen that took up an entire wall. When Dad used it to give presentations to clients, they had to crane their necks to see everything.

After giving the file a quick virus scan, I downloaded the game and had it installed on our home theater system in a few minutes.

"Is it ready? Is it ready?" Melanie squealed.

"Not until you stop asking."

She moved her finger across her lips like a zipper, so I started up the game.

It opened with an elaborate CGI movie about a fantasy world under an apocalyptic threat. Typical JRPG stuff. Once the gameplay started, Melanie watched me maneuver the sword-wielding hero through a tutorial where I had to fight some low-level monsters. I always thought it would be fun to be one of those heroes, just going around fighting monsters all day and finding cool treasures without having to worry about college applications or absent parents.

"There's a chest! Open it!" Melanie shouted, pointing to a hidden treasure chest in the corner of a dungeon.

"Geez, calm down."

"But I want to know what's in it!"

"The game just started. It's probably a potion or something."

I moved the hero to the chest, but when I pressed the action button, the screen turned fuzzy, causing the image to blink in and out. The game's soundtrack started skipping, which was pretty jarring with our surround sound speakers blasting from all sides of the room.

"What happened?" Melanie whined.

Why does she think I know everything?

I shook my head. "How should I know? It's an early copy. They're probably still working out some bugs."

She bounced on the couch cushions. "But I want to know

what was in the chest!"

"Let me see if I can check the coding. Maybe I can mod it to overwrite the bug. Dad showed me how to do this once."

I reached for my laptop and started to enter the password. Suddenly, the screen blinked back into focus, and the game continued as normal. An item notification appeared with a picture of a giant CGI ring and the words "Obtained Ring of Hope."

"Looks like it's working again. I guess that's what was in the chest." I shrugged.

Melanie pointed to the screen with excitement. "Spero, that's the ring Dad gave you!"

"What? It can't be. Why would that be in the game?"

I glanced down at my finger, where I wore the family heirloom that I had never taken off since Dad passed it down to me. He was convinced it was magical. I remembered the story he told me about how a woman with pink hair showed up out of nowhere and gave it to him, claiming that it would bring him good fortune. Then he said she vanished into thin air. That part was a little hard to swallow.

According to him, he was offered a billion-dollar deal to open Star Tech right after he put it on. A few years later, he and Mom got the son and daughter they always wanted, despite their busy schedules. The sapphire in the middle of the ring had a tiny engraving of a four-pointed star surrounded by a sun and crescent moon that my dad turned into his company logo, which perfectly matched the CGI ring in the game.

"It does look similar," I admitted.

Melanie wrapped her tiny fingers around mine. "It's the same ring! Dad was right. It is magic."

"Just because it looks like the one in the game? I don't think so, Mels."

"What does it do? Read the item description!"

I sighed and opened the menu, knowing there was no use arguing with her. Looking in my character's inventory, I located the "Ring of Hope."

"It says it's a magical relic created by the sorceress Estella to foster the essence of hope. What the heck does that mean?"

Melanie's eyes lit up. "Maybe you're the essence of hope! Do you have any cool powers like the hero in the game?"

Kids will believe anything these days.

"I'm not a video game character."

"I know that, silly! You're my brother."

There she goes being cute again.

"Come here, you!" I tickled her stomach, making her burst into giggles.

She laughed. "Stop it!"

The game's soundtrack started skipping again. We looked up. The CGI image of the ring grew so big that the sapphire looked like it was burning a giant hole in the wall. The next thing I knew, the ring on my finger started burning. I clutched my hand.

"Ow! What the?"

Melanie stopped laughing. Concern filled her blue eyes. "Spero?"

I met her gaze. "It's my ring."

I tried to pull it off, but it wouldn't budge. It was as if it had merged with my finger. Then, a blue laser beam shot out of the image on the screen into my ring, pulling my hand and the rest of my body toward it. I tried to resist, but it felt like my hand would rip clean off if I didn't go along with the strange force. Clasping my hands together, I winced as I was dragged across the floor of our theater. The friction from the carpet started rubbing uncomfortably against my jeans.

"Is this part of the game?" asked Melanie.

"I don't think so."

Melanie tried to grab my hand, but I pushed her away. If the ring was burning my finger, it would probably hurt her too. I floated into the air toward the middle of the screen. It felt like I was hanging off a monkey bar. My legs dangled beneath me.

"I didn't know our theater could do that!" she gasped.

I threw Melanie my phone. "Mels, call Dad! Tell him what happened."

My ears started ringing as the image on the screen blurred into beams of light that pulled me in like a portal from an anime. The sensory overload made it hard to think straight. Part of me was convinced that this was all a dream and that I would wake up any second, but the shaking I felt all over my body told me otherwise. People claim you can't even feel a little pinch when you're dreaming, and this felt like every inch of my body was being pinched. If I got out of this alive, I was going to send a strongly worded reply to whoever sent me that email and possibly involve a few lawyers.

"Spero!" Melanie cried. "Come back!"

It was no use. The lights on the screen blinded me as they pulled me toward the other side. Poor Melanie was going to be all alone now. Her shouting and cries grew distant, but I could still hear her from somewhere far away. Hopefully, someone from the staff would show up when they heard the commotion.

"Don't give up on me!" I shouted. "I'll find a way back!"

Then I was sucked into the screen, and my whole world faded away.

Three

Amoura

My perfectly practical father was the last person anyone would expect to marry a magical angel from another world. Mother and Father could not possibly have been more different, yet they could not have loved each other more.

The three of us had gathered at the creek the summer I turned eight. Mist flowed through the air like magic. The sun shone brightly, making our quiet neck of the woods feel like a painting in a fancy chapel. On days like this, I felt as though I could do anything as long as I had my parents at my side.

"Look at me!" I squealed.

I dove with a satisfying splash as water droplets danced around me, sparkling in the sunlight. Humming filled my ears as the water flowed in and out of them, adding to the dreamlike feel of the morning.

"Mama, Daddy, come join me!"

Then Mama's warm smile melted into a frown. She clutched her ear in alarm, though everything around her looked peaceful. In a panic, she leaned over and whispered something to Father. His gentle expression melted into one of concern. Mama wandered off into the woods. I wanted to chase after her when Father came over and scooped me up out of the water like a sack of wheat.

"We have to head home now, sweet dove."

"Daddy, I wasn't done playing yet," I huffed. "Where are we going?"

"Your mother needs some privacy. She will explain everything soon."

Even at my tender age, I knew there was more to the situation than they had let on. I always wondered if Mama's powers gave her some sort of tie to royalty, like in fairy stories. Mayhap there was a magical kingdom somewhere that looked to her as its queen, making me its princess. Or perhaps Queen Elizabeth had given her a secret task due to her special powers.

"Is she doing an important secret mission for the Queen?"

He chuckled. "You have such a wild imagination."

"I bet it's something magical."

He tapped me on the nose. "You know the most magical place your mother can be is here with us."

My small hand clutched his large, calloused one, and we walked home together in silence. There was no doubt in my mind that Mama would be home soon. She'd never leave without saying goodbye. Later that day, a bright light appeared in our cottage while Father prepared some freshly harvested turnips for our dinner. I peeked around the corner and saw traces of white feathers on the ground, signifying that Mama had used her magic to travel. Then I saw her float to the ground on a large pair of feathered wings like an angel who had come down from Heaven to bless our family.

Her silvery-blue hair fell to her ankles as her wings faded away. Its color shifted to a pretty shade of blonde in public to avoid suspicion, but she could always be her true self around us. She was wearing a regal pink, otherworldly gown with draping chiffon sleeves and shimmering accents. It made her look like a stranger compared to the simple peasant dresses she normally wore on outings. I stayed quiet and hid in the shadows, hoping I might hear more secrets about the mysterious place she came from.

"You're late," said my father, without looking up from his frying pan. "I thought you would be back hours ago."

Her eyes were red and puffy. "Darling, forgive me."

Father looked up, realizing from her chagrin that she wasn't apologizing for her tardiness. Something was horribly wrong. He dropped the turnips and ran to her, clutching her long, delicate fingers in his. Whatever had happened in the woods must have been more significant than any of us realized.

"Why are you dressed like that?" he asked.

"I must return to Imperium."

"For how long?"

Her lower lip trembled. "I could not say."

A look of alarm crossed Father's face. "We need you here. Whatever it is, we can fix it together as a family."

"I'm afraid this isn't something that we can fix. This world is in danger. My sisters in Imperium need my help."

"Then take me with you."

Mama shook her head as silvery tears dripped down her cheeks. "You need to stay here and care for Amoura. There are many dangers where I'm going. She would get hurt."

"She'll be more hurt if she loses you."

A sinking feeling entered my gut. There was no use hiding anymore if I wanted to know the truth. I spoke up, revealing myself from around the corner. "Mama? You're not really leaving, are you?"

Mama scooped me up into her arms. She ran her fingers through my scruffy brown locks like a soft fur brush.

"My precious angel, I want you to know that I will always love you."

I leaned against her. She always smelled of cinnamon and roses. "I love you too, Mama. Your dress is quite pretty. I like your hair like that."

"Do you like my pendant too?"

"Oh yes, 'tis lovely!"

Another tear rolled down her face as she removed her enchanted pink pendant and placed the long chain around my small neck. "It's yours now."

I ran my fingers over the smooth, shimmering surface and looked back up at Mama. "If I don't take it, will you stay?"

Her green eyes darted away. "I'm afraid it is not that simple."

I leaned closer to her. "But I'd rather have you than your necklace."

Her comforting arms wrapped around my slight form, filling me with warmth and security. "I know, sweetheart, but right now, this is all I can offer. Make sure you never take it off. It will protect you from harm. Be a good girl and listen to your father until I see you again."

I tilted my head toward her. "Will you come back soon?"

She set me back down. "I hope so."

I clutched the pendant. "Then I'll wish on it every day to bring you back home until I see you again!"

Mama bent down and brushed her lips against my forehead. "You do that, my dear. Maybe one day your wish will come true."

She stood up and entered my father's open embrace. "This is it, my love. I've cherished the time we had together, and I wish we could have had more."

He pulled her against him as though refusing to let go. "I pray you, Solara, you must reconsider. There has to be a way you can aid your sisters without leaving. You've always said that nothing is more important than family."

"I'm sorry, darling, but they are my family too, and they need me now."

"Please," he begged. "Think of Amoura."

"I already have. She is the reason I must do this. I must protect this world for her sake, and yours as well."

After giving him a gentle kiss, she stepped out of his arms. I watched her disappear in a silvery-blue light. Mama left our lives forever that day. My pendant and the secrets within it tethered me to her and her magic, but only from afar. I never stopped wishing it would somehow bring her back, or at least allow me to contact her. If it could heal wounds, why could it not also heal my broken heart?

* * *

The splendid gray stone building shone in the sunlight like a freshly polished gem as scholars bustled in and out of the new library, eager to fill their minds with words of enlightenment. When Father opened the door, the scent of fresh parchment danced on the breeze that whooshed out alongside an old man clutching a stack of leather-bound tomes. The interior of the building seemed to stretch as far as a wheat field, with its white marble floors and shelves upon shelves of newly bound books with golden edges and embossed titles. Father and I squeezed our way through a large crowd of people.

"Set your hopes not too high, Amoura. I think none but your mother knew about Imperium."

I brushed my calloused fingers along the smooth spines of the books on a nearby shelf.

"If she came from there, mayhap someone else did too. And mayhap they wrote about it."

"You speak a great many mayhaps."

I skipped past several books written in Latin, a language that only scholars understood. Narrowing my gaze at the letters on the spines, I took my time trying to decipher the English titles. It was hard work, but I knew it would be worth it in the end. Several people came in and out of the library as I scoured through titles. My efforts came to avail when I discovered some books about farming and pulled out one or two that might have some good tips for Father.

Wandering past books about fashion and royalty, I finally came upon a section about other known kingdoms and lands. If there was a book about Imperium, it would be there. I savored the unlimited power of knowledge hidden within their pages. A thick, heavy book listing every known country rested on a high shelf. I reached up, digging my fingers under the spine to pull it toward me.

Father saw me struggling and pulled it out, placing it on a table where a huge cloud of dust puffed out from it. Dust clogged my lungs. I fanned it away with my hands until my coughing fit ended. Once the air had cleared, I opened the cover and began flipping through a series of maps. The tiny printed words were difficult to discern, forcing me to squint at them while I recalled the letters of the alphabet in my head.

"This may take a while. Help me look, Father."

He sighed and browsed the shelf behind me. In my slow but steady progress perusing every book that might be relevant, I lost track of how many hours had passed. The crowd thinned out as the last bit of daylight faded away through the windows, making it impossible to keep reading.

Father put the last book back on the shelf. "Let's not tarry, sweet dove. There's work to be done. We can come back another time."

"But we're so close! I know it to be nigh!" I insisted.

I just knew there was something we were missing. I thought of Mama and how much she loved me. She couldn't have stayed away for so long by choice. Something must have happened. My thoughts seemed to trigger a reaction in my pendant. A faint pink beam emitted from the gem and landed on a book in the corner of a shelf that I swore I had already looked at. In the dim light of the pendant, I could just make out the word "Imperium" embossed on the spine.

"Over there! This is it!" I grabbed the book.

Father frowned. "How can you even see in this light? It's dark as pitch in here."

I clutched my hand over the pendant covering my heart.

"Mama revealed it to me."

As I opened the cover of the book to the first page, the warmth of the pendant heightened to a burning blaze. Not wanting to alarm Father, I did my best to hide my discomfort. I was so close to finding the truth. In the faint pink glow, the narrow text in the book hardly even looked like letters. It was as though I was looking at some sort of foreign symbols, and those symbols glowed with an ominous light. Something told me this wasn't an ordinary book.

Father's hand weighed down on my shoulder. "This is an ill omen, Amoura. Your necklace has never lit up that bright before."

An unnatural force flowed through my body and pulled me toward the book. The page grew bigger and bigger until it opened into some sort of great maw. It was as though a pair of invisible hands were reaching out and drawing me within, pulling me out of Father's grasp. I kicked and screamed, but the force continued to draw me in. Father clasped my hand and pulled me as hard as he could, but it was no use.

"Amoura, you must fight it!"

I tried to grasp his hands, but it felt like I was going to be ripped in half if I kept holding on. "I'm trying!"

Our hands were forced apart. He stretched out his fingers as far as they could go. "I will not lose you, too!"

My world faded quickly. One moment, he was right in front of me, and the next, it was as though he was across three fields. The sound of rushing winds filled my ears, and the fatigue I felt when I used my pendant set in tenfold. Yet, it wasn't coming from Mama's magic this time. This was something else, an outside force that wouldn't let me go. I took one last glimpse at my father's panicked face.

"I shall find a way back to you! I promise!" I gave one final desperate yell as the page consumed the rest of my body. The cover of the book closed on top of me, trapping me inside.

Four

Spero

The loud humming sounds and forceful tugging on my body finally stopped when I crashed onto a soft mound of dirt, allowing me to get a grip on my surroundings. This place didn't look like a video game, but it didn't look like a regular forest either. This was a fantasy world if I had ever seen one. Was my dad testing some sort of new virtual reality tech on me? If so, there were definitely some bugs that needed to be worked out before putting it on the market.

A jarring shade of fuchsia swirled through the sky. Fluorescent-colored branches swayed in the wind on trees that looked like something out of a stop-motion movie. A sweet scent filled the air, which sparkled with a strange thickness.

Getting pulled into the portal created the same rush as a high-speed roller coaster at a theme park, and I needed a few minutes to regain my bearings. I stood up and pounded on my ears a few times until the ringing stopped. Before I could fully steady myself, something large and heavy fell on my head. I collapsed back onto the ground.

"Hey, what gives?!"

I pushed the surprisingly soft object off me before realizing it was a person—a girl, at that. Shoot! I hope I didn't hurt her. She rolled over and groaned, as though she had just gotten off the same ride. Her soft features and graceful demeanor reminded me of a princess from one of those old animated movies before they got all dolled up. Her old gray dress was laced up in the medieval peasant style and looked like it belonged at a Renaissance Faire, although I could tell it had seen better days. Was she a cosplayer? That didn't seem right. Most of the cosplayers I knew kept their costumes in pristine condition for conventions. Maybe she was some kind of actress, like Mom.

"Are you all right, Miss?"

"Is this Imperium?" she moaned, rubbing her head.

She had an old-fashioned British accent that reminded me of the historical dramas on the BBC.

"Sorry, but I have no idea where we are. I got pulled in here through some sort of portal."

She shot upright like a bolt of lightning. When I finally managed to get back up, I extended my hand to help her to her feet, but she beat me to it. I guess she wasn't the type to sit around playing video games all day.

"That's exactly what happened to me! Was it also through a book?"

I shrugged. "Video game."

Her head tilted, an innocent expression forming on her

delicate face. "I beg your pardon?"

"The portal. It was in a video game."

When did I forget how to speak in complete sentences?

"What's a… V-D-O game?" She scrunched her eyebrows.

What's wrong with this girl?

"Where are you from?" I asked in the most nonthreatening voice I could muster. I hoped she wouldn't hold a grudge for my shoving her, but in my defense, she did fall on top of me.

She fidgeted with her long brown hair. "Why, England, of course. What about you?"

I considered not answering her at all. Something very weird was going on here. Maybe this was some kind of phishing scheme. Yet, her bright green eyes gazed at me with such vivid curiosity that I had to say something.

"America. More specifically, the Silicon Valley."

The same innocent expression appeared again. "I've never heard of that kingdom."

Could she be a character from the virtual reality game world? She didn't behave like an NPC, but who knew what kind of crazy AI technology was being tested these days? Maybe I should try a different approach. Her present-day knowledge was nonexistent, and she was dressed like someone from hundreds of years ago.

"Um, maybe I should be asking *when* are you from?"

She raised an eyebrow at me. "That's a silly question. 'Tis the Year of Our Lord 1590."

I studied her face for signs of sarcasm. "You're trolling me!"

"I hope not. Aren't trolls supposed to be dangerous?"

I crossed my arms. "Okay then, who's the king of England in 1590?"

A glint of amusement filled her eyes. "Surely you jest.

Everyone knows the current sovereign is Queen Elizabeth."

I probably shouldn't have asked a question I didn't know the answer to.

I shrugged it off. "Maybe you were just paying more attention in history class than me."

She gave me a strange look. "How would I possibly take a class? I'm a peasant and a girl."

Is she serious?

"That makes no difference in the 21st century."

Her intense green eyes lit up like stars. "By the saints! Are you truly from the future? Can you tell me about it?"

Get a hold of yourself, Spero. You don't have time to get distracted by pretty girls.

"Maybe later. First, I need to figure out where we are and how to get back to my sister."

Her innocent expression turned thoughtful. "I think I can help with the first part."

Maybe she isn't so useless after all.

"You know where we are?"

Her fingers brushed over a big pink jewel hanging around her neck that looked out of place with her raggedy dress. "I believe this is Imperium, a land of magic."

I raised an eyebrow. "And how does one get out of Imperium?"

"That I know not."

Then again, maybe not.

"I thought you said you could help!"

"I did!" she huffed, stomping her soft shoe in the dirt. "I told you where we are."

"I don't have time for this. I've got to get back."

I turned around to explore the forest. Her soft footsteps

echoed close behind. Every instinct wanted me to tell her off, but when I looked back, she was gazing at me with tender concern that made me instantly forget all my doubts about her.

"You must care about your sister very much."

"Of course I do!" I snapped. "She's family. She's just a kid, and she's all alone."

"I'm sorry. I wish there were something I could do to help."

Why would she want to help a complete stranger?

"Don't you want to get back to England too?"

She gave me a conflicted look. "Eventually, but my father can take care of himself for a while. I believe my mother is here somewhere, and I need to find her."

"Is she in some sort of danger?"

"I think so. She's been gone a very long time."

The sadness in her eyes was overwhelming. I pushed my suspicions about her being some sort of con artist to the back of my mind. She needed help, and at the moment, so did I.

"I'm sure she's okay. We'll find her. Don't worry."

"Why are you so sure? Moments ago, you didn't even know where we were."

I shrugged. "I just have a sense about these things. Call it intuition. I'm Spero, by the way."

I held out my hand.

The girl stared at my hand as if she didn't know what to do with it and gave me a regal curtsy. "Well met, Spero. I'm Amoura."

"That's really pretty," I said before I could stop myself. "Very unusual."

"I've never heard of anyone named Spero, either. Is it common in the 21st century?"

"No. It's Latin for hope. My dad's kind of a nerd. Leave it to him to use a dead language to name his firstborn."

She furrowed her brow. "Latin isn't a dead language. Half the books in the library were written in it."

Still dead set on the whole 1590 thing.

"Anyway, famous people always give their babies weird names. Apple, Bear, Bird…"

She looked intrigued. "Your parents are famous?"

Me and my big mouth.

I finally had the chance for someone to think I was a normal person, and I blew it. What was it about this girl that made it feel like I could tell her anything?

I did my best to backpedal. "That, uh, depends on your definition of famous."

She sighed. "At least you know they're safe."

"Yeah, safe, and far away from us. Why don't I help you find your mom? I might know a thing or two about what it's like to have absent parents."

Amoura gave me a hopeful grin that lit up her doll-like face. The more I spoke to her, the more I started to forget about my pampered life back home.

"Where should we look first?" I asked.

"That's awfully kind of you, but I haven't the faintest idea where she might be. All I know is that she went back to Imperium."

"I guess that's a start."

I searched the open wilderness around us, trying to find signs of civilization. I wished I could just open the world map and read directions to the nearest town like in a video game. If it wasn't for the pink sky, overgrown polka-dotted flowers, and weird shimmering mist in the air, we could have been standing in a regular forest. A bird flew over us with shimmering golden wings and a long tail that flowed behind it like a waterfall. Amoura gazed at it, her eyes sparkling like stars. This place seemed just as foreign to her as it did to me. The mystery of these woods increased with each step we descended deeper into them.

"How much do you know about this place, anyway?" I asked her.

She twitched as though she was so lost in thought that she forgot I was there. "Not much, I'm afraid. I know it's magical."

"That's the understatement of the year."

After some wandering, I found an entrance to a cave hidden behind some long, floral vines. Most caves in RPGs lead to dungeons containing secrets that advanced the plot, so maybe we'd find a lead here. They also usually contained deadly monsters. Hopefully, this one wouldn't have any.

"Amoura, I think I found something!"

She raced toward me. "What is it?"

Her excitement was infectious, causing my heart to skip a beat.

"There might be some sort of secret passage through here. Maybe it'll give us a clue to finding your mother or a way back."

Her face lit up. "That's amazing, Spero! Thank you."

Amoura followed me into the cave. Darkness loomed over us, forcing us to feel our way past the entrance. I don't know why I wasn't expecting a cave to be dark, but video game dungeons usually have at least enough light to navigate. A faint blue glow below me caught my attention. Moving my hand around with the glow, I realized that my ring had essentially become a flashlight. Amoura had a pink light shining over her heart, where her necklace rested.

"Cool," I said. "It looks like we have built-in flashlights."

"Built-in *what?*"

Right, I forgot about the time-travel thing.

"Er, torches?"

Amoura held her necklace over the ground in front of a forked pathway. "Spero, I think I found some tracks leading this way."

The pink glow revealed some imprints in the dirt, but I couldn't tell if they were footprints or potholes. It was becoming clear that Amoura was more than just a pretty face.

"You know how to track?"

"My father is a farmer," she replied, as though that explained everything. "I cannot fathom how many times we've had to chase down runaway livestock."

"That's neat. I'm decent at coding, but I don't know very much about surviving in the wilderness."

The tracks led us down a narrow path where we heard a shuffling sound echoing from around a corner. Placing my finger against my lips, I gestured for Amoura to be quiet. We glanced around the corner. A colossal beast with a scorpion's tail, lion's body, and a beast-like face stalked the grounds. I recognized it as a manticore from the monsters I'd fought in video games. Even though we were being quiet, it didn't take long for the predator to lock onto us thanks to our glowing jewels.

Why didn't this thing come with an off switch?

With a loud growl, the beast stomped in our direction, probably looking for a midday snack.

My breath caught for a moment. In video games, monsters weren't scary. If you lost, you could just start over again.

The adrenaline surge of defeating a difficult boss could not compare to the pounding I felt in my chest as the manticore loomed over us. I could feel drops of saliva hit my face when it growled, and it smelled like a zoo. If we didn't get out of here quickly, there might not be a second chance. Amoura's eyes widened with fear. She stared at me as though silently begging me to come up with some kind of plan. There was only one thing I could think of to do, a strategy I often used for monsters that were way above my level. I grabbed her hand, and we high-tailed it back to the exit.

Unfortunately for us, the monsters in this world don't stop chasing when you exit a dungeon. We struggled not to get tangled in the vines at the mouth of the cave and made it out just in time for the beast to follow us into the uncanny-looking wilderness of this strange world. What were we supposed to do now? We were completely unarmed. Amoura and I ran through the trees until we thought we might collapse. Well, *I* thought I might collapse. She seemed to have enough stamina to go for miles.

"Spero, look!"

While I was still trying to remember how to breathe, Amoura pointed to a glittering crystal palace that looked like it came right out of an illustration from a fairy tale. It shimmered with a soft bluish-purple glow, reflecting rainbows in the sunlight. I would have settled for an abandoned shack, but this place was exquisite. It was taller than the Empire State Building and more extravagant than a theme park display.

I struggled to keep up with Amoura as we raced to the gate, the manticore hot on our trail. Just before we reached the grand arched doorway, it opened from the inside. A woman with long lavender hair, dark skin, and a deep purple velvet dress hugging her curvy figure stood in the entryway. With a wave of her hand, purple sparks flew at the manticore as it raced toward us. The sparks crashed into it like bullets. Upon contact, it flopped over onto its back and shrank down to the size of an ant. She must have been some kind of high-level wizard to wield such powerful magic at the flick of a wrist.

"Get in, quickly!" the woman scolded us as though we were children. "I've been expecting you. We have much to discuss."

Five

Amoura

As I followed the mysterious woman into the sparkling castle, the questions I had hoped the library would answer multiplied tenfold. Who had sent me here? Why had Spero been sent with me? Did Mama have something to do with all of this? Maybe this woman would provide the answers I sought. My head grew heavier with each step I took through the grand corridor.

My breath caught as I took in the fantastical splendor of the grand lobby with its marble floors that glinted with the colors of precious metals and fine jewels, befitting royalty. My surroundings reminded me of the time Lady Margaret yelled at me for trying to sneak onto her and Lord Thomas's estate as a child out of curiosity for what the home of a noble looked like. A twinge of guilt set in for imposing upon this magnificent palace despite the open invitation we received.

The woman stared at me with an intense gaze. She had

skin the color of the night sky, contrasting with my mother's complexion, which reminded me of a sunset. Yet, her features bore an undeniable resemblance to hers in the shape of her face, the way she carried herself, and the silver shimmer in her lilac hair.

Her soft, gentle voice reminded me of a whisper on the breeze. "Amoura, it's a pleasure to see you here in the flesh. I've waited a long time to meet Solara's progeny."

At the mention of her name, my heart pounded so hard that I found it difficult to breathe.

"You know my mother."

It wasn't a question. My mother's familiar scent of cinnamon and roses wafted through the air. I knew she was somewhere near.

The corners of her burgundy lips curled into a smile. "Of course. She's my sister. Come, give your Auntie Caliga a kiss."

The racing in my heart grew so loud I could hardly hear myself think. "Verily? Forsooth?"

My vision blurred with tears as my hopes and dreams came to fruition at last. This woman was my family. I wrapped my arms around my aunt's slim, yet voluptuous figure. Joyful tremors radiated up my spine and escaped as pearls of tears from my eyes as I embraced her for the first time. She ran her fingers through my hair like Mama did the last time I saw her. Her hands pivoted to my shoulders as she studied my face.

"You have her eyes."

My tears flowed harder. After so many years away, most people in our village didn't remember Mama, and now my own aunt saw a part of her in me.

Spero cleared his throat, reminding us he was still in the room.

"Amoura isn't the only one missing her family right now." Caliga's warm smile melted into a studious expression. "Right. Come with me. There isn't much time."

My aunt led us down a long hallway covered by a rose-colored carpet and tapestries of fantastical imagery of creatures from the bedtime stories Mama used to tell me. We followed her up a tower with a spiral staircase. The crystal walls reflected rainbow-colored shimmers onto the stairs as we climbed.

"You know, I don't really appreciate being ripped from my home with no warning," Spero chided as we circled up the tower. "I think that goes for both of us."

Spero's words cut through the air like a knife. Yet, I found myself unable to share in his affliction. He glanced at me, but the unicorn imagery on the stained glass windows held my full attention. Mama once told me that these beautiful creatures protected the forests. I wondered how much truth her words held.

Caliga seemed to float up the stairs as her elegant dress swayed over each step. "Believe me, I would not have brought the two of you here if I didn't have a very good reason."

Spero continued ranting. "I should have realized that email looked sketchy. You're the one who sent me that game, aren't you?"

Her footsteps echoed off the walls of the tower. "Locating you was not easy."

A sinking feeling entered the pit of my stomach as I considered Spero's words. "There never was a book about Imperium in the library, was there?"

She stopped at the top of the staircase. "Your discovery brought us together. Isn't that what you wanted?"

"Aye, but you did separate me from my father."

Her shoulders sagged, disrupting her statuesque gait. "I'm afraid it couldn't be helped. This is a matter of the utmost importance."

My aunt led us through a stone doorway into a dark room with no windows. Deep purple velvet curtains that matched her dress hung from the walls. The cold, black floor held five stone pedestals with intricate designs carved into them. Four were empty. A glowing ball of crystal floated several inches above the central pedestal. She claimed her spot behind the ball and waved her hand over the smooth, clear surface. A soft white glow surrounded it at her approach.

"Now, my children, I shall reveal your destiny."

Everywhere she touched, images formed inside the ball, suspended by dancing lights. I'd never experienced anything like it before. It was a miniature theater that could fit in one's pocket. The glass revealed a thriving magical realm with enchanting creatures dancing in the brightly glowing forests. Some had glowing wings, and others had glistening tails made of fish scales, just like in my mother's stories. A beautiful, color-changing jewel shed a bright light above them like the sun itself.

"Imperium was once a peaceful land, filled with magic and wonder. All who came here found only joy and eternal life thanks to the magic of the enchanted crystal and the loving guidance of the three sorceresses who watched over it: Mistress Solara, Mistress Estella, and myself, Mistress Caliga."

Three women's silhouettes appeared above the magical creatures in the image. The fairies and other creatures bowed down to the women as one would when approached by the queen.

"However, this peace was only temporary. One day, Mistress Estella decided that she no longer wanted to share the crystal's power with her sisters and the rest of Imperium. In an act of pure greed, she shattered the crystal into its four original elements—fire, earth, water, and air."

The projection of one of the sorceresses grew larger than the rest, spreading a dark shadow over the magical land. She reached up and grasped the crystal from the sky, expelling its light and smashing it to pieces. When she opened her hand, four shards flew beyond the boundaries of the image projected in the ball. The wicked woman's silhouette grew larger until her face was the only thing visible in the magic crystal, and she gave a horrible, crackling laugh.

Caliga's voice grew somber. "Without the crystal's light, the beings of Imperium grew weak, and the land became flooded with monsters like the one you encountered today. Soon, this world will fade away. Since it is connected to the life force of your own world, it won't take long before the Earth is affected as well."

"How awful!" I cried.

All my life, I did everything I could to help as many people in my small village as possible. Now that I had found the place Mama came from, I needed to protect this place as well. Mayhap this was meant to be my mission all along.

"Hold on, Amoura," Spero spoke up, but Mistress Caliga did not let him continue.

"In order to prevent Mistress Estella from causing more damage, the crystal shards have been sealed behind four labyrinths matching their elements and are guarded by dangerous beasts. Do not be fooled by their docile appearance. Their disguises are meant to confuse their victims."

"Why don't you just zap them like you did that manticore?" Spero interrupted again. "You're powerful enough."

There was a notable twitch in Caliga's eye at the interruption. Why couldn't Spero see how important all of this was?

"If you let me finish, you will learn exactly why. I see some of you are better at listening than others."

She waved her hand over the crystal ball again. Symbols for fire, water, earth, and air appeared along with a lock symbol covering each one.

"In her desperation to protect the worlds, Mistress Solara cast a spell, tethering the essences of hope and love in their purest forms as the key to unlock the labyrinths. Spero, you are the essence of hope. And you, Amoura," she said, turning toward me, "are the essence of love. Only the two of you can enter the labyrinths and recover what was lost."

I clutched my pendant. Its warmth radiated in my chest. "I knew she was in some sort of trouble. If only she had found a way to contact me sooner."

Caliga's violet eyes were heavy with the desperation of two worlds. "It took me years to find a way to bring you both here. Your mother chose you specifically for this mission."

The urgency of her words filled every fiber of my being. This was the missing truth I had been searching for. Mama had sent for me after all these years to save her people. This was why she never returned. I needed to do this for her. Half of me belonged to Imperium, and it was vital that I kept it safe.

I gave her a resolute nod. "I understand. I shall do it."

"Now, wait just a minute!" Spero interjected. "Do you really just expect us to take your word for all of this? I didn't see anyone suffering when I got here. How do I know you haven't told this same story to countless other victims who didn't survive the journey?"

"Take heart, Spero," I said. "Why would she lie about something like this?"

He crossed his arms. "Come on, Amoura! You can't possibly be that stupid."

"I beg your pardon!" I huffed.

Apparently, they stopped teaching people manners at some point in the future.

"Don't they have con artists where you come from? How do you even know your mother was the one who cast this spell?"

"You can always try asking her," said Caliga. "Although I doubt you'll get an answer in her current state."

My heart skipped a beat. "Can you tell me where she is?"

Caliga's hands fell to her sides. "I'm afraid Solara's spirit is gone from this world. She was so brave trying to stop our sister, but it wasn't enough. Her body rests at the top of the North Tower. I would have brought her back long ago if I had access to the labyrinths like you do. Only the crystal has the power to awaken her. It's up to you now."

My breath caught in my throat. Mama's spirit was gone? It simply couldn't be true. I felt her presence watching over me all these years. I pressed my hands against my pendant as my lip began to quiver. It must have been a mistake.

"I wish to see her. Take me to her."

"As you wish, my dear. If you head back down the way we came and make a left at the statue, you'll find the staircase to the North Tower."

I raced out of the room without a moment's hesitation. With my heart thumping in my chest, I ran past a statue of Mistress Caliga, Mama, and another woman who must have been Estella. Winding staircases filled the palace, but there was no sign of life anywhere. It was a bit eerie. I tried to calm my pounding heart as I made my way up the long staircase leading to the top of the northernmost tower.

There, floating in a round chamber, was the glowing, lifeless form of the woman I would have given up everything for. She had waited for me all this time, frozen in slumber. My heart felt as though it had split in two. After all these years of searching, the burden of awakening her fell upon my shoulders. I could not let her down.

Six

Spero

A moura ran off before I had a chance to stop her, not that she would have listened to me, anyway. She seemed dead set on falling into whatever trap we'd been pulled into. There was something I didn't like about this woman. She was toying with Amoura's emotions, and that girl was as innocent as they come. Besides, none of this was my problem. I had to figure out how to get back to Melanie. The staff didn't understand her like I did.

"Look, lady, you might have Amoura wrapped around your little finger, but you can't fool me. Why don't you do both of us a favor and send me home?"

She narrowed her eyes at me. "You would dare put the lives of two worlds at stake just for your own personal sense of comfort? You are this world's last hope."

I crossed my arms. "You claim to know so much about our worlds, yet I haven't seen a single thing I recognized in that low-budget light show ball of yours. I've seen better effects in '90s CGI movies."

The corner of her mouth lifted into a devious smirk. "You wish to see something you recognize?"

"I'd like to at least see you try."

"Very well."

She waved her hand over the ball. There, huddled on the couch in our lobby, was Melanie, crying to a police officer. The stone-faced, middle-aged cop jotted down notes on a Star Tech tablet, unaffected by my sister's distress. My pulse quickened as heat rushed through my body. My hands clenched into fists.

"If you hurt her, I swear…"

Caliga tapped the ball, and the image faded. "I have no interest in her, I assure you. However, if you want to see her again, you will do as I ask."

"And if I still refuse?"

A purple glow surrounded her. "Do you know to whom you are speaking? I am one of the three sorceress guardians of Imperium. It is an honor just to stand in my presence."

She raised her hand, releasing sparks at my chest. Pain pulsed throughout my whole body. My muscles locked up, causing me to fall to the ground. The more I tried to move, the worse the pain got. Finally, I stopped fighting it. After an agonizing minute, the horrible sensation went away.

"Do not test me, boy."

I took several deep breaths as the sweet sensation of movement returned to my body. "One more stunt like that, and you'll have to find someone else to do your dirty work for you."

She made a sound that was somewhere between a laugh and

a snort. "Good luck finding a way back on your own."

I backed away to the door. "We'll see if Amoura still wants to help you after I tell her about this."

* * *

I raced out to catch up with Amoura, shaking off the stiffness from that awful spell. The statue that Caliga directed her to was of three sorceresses. One of them looked like Caliga, which probably meant that another one was Amoura's mother. Though they all resembled each other, I guessed she was the one with the warmest smile. Someone as sweet as Amoura could never have come from someone as callous as Caliga. I had my doubts that they were even really related.

Another thing I noticed while feeling returned to my joints was the logo for Star Tech plastered all over the castle. I guess it wasn't always my dad's company logo since he copied it from the ring he gave me, but it was still weird seeing a famous corporate logo in an RPG-like fantasy world. The star, moon, and sun symbols were probably supposed to represent the three sorceresses, but they worked well as a logo. It was simple, clean, and eye-catching. My dad used to hand out tons of merchandise with it at conventions. I was accustomed to seeing it on hats, t-shirts, mugs, and all kinds of other swag, not plastered all over the walls of a castle.

The spiral staircase to the North Tower was even bigger than the one Caliga brought us to. The final effects of the spell were still wearing off, making the climb pure agony, but I had no desire to stick around with Caliga while I waited for it to wear off. I stopped for a minute to catch my breath and then huffed my way up to the top.

The stairs ended in an empty room with a jade marble floor accented by golden threads. In the middle of the room was a cylindrical pink force field. It made a low humming sound, like an old hard drive trying to load a large file.

A woman floated lifelessly in the middle of it as though she were suspended in a cloud. It looked like I had guessed right about which sorceress was Amoura's mother. A peaceful smile complemented her warm brown face. Long, shimmering lashes shrouded her gently closed eyelids as though she were taking a light nap. Her pink chiffon gown and long blue hair spiraled around her like smoke curling above an open flame.

Amoura stood inches in front of the chamber. I walked up behind her.

"That isn't something you see every day."

Then I saw her face. Her green eyes had turned red and puffy, tears streaming from them as though her whole world had ended. Of course she was upset. This was her mother. How could I make a joke at a time like this?

I'm such an idiot.

"Mama…" she whimpered, raising a cautious hand toward the force field.

"You shouldn't touch it," I warned her. "It could be danger-ous."

She turned to me with fire in her puffy red eyes. "My mother is not dangerous!"

Her necklace pulsed with a thick pink light that flooded half the room. Why could I never say the right thing around this girl?

"There's still a way to save her, you know," echoed the voice of our captor from behind us.

In a dramatic flash of purple smoke, Caliga materialized at

the entrance to the room. She seemed to enjoy flaunting her otherworldly powers in our faces.

I glared at her. "How come you got to take the shortcut?"

"What must I do?" Amoura regarded Caliga, clutching her necklace.

"Enter the four labyrinths and restore the crystal to its original shape. It alone has the power to save Mistress Solara."

I placed my hand on her shoulder. "Amoura, I know you're upset, but you shouldn't trust her."

She ignored me.

"I'll do it on one condition."

This was getting interesting. Amoura didn't come off as the type of person who liked to include fine print in her contracts.

Her voice wavered through her tears. "Send Spero back whence he came. His little sister waits for him."

I stared at her in shock. She had an opportunity to recover her long-lost mother, and all she could think about was my family? This girl was full of surprises. Even though I was concerned about Melanie, she had an entire staff taking care of her back home. She'd be okay. Amoura, on the other hand, was stuck doing this lunatic's bidding. Without someone to guide her in the right direction, who knew what this woman would be capable of making her do? A peasant girl from the Middle Ages wouldn't stand a chance against someone like this. Heck, I barely stood a chance against her, but I at least had to try.

"Amoura, no," I stammered.

Caliga pursed her lips. "I'm afraid I can't do that. You alone cannot enter the labyrinths. The conditions for unlocking the seal are very specific. It requires both the essence of hope *and* the essence of love."

I glared at Caliga. "Then I guess it's your lucky day."

Amoura made a sharp intake of breath from behind me. "Spero, you need not do this."

I turned to face her. "I can't let a naïve crybaby like you fall for this woman's scams. If you're going to save your mother, you'll need someone who knows what they're doing."

I wanted her to defend herself or yell at me —anything to get her to stop crying. Instead, she continued to stare at the woman floating in the tube. Her eyes had turned so red and puffy that I could barely see the green in them anymore. She looked so pitiful that I couldn't help feeling sorry for her.

I decided to take a risk and wrapped my arms around her shoulders. There was hardly anything to her. Did she even eat back home? Instead of pushing me away, which I honestly wouldn't have blamed her for, she leaned into my chest and sobbed into my hoodie. Her tears leaked through to my shirt underneath. I could feel her trembling in my arms. Her frail form grew heavier as she leaned into me harder. Finally, her breathing slowed, and she let go. She refused to make eye contact with me after that.

"Come with me," Caliga commanded after Amoura had calmed down. "You'll need weapons to defend yourselves against the beasts."

Caliga let us take the shortcut this time. With a wave of her arms, the surrounding tower disappeared. Like an iris transition from an old cartoon, a new room faded into view around us. A quick bout of nausea passed through my stomach as my brain processed the transition to a new location without movement, similar to playing a VR game for the first time.

We materialized in an armory covered with every type of weapon I had ever seen in a video game—swords, maces, flails, crossbows, even some rifles. Every single weapon was forged from the same sleek-looking black steel that seemed to repel all light.

"All of these weapons are unbreakable and will never miss their mark," she explained. "Choose wisely, for you will need a powerful tool to recover the crystal shards."

Amoura looked around like a deer in headlights. Everywhere she turned, a new expression of horror filled her face. "I don't believe in violence."

"I should have suspected the essence of love would be a pacifist," Caliga groaned. "Are you not willing to fight for your mother's life?"

"Of course I am, but surely there's another way."

"This is the only way. You must choose a weapon if you want to have any hope of restoring her. I'll be back in my scrying room if you need me."

She vanished again. I hoped we could find our way back on our own so I wouldn't get another taste of Caliga's magic. In the meantime, I needed to cheer up Amoura, which should be a lot easier without her looming over us. I grabbed a sword and swung it around playfully.

"Come on, Amoura, maybe it'll be fun. Think of it as a game."

She crossed her arms. "Destruction isn't a game."

She still refused to look at me, probably embarrassed about the scene she had made earlier. I scanned the room and found a lightweight crossbow. Maybe she'd be more willing to fight if she didn't have to be close enough to see her target's face.

"How's your aim?"

Her hands fell back to her sides. "Not bad, I think."

I handed her the crossbow. "See if you can hit that target across the room."

I pointed to a target in a corner next to a group of scarecrows and some punching bags. Her hands shook.

"I will not shoot a living target."

"I'm not asking you to. Just show me how well you can aim."

She sighed. "Very well, but this doesn't mean I will fight."

She fired a bolt that hit the bullseye perfectly in the center.

"Wow! Where did you learn to shoot like that?"

"I've been to a few archery competitions in my day." There was a surprising hint of smugness in her voice.

"Just take the crossbow with you. Maybe it'll come in handy for something else. You certainly know how to use it."

Amoura sighed. "Perhaps, but I will not use it to harm a living being."

She took the leather belt that was attached to it and fastened it around her waist.

"Don't worry. I'll handle all the fighting."

She cocked an eyebrow. "And what experience have *you* with battles?"

I smirked. "Plenty if you count video games."

"Is that like jousting?"

"Not really. You mostly sit around and press buttons."

"How is that supposed to help us?"

"I don't know. We'll figure it out later. Are you coming, milady?"

She winced at the title. "You needn't treat me that way. I'm not noble like you."

"What makes you think I'm noble?"

She began counting off reasons on her fingers. "The famous parents, the complete brazenness you showed Mistress Caliga despite her obvious superiority, how comfortable you look wandering the halls of an extravagant palace, among other things."

"This place is pretty cool, but it isn't too different from a fantasy game or movie."

The look she gave me told me I wasn't doing much to plead my case.

"Fine," I admitted. "I guess I'm better off than most people, but that doesn't make me better than them."

"It doesn't?"

"In the future, everyone is treated equally regardless of their status."

Amoura gave me a thoughtful look. "Mayhap you aren't like most nobles I've encountered."

"I'll take that as a compliment."

Hoping to avoid another encounter with the shadow lady, I navigated our way out of the armory. There was another annoyingly long flight of stairs. Once we exited the tower, it led us back to the same lobby where we had found all the other towers. From there, it was easy to find the front gate. Although it would have been nice to get more hints about where we were going, I didn't want Caliga to use more of her manipulation tactics on Amoura. If we wandered around for long enough, surely we'd find the labyrinths eventually.

Seven

Amoura

Imperium was all the things I had imagined it to be from my childhood fantasies. The air smelled of honey and lilacs. Flowers of every shape and size glittered in the trees and the bright turquoise grass. There weren't many signs of civilization, but the wildlife we did see was like something out of a dream. Birds danced with ribbons of color hanging from their tails, and tiny chipmunks scurried past with big, intense eyes.

A tree with upside-down white blossoms in the shape of bells spilled glittering dust into our hair. Spero patted his head in an attempt to rub it out.

"Something's not right about this place. Don't you feel it too?"

I brushed some specks of shimmering dust off my sleeve and watched them float delicately to the ground.

"I think 'tis beautiful. If you truly believe something is

wrong, that is why we were sent here to fix it."

Spero blocked my path, forcing me to make eye contact with him. "Look, Amoura. I know you want to believe what Caliga told you back there, but I'm telling you, she's not who she says she is."

I shot him a challenging look. "She isn't really my aunt?"

His eyes darted back and forth. "No. I mean, maybe. I don't know. But you didn't see what she did to me back there! She cast some kind of hex on me."

I raised my eyebrow. "You appear not hexed to me."

He obscured his face with his hand. "It wore off. That's not the point. What if she wants this crystal to do something awful?"

"Care you to elaborate?"

"I don't know… Make everyone her slaves?"

Growing tired of his cynicism, I walked past him. Though his heavy breathing revealed his struggle to keep up, he remained at my side.

"Mistress Caliga is already one of the three monarchs of this land, as I'm sure you've seen from the statue in the palace. The people of this land are already bound to her, and you would do well to refer to her by her proper title if you wish to avoid being hexed again."

He threw his hands up in the air. "You are impossible!"

"It takes one to know one."

Why would Mama send someone like this to help me with my mission? Maybe there was some sort of mistake, or this was all a test. I tried to convince my aunt to send him back, but he remained steadfast for some reason I failed to comprehend. If he were truly so against all of this, why was he still helping me?

We wandered in silence for the next few hours until the sky turned a dark shade of violet. It was clear neither of us could go much further without resting. Spero's frustration melted into a look of relief when I stopped, allowing him a much-needed break.

"We need to find a place to sleep," I said. "We can search for the labyrinths more on the morrow."

Spero's eyes darted around the empty forest. "You don't think Imperium hosts any inns, do you? I haven't seen any signs of civilization since we got here."

"I think we're going to have to make camp."

He looked even more uncomfortable with that suggestion. "Are you sure that's our only option?"

He was probably accustomed to sleeping in a castle with servants who fetched him meals throughout the day. Perhaps I should have asked my aunt if she could have made accommodations for us at the palace, but he was in such a hurry to leave that there was no time. Had she truly placed a hex on him? Why would she do that? All she wanted was to save Imperium.

"Not used to sleeping outside, are you?"

Spero ran a hand through his slick yellow hair and gave me a sheepish grin. "I went camping with my dad once. I just… didn't like it very much. There were bugs and poison ivy, and he was always checking in on his job. It felt like he was only with me out of obligation."

Perhaps this was what caused Spero to be so untrusting of people. A twinge of sympathy washed over me. Father always made sure to devote as much time to me as possible, no matter how much work he had on the farm.

"Then it's a good thing your father isn't here now."

That didn't assuage him. "It isn't just that. Don't you feel weird about camping out in the woods with a strange guy you just met?"

I smirked. "You're not *that* strange. If Mama chose you to aid me with this mission, then you have my complete trust."

"That's exactly what I'm talking about. You need to stop being such a pushover, or you're going to get yourself killed."

"Who, pray tell, are you calling a pushover?" I huffed. "If I recall correctly, you were the one who turned down the opportunity to return home when you had no obligation to help me or my aunt."

He crossed his arms. "I had to. You wouldn't survive in these woods for one hour by yourself!"

"Is that what you think? That I'm some sort of needy child?"

"You are doing all of this just to get back to your mother."

I threw my arms in the air. "So be it! If you're so certain you can handle everything yourself, then you prepare the campfire for us."

He gave a confident grin that didn't quite reach his eyes. "One campfire coming up."

My hunch was correct. I could see he had no idea what to do. He grabbed the two tiniest twigs in the forest and began rubbing them together to absolutely no avail. Relishing his failure, I put my hand on my hip and tapped my foot as though I was waiting for something to happen.

"Well?"

He sighed. "Fine, you got me. This isn't my area of expertise."

I gathered some sticks under a nearby tree and playfully whacked his head with one of them. "You nobles are all the same."

"Hey, I thought you said I wasn't like other nobles!"

"Perhaps in some ways."

I built the base for the fire and found some larger twigs to form a plank. Then I blew on it until it ignited with a healthy glow. Warmth radiated through my chest, reminding me of home. The fire was fuchsia, like the sky of Imperium. So many things were different about this world, but there was a part of me that would always belong here. This was my mother's home, after all. Spero and I gathered some moss and giant flower petals to soften the ground, and he made himself comfortable on the opposite side of the campfire.

"Good night, crybaby," he mumbled.

"Good night, Lord of the Campfire."

* * *

I woke to an annoying buzzing sound. Something tickled my skin like a fine-haired brush. I rubbed my eyes. When I opened them, a tiny pixie hovered above my face. Her dark hair and pointed ears glowed in the morning sunlight. She wore a dress made of pink flower petals. Her pointed wings hummed like an insect, spilling glittering dust all over my dress.

"Rise and shine!" she sang in a high-pitched voice.

I rubbed the dust off my face and sat up next to the now extinguished campfire. Spero was still asleep. He must not have been used to waking up at dawn like farmers did.

"Who are you?" I asked the pixie.

"My name's Fey! Mistress Caliga sent me here to help you on your quest!"

She was a bit too cheerful for such an early hour.

"She did? That was kind of her," I yawned.

Spero rolled over.

"Should I go wake him, too?" asked Fey.

"I'm awake," he mumbled without opening his eyes.

"Spero, look!" I exclaimed. "'Tis a fairy."

That did the trick. He sat up and rubbed his eyes. "For real?"

"It's a pleasure to meet the heroes who are fated to save the realm!" Fey exclaimed, buzzing over Spero. "Mistress Caliga asked me to test your skills, so I found a baby dragon whose wing got stuck in a tree! If you work together, you can save it and improve your, er… What did she call it again? Collaborative problem-solving?"

She seemed far too excited to be speaking about an injured creature. My chest tightened as I imagined how scared it must have been, stuck there all alone.

"The poor dear," I replied. "We should help it."

"Great! It's just this way!"

Fey began to fly away, but Spero didn't budge.

"What is this? A test? Are we in school now? And she sends a fairy to guide us instead of coming here herself? We're not interested."

I stood up. "Spero, we should help."

Spero got up and brushed away the remains of the campfire. "We don't have time for side quests, Amoura. The sooner we restore the crystal, the sooner we can get back to our families. Who knows how many more tests your aunt is going to give us before she tells us where to find the labyrinths? This isn't a vacation."

Fey buzzed over him.

"But a creature is hurt!" I cried.

She flew back over me, kicking her feet in the air. "This is no good. You need to get along if you're going to save Imperium together."

Spero crossed his arms. "It's just a test! For all we know, Caliga is the one who put it in that situation."

"Even if that's true, 'tis our duty to help," I insisted.

"Is it? I don't remember signing any contract."

Fey darted around us in circles. "Mistress Caliga isn't going to like this very much."

"Why should I care what she likes?" Spero huffed. "I'm here to restore the crystal and return to Melanie. She's been alone for too long as it is."

Why did he have to make this so difficult? I understood that he missed his sister, but he still agreed to help. What sort of future did he come from, where everyone was in such a hurry all the time?

I kicked some dirt and moss in Spero's general direction. "If you're not going to help the dragon, then I shall do it myself."

"Fine! I never needed your help, anyway."

I crossed my arms and squinted at him. "Thou dost vex me!"

"Then go be vexed somewhere else!" He turned and went in the opposite direction.

"Oh dear," chimed the pixie. "This isn't going well."

"Just take me to the dragonling."

"But…"

"Do you want my help or not?"

Fey sighed and flew into the woods, past some giant red-capped mushrooms. She stopped by a tree with bright orange and yellow flowers hanging from it like streamers. Halfway up the trunk, a small lime-green creature with an adorable face hung off the tree from a barb in its wing. It made a horrible wailing noise that cut through my heart like a knife.

"You poor creature."

I clung to the rough bark of the tree and climbed a few feet up to reach the dragonling. A protrusion in the bark pierced through the lavender lining on the inside of its wing, causing it to get hopelessly tangled in the trunk of the tree. Keeping my grip on the tree with one arm, I carefully removed the pieces of bark that held its wing in place. The dragon wailed louder, blowing sparks at me that dissipated in a transparent pink light from my pendant. I loosened it just enough to free the creature, but it didn't look like it would be able to fly for a while. Cradling it under my free arm, I carefully made my way back down the tree.

When I landed on the ground, the dragonling looked at me with piercing black eyes and reached out with a small, clawed hand. I grasped it, and the tiny claws wrapped around my finger. The baby animals I helped birth on the farm never looked this cute. It squirmed in my arms from the ugly-looking gash in its wing. Gently setting the dragonling on the ground, I brushed my fingers over its wing and attempted to activate my mother's pendant. The familiar warmth of its healing power flooded my chest. Slowly, the gash on its wing closed into a scar, causing it to shrivel around it.

"I'm sorry," I said, "but this is the best I can do. Think of it this way. Now you shall have a special wing that isn't like any other dragon."

He tilted his tiny face toward me. The corners of his mouth curled into a smile. He winced a bit as he flapped his special wing that lifted him a few inches off the ground before the erratic flapping failed to keep him aloft. I reached out and caught him, cradling him in my arms. He blew more tiny sparks at me.

"Watch it, Sparky. You do not want to set anyone on fire."

He made a gleeful cooing noise in response to the nickname. "You like that? Very well, then. From now on, I shall call you Sparky."

Sparky squealed with excitement and blew sparks up toward the sky. I gazed in that direction. A loud screech rang out from high above. Looming over us was a full-sized dragon with thick scales the same shade of green as Sparky's. Was this dragon cross with me for handling its kin? Every instinct I had told me to flee, but the heavy use of my magic had affected my reaction time. I froze in terror, my heart racing as Fey darted away in a panic.

Eight

Spero

Amoura was so frustrating. How was I supposed to help her if she couldn't even help herself? We would never be able to rescue her mom and get out of here if she went running off every time someone's cat got stuck in a tree. Maybe it would be easier to gather information about the labyrinths without her getting in the way. This whole situation was bizarre. If I were really trapped in a video game, why would Caliga have been able to summon an image of Melanie in her crystal ball? We didn't have any indoor security cameras that I knew of. Something else was going on, and I didn't like someone as innocent as Amoura being involved.

I passed by some more birds and forest critters, but found it odd how few signs of sentient life there were around here. Fey was the first native I'd seen who could speak English since we left the palace. If Mels came here, she probably would have gotten a kick out of all the untapped mysteries to explore. She also probably would have gotten into a lot of trouble. I wondered what she was doing right now. I hoped she found a way to take her mind off my disappearance.

After wandering through the woods for a while, I came across a glade with a silvery waterfall pouring into an enormous lake of crystal-clear water. Rainbows reflected on its surface. Exhausted from all the walking we did the day before, I helped myself to a drink and felt instantly revitalized. This must have been like a healing spring from a video game, though helpful creatures like fairies or mermaids usually surrounded those.

"How are you able to hold yourself upright like that?" asked a voice coming from the lake.

A young woman with long green hair and gilled ears swam toward me. Her body was adorned with peach-colored seashells that complemented her caramel skin. When she got closer, I realized she was propelling herself through the water with a turquoise tail covered in shimmering scales. She pulled herself onto a rock in the middle of the lake and began preening her seaweed-colored locks.

My jaw dropped open. "You're a mermaid!"

"Naturally. Aren't you a merman? Why do you have two tails?"

Great. Another NPC.

"You've never seen a human? What about your sorceress guardians? They're human, aren't they?"

"Those are sorceresses, not humans. They can appear in whatever form they like. They usually have fish tails like us when they visit our home."

I gazed into the shallow-looking spring, trying to determine how deep it went. The clear blue waters extended down a long rock wall until they became too fuzzy to see beyond.

"You live in the water?"

She glanced down at her reflection. "Where else would we live? Your kind isn't very bright, is it?"

She wrapped a piece of seaweed around her hair to form a ponytail and adjusted it to different positions on her head. "Tell me, human, do you think my hair looks better like this or like this?"

I blinked at her. Were all mermaids this vapid? She was pretty, but in a cartoony way, not a classic beauty like Amoura.

"Uh, you look fine either way. Can I ask you something, Miss Mermaid?"

"It's Katrina."

"Katrina. I'm Spero, one of the heroes your sorceress chose to restore the crystal. Do you happen to know if there's a labyrinth nearby? Maybe one containing the water shard?"

Katrina played with her hair some more. "My father did send some guards to investigate a mysterious cave that appeared not too long after Mistress Solara entered her enchanted sleep, but no one was able to open it."

If the labyrinths formed at the same time Amoura's mother was cursed, that would follow Caliga's story about how she was defeated while trying to stop Estella from destroying the crystal. I wondered how much the people in Imperium knew about it. Maybe this was my chance to get some answers.

"What caused Mistress Solara to fall asleep? Do you know?"

Katrina pulled a pearl out of a small bag and braided it into her hair. "If you ask me, I think she fell asleep out of boredom from spending so much time in that terrible world without magic. It sounds like a dreadful place. Ever since she left, the sea monster population has been spreading like tidal waves."

"That does sound like a problem. Restoring the crystal might help. Can you tell me where this cave is?"

"I can show you. It's about two hundred leagues east of here."

She dove off her rock with a splash.

"You mean it's underwater?"

"Where else would the water labyrinth be?"

Why is this place filled with girls who want to make everything difficult?

"You wouldn't happen to know of a spell that could turn someone into a merperson like you, would you?"

"I'm a mermaid, not a sorceress. Why would I know how to use magic?"

I sighed. "Never mind, then."

She filled a small clam with some water and tried to use it as a mirror. "Do you mind? You're in my light."

This was getting me nowhere. I headed back into the woods when a beam of light shot at me. When it got closer, I realized the light was dripping over dirt, creating a path of sparkling glitter.

Fey darted around me in circles, wearing a panicked expression on her tiny face. "Thank goodness I found you! Amoura's in trouble. You have to come quickly!"

A sinking feeling entered my chest. I should never have left her alone. She was way too gullible.

"Where is she?"

Fey ricocheted back the way she came. "This way! Hurry!"

I raced to keep up with the trail of sparkles behind her while she explained the situation.

"She went to help the dragonling, but then its mother

showed up. She's a big dragon with really sharp teeth and flaming hot breath."

"I get the picture," I huffed, reaching for my sword.

As we got closer, I saw the large, ferocious dragon Fey had described swoop down from overhead. It was covered in hard emerald scales, had enormous barbed purple wings, and, judging from the growl it made that echoed throughout the forest, a voracious appetite. It swooped down toward a tree, where Amoura was cradling a baby dragon in her arms. Sweat poured down my back as I imagined the mother dragon swallowing her whole in one gulp.

"Amoura!" I shouted.

The dragon landed in front of them and took a deep breath, ready to fry its baby's captor to a crisp. Summoning all my strength, I leaped toward Amoura, tackled her to the ground, and rolled away just as a huge blast of ruby-red flames caught the tree behind her. I could feel its heat singeing the hem of my jeans. The baby dragon fell out of her arms, rolling into the dirt. Its vengeful mother scooped it into her massive claw. I backed away from Amoura once I could tell she was safe.

"Are you okay?"

She cradled her forehead in her hand and blinked at me a few times, clearing the foggy haze from her eyes. "Spero? Whence did you come?"

"Fey found me and told me about the dragon."

She clutched her pendant. "I think you just saved my life. I wasn't expecting you to come back for me after that fight we had."

I shrugged. "You know how brazen we nobles are."

The dragons screeched at each other, having some sort of private conversation in a language I couldn't understand. The baby darted toward Amoura in an erratic flight pattern and spread open its claws as though guarding her from its mother. The larger dragon glared at us, but didn't attack. She gave Amoura a reluctant nod of approval, then scooped up the dragonling in a massive talon and flew away.

"They're sparing us?" I asked in disbelief.

Amoura's face lit up with a warm smile. "It's probably because I helped her child. I think this is her way of thanking me."

I adjusted my sword on my back. "By not eating you for lunch? Way to show some gratitude."

She gazed upward, following the dragon's trail with her eyes. From this distance, it could have been confused with an airplane.

"Mayhap we'll see them again. Sparky was so precious."

I furrowed my eyebrows at her. "Sparky?"

"The baby."

Is this girl for real?

"You *named* it?"

"I had to call it something! After all, there was no one else around to talk to."

Ouch.

Fey darted back and forth between us. "Well, it looks like my work here is done. I'll go report to Mistress Caliga that you're working together again. See you!"

I held up my hand. "Not so fast."

She hovered over me, slowing down enough that I could see her tiny face. "Yes?"

"Why did she send you to look after us? Does she not believe we can do this on our own?"

A hint of fear appeared in the ordinarily cheerful pixie's

glowing eyes. "Restoring the crystal and waking Mistress Solara is very important to Mistress Caliga. To all of us, really. The magic in Imperium has been unstable ever since Mistress Solara left for Earth. She went into a magical stasis as soon as she came back. There have been so many monster attacks since then. We've hardly had a chance for reprieve. Plus, Mistress Estella's gone missing, so she hasn't been much help either."

Amoura fidgeted with her hair. "Wasn't she the one who destroyed the crystal?"

Fey clasped her hands, kicking up dust in the air. "I doubt that. It was her invention."

I glanced at Amoura. Her eyes grew heavy as though she didn't know what to make of this information.

"See?" I said. "I told you something wasn't right about that story she told us."

Suddenly, Fey started convulsing in pain.

Amoura clutched her pendant. "Are you all right?" she asked.

"Sorry!" Fey shouted, blinking with an unnatural purple glow. "Gotta fly!"

She zipped away, leaving Amoura and me even more perplexed.

"That was weird, wasn't it?" I asked.

She ran her fingers through her long brown hair. "'Twas peculiar. I admit I don't entirely understand everything that's going on here, but it sounds like the citizens of Imperium need my mother to awaken just as much as I do. Are you still willing to help?"

I took a deep breath. "I was always planning on helping you. I lost my temper back there when I found out Caliga sent someone to spy on us. I'm sorry for abandoning you."

I tilted my head toward the ground, not wanting to see her reaction. She probably hated me.

"I'm sorry, too."

I looked up. Her intense green eyes were filled with sincerity. "After learning about Estella and the crystal just now, I believe there is more to the story than my aunt let on. I know not whom to trust."

I held out my hand. "You can start by trusting me. Truce?"

She stared at me for a moment and then nodded. Her calloused fingers pressed against mine as she shook my hand. I wasn't prepared for the way my heart started racing at the warmth of her touch. Pulling away, I decided to change the subject.

"I found a lead on the water labyrinth, but it might be a challenge to get to."

Amoura took a step back, looking almost disappointed. "Where is it? We should collect all the shards as soon as possible, like you said. The sooner we restore the crystal, the sooner I can see my mother again, and you'll get back to your sister. I know how important she is to you."

I gave her a grateful nod. "Thanks for understanding."

"Take me there. I'll be right behind you."

I led her in the direction of the waterfall. "How good a swimmer are you?"

Nine

Amoura

My mind churned like butter. Part of me longed to throw caution to the wind and embrace this world I had longed to find for half my life, yet I knew I should be practical, as Father would say. I wanted to trust Spero, especially after he had just saved my life, yet that would mean placing myself at odds with my newfound family. Back home, all I needed to do was tend to the animals and sell fresh produce. Now, an entire world depended on me.

I pushed aside some hanging vines covered in delicate pink blossoms as I followed Spero through the vibrant forest. Our footsteps marred the untouched moss that carpeted the rich soil below our feet as though we were imposing on sacred ground. To assuage my misplaced guilt for merely existing in such an ethereal place, I decided to strike up a conversation.

"What made you decide to come back? I thought I was just slowing you down."

He turned to face me. "Actually, Fey told me you were in trouble. But you wouldn't have been if I had just gone with you. We need to see this thing through to the end so I can get back to Melanie."

"Is Melanie your sister?"

"Yeah."

A charming glint appeared in his eye whenever he mentioned her. He acted so callously most of the time, but not when it came to his family. Maybe his devotion to his family did not differ so much from my own.

"I pray we both get what we desire by the end of all this."

His mouth widened into a confident grin. "I'm sure we will, as long as we stick together."

His steadfastness was infectious. I longed to believe him with every fiber of my being. It was no wonder Aunt Caliga called him the essence of hope.

Spero led me through the woods to a beautiful glade. A sparkling waterfall seemed to spin pure silver into a crystalline lake. I was amazed that he had been able to discover such a treasure in the short time since we had parted ways. I took a deep breath, inhaling the refreshing air that smelled of sea salt and mint.

"Drink some water from the spring," he suggested. "It'll make you feel better."

I cupped the silvery water between my hands. A cooling sensation washed over me as all my aches from climbing the tree vanished in an instant. I had never thought of water as sweet before, but this drink reminded me of the apple pies Mama used to bake with me.

"By the stars! Spero, how did you find this place?"

He shrugged his shoulders. "I was looking for you, and I

just kind of stumbled upon it. My mermaid friend should still be around here somewhere to show us where to go next."

"Mermaid friend?"

For some reason, the thought of Spero befriending a mermaid while we were apart made me uncomfortable. Mermaids were rumored to be unnaturally beautiful creatures who liked to lure sailors to their doom for fun, and I didn't want to lose him so soon after we had made amends. Ripples appeared on the lake. The head of a woman with lime-green hair popped out. She grimaced when she looked at my feet.

"Is this your friend?" she asked Spero. "She doesn't have a tail either! What sort of strange company do you keep?"

I glanced at Spero to see if her beauty had lured him into a trance, but the warmth his face held when he mentioned his sister had all but vanished.

"Katrina, I'd like you to meet Amoura, the other hero of Imperium. Amoura, this is Katrina."

I gave my best curtsy. "Well met, Katrina."

She huffed at my polite gesture. "Just because you have an unusual-looking tail doesn't mean you have to flaunt it."

"We need directions to the cave you told us about," said Spero. "Is there a way to get near it on land?"

Katrina looked thoughtful. "It's pretty far from here. I doubt you can make it without gills."

"This is a magic spring," I pointed out. "Maybe it'll give us magic healing powers?"

Without any warning, Spero removed his thick, hooded shirt to reveal a short-sleeved shirt underneath and dove into the water.

"We'll never know until we try."

"I didn't mean you should begin stripping and jump in!" I

gasped.

A blue aura surrounded him as he submerged his head in the water. I stared at the ripples appearing over the spot where he went under and waited with bated breath.

"You need to check on him," I told Katrina. "He's been down there too long."

She gazed at her reflection in the water. "Why should I? He's *your* weird-looking friend."

"He is *not* weird-looking!" I retorted.

Before I could go into a full panic, Spero's form rose toward us through the clear waters, emerging with a splatter of cool droplets landing on my face.

"Thank the saints!" I exclaimed. "We were so worried."

Katrina tried to push away the ripples that had formed on the surface. "Speak for yourself."

"It was like there was a bubble of air around me the whole time," Spero explained. "I think it was coming from my ring. I'm not sure if it would work for you. Maybe if we held hands the whole time…"

I reached for my pendant. "You're not the only one with an enchanted jewel."

My heart called out to Mama's spirit. After removing my shoes, I dipped my foot into the spring, shivering at the coldness of the water on my toes. Submerging myself further, my dress grew heavy, pulling me deeper. Once my head went under, a warm pink light surrounded me. Just as Spero had said, it felt no different from walking and breathing on land. The stone walls of the spring tapered down into a vast open sea. The calming waters soothed my nerves. I swam back to the surface, where a worried Spero looked as if he was just about to dive in after me.

"My necklace works the same way as your ring. It was wondrous. I'm eager to explore the depths of Imperium."

Spero nodded. "Then it's settled. Katrina, lead the way."

"All right, but I can't promise my father is going to let you into the labyrinth."

"We'll cross that bridge when we come to it."

The grouchy mermaid dove into the water. Spero took my hand even though I had already proven it wasn't necessary, and we floated down after her. The peaceful world below created a reprieve from my worries as lights danced around us in slow motion. Katrina was doing little to accommodate our lack of tails. Thankfully, the combined powers of our jewels made us feel lighter, allowing us to keep up with her by propelling ourselves through the deep by kicking our feet in unison.

The underwater world extended far beyond the shallow walls of the spring. Rocky passageways led to other channels throughout Imperium that weren't visible on land. The merfolk had free rein to travel anywhere in the waters below. Fish shimmered in every color of the rainbow, and beautiful coral structures of all shapes and sizes in pink, teal, and violet flourished around us.

A palace made of opalescent seashells shimmered in the distance, glowing in shades of pale pink and sea green. A mermaid with brown skin and a dark blue tail pushed past us, rushing toward the palace, forcing Spero and me apart. Without the added power of his ring, my body grew heavy against the current. I kicked harder, increasing my force to keep up with our previous speed. Katrina gained momentum ahead of us. Spero came back over and took my hand.

"That was rude. Are you okay?"

I nodded. "Why was she in such a hurry?"

Spero pulled me behind a rock, pointing in the direction the mermaid had come from. "I think that's why."

A large serpent slithered through the depths straight towards us. It had dark purple scales, black fins, and several rows of sharp, pointy teeth. Tendrils of lightning blinked off a narrow antenna extending from its angry face.

"What is that thing?" I whispered.

He shrugged. "Some kind of sea monster, I guess."

We were trapped. If we swam away from the rock, it would chase after us. If we didn't, it would be too late to escape. I looked around frantically and noticed a large colony of bright red fire coral that we had passed along the way. If we could lure it over there, it would be stunned long enough to get away.

I turned to Spero. "See that coral colony over there?"

"Yes. Do you have a plan?"

"I think so. When it gets close to us, you swim around it to the right, and I'll swim to the left. That should entrap it."

He nodded. "Good thinking. We'd better act fast. It's getting closer."

A horrible screech rippled through the water around us. I gestured to him, and we swam along the designated path. I could hear lightning crackling behind me from the serpent's antenna. The water grew thick with the vibrations of its movement. Spero swam a bit slower than me, so I adjusted my speed to match him, timing it so we would split just at the right moment. The serpent was gaining on us. I darted to the left of the coral just before it could snap at me with its fearsome maw.

Spero and I met back up on the other side of the colony.

The serpent slammed into the fire coral, writhing in agony. Strings of lightning surged up and down its body as its antenna reacted to the toxins in the coral. I held my breath until the thrashing finally stopped. It accepted its fate and slumped over in the coral.

"That was brilliant," said Spero.

"That was close," I replied.

Katrina doubled back toward us. She swam around the fire coral, completely ignoring the unconscious serpent. "You humans are so slow. Why'd you stop?"

Spero crossed his arms. "Oh, I don't know. Maybe because we didn't want to get eaten by a giant sea monster?"

She glanced at the unconscious serpent. "Yes, those have been popping up more than usual lately."

"And you didn't think to tell us?"

She shrugged. "You didn't ask. Do you want me to show you the rest of the way or not?"

Spero looked too angry to respond, so I took the initiative. "That would be lovely. We thank you."

After making our way through a narrow passageway that forced us to temporarily part ways again, we came to a large rock guarded by a muscular merman with an emerald green tail, gold adornments on his chest, and a messy green bun on his head.

Katrina regarded him with familiarity. "Hey, Pops."

The gruff-looking merman spoke with a surprising amount of affection. "Angelfish, what are you doing back so early? It isn't low tide already, is it?"

"No, but I ran into some weird land walkers, and they want to enter the cave for some reason."

He guffawed as though that was the silliest thing he had ever heard. "Don't they know no one can get in here? If we knew how to break the seal, we would have done it already. Ever since this cave appeared, the tides have been out of whack. Whirlpools have been appearing in strange places, and sea monsters have been rampant."

"That's exactly why we're here," said Spero. "We came to restore the crystal for Mistress Caliga. We also stopped a dangerous sea monster on the way over."

The guard gave us a suspicious look. "Why isn't Mistress Caliga with you then?"

"Maybe because she's a lazy—"

"She was preoccupied," I interrupted, hoping to avoid an international incident. "If we can enter the labyrinth, will you let us recover the crystal?"

"Sure, but like I said, no one can enter here, especially with those silly-looking legs of yours."

A large rock blocked the entrance to the cave. Strange symbols covered its surface. Spero placed his hand on it. Glowing blue symbols spiraled in a circular pattern around it.

The guard was impressed. "That's never happened before."

Spero nodded to me. I placed my hand next to his. Pink symbols spiraled around the blue ones in a complex pattern. Once the rock was covered in the glowing runes, it crumbled, leaving the entrance wide open.

"Well, I'll be," the guardian gasped. "Looks like the land walkers have a trick or two up their fins, after all."

Spero and I entered the cave. Pressure exploded in my chest from the swift change in environment, causing me to gasp for air. It was as though we were walking on dry land again. I stabilized my breathing as Spero did the same. The water behind us shimmered away into nothingness, leaving us stranded in the empty room. There was no turning back now.

I turned to Spero. "Are you ready?"

He flashed me a confident grin. "Let's do this."

Ten

Spero

The dry air of the labyrinth slammed into my throat like a semi-truck. It took a minute to adjust to the new atmosphere. The underwater world fizzled out behind us. We needed to find the exit to this place, or we'd be trapped. The room we entered reminded me of a cross between an aquarium and an ancient temple. Glowing blue and white shimmers danced over the glass floor like ripples. A bright light burned my eyes, making it impossible to look directly up. When I could breathe normally again without the aid of my ring, a strong saltwater scent filled the air.

I couldn't tell if we were still underwater or back on land, but that didn't matter as long as we stuck together. No matter what happened, I wouldn't leave Amoura's side again. I stayed close to her as we made our way down the eerily quiet hallway, our footsteps clinking over the glass floor.

The end of the first passageway led to a fork that split into three separate directions.

"What do you think?" I asked. "Should we try going straight through?"

She shrugged. "It's up to you. You're the V-D-O game expert."

I rolled my eyes at that, but she wasn't entirely wrong. This did look like a trial from a video game. I took a cautious step forward and immediately reared back to check for traps. When nothing happened, I gestured for Amoura to follow me. We approached the fork at the end of the hallway. I held my hand in front of each path, and nothing happened.

"It almost seems too easy," I said.

Amoura stifled a laugh. "You tarry as though waiting for something to happen. 'Tis merely a hallway."

She stepped forward, and a strong jet of water pushed her down the path to the right.

"Amoura!" I shouted.

The moment I stepped forward, a jet of water sprayed at me, forcing me down the left path. No matter how much I tried to fight it, it formed a powerful wall that pushed me in the opposite direction.

"Spero!"

Her voice echoed in the distance, barely audible through the sound of rushing water. Gazing through the cascading jets, I could discern her blurry silhouette that grew distant as the force of the jets continued to separate us.

"Amoura!" I shouted back. "Can you hear me?"

Her voice echoed from somewhere far away. "I'm here!"

My mind flashed back to Melanie's voice screaming for me from the other side of the portal. I couldn't let Amoura down too.

"Meet me on the other side!"

The stream finally dried up, leaving me drenched on the floor of a room containing a series of circular tubes that reminded me of totem poles with three stacks of rotating images. I'd played a lot of games with puzzles like this before. The trick was to spin the images until they lined up in the correct order. My sneakers slipped on the marble floor as I tried to get back to my feet, wringing water out of my t-shirt.

The first puzzle had three stacks of images with profiles of people's faces. The series of images on the top row contained a man with a long beard and crown, followed by a siren-like creature with white hair and pointy teeth. The last rotation revealed Caliga's sleazy mug. It was impossible not to recognize her shadowy complexion and lavender hair. Considering where I was, this was probably a test to identify the three sorceresses. I rotated the second portion until it revealed the beautiful woman I had seen floating in the chamber earlier, with blue hair, copper skin, and the same intense green eyes as Amoura.

As for the third sorceress, I'd never seen her face aside from the statue at the palace, which was stone gray. I glanced down at my ring and recalled the story my dad had told me about the pink-haired woman who mysteriously disappeared after she gave it to him. Was it possible that she was Estella, the third sorceress? The first image on the bottom row was of a young boy. I twisted it to reveal a woman with silvery skin and sleek black hair. One more rotation revealed a portrait of a pale pink-haired woman with small spectacles over her narrow eyes. When it clicked into place, the pillar lit up. The sound of gears turning echoed from somewhere nearby.

The second pillar was easy to solve. It was a blown-up

version of the Star Tech logo, which I'd assumed was also the official crest of Imperium. If it hadn't been for my ring or the tons of corporate merchandise we had at home, it probably would have been harder to solve. There were different variations of the star symbol with five or six points instead of four, and other icons to replace the sun and moon, like hearts or flowers, that all seemed to fit the overall design. I rotated the pillars to form the correct logo. With a mechanical click, the pillar lit up.

The stone door behind the pillars had blue waves carved into it like hieroglyphics. It slid open with a rough rumbling sound after I had solved the puzzles. I followed the path on the other side to a chamber where Amoura waited for me in front of another stone door with a similar design. Her face lit up when she saw me. Relief flooded through my shoulders, allowing me to relax for a brief moment. I didn't realize how worried I had been.

"Spero, thank the saints! I was afraid I'd lost you."

I flashed her a cocky grin. "No reason for that. I'm the video game master, remember?"

She frowned at the next door, which had a similar pattern carved into it. "It looks like this is the only room we haven't been to yet. Do you suppose the crystal shard is in there?"

"Only one way to find out."

I tried to shove the door open, but it wouldn't budge.

"Maybe there's another puzzle we missed," I said.

Amoura took a cautious step forward.

"Mayhap it's like the door at the entrance."

She placed her hand next to mine. The same pink and blue symbols we saw outside the entrance began spiraling into the center. The door vanished in a bright light, leading to an empty white room.

"There sure are a lot of empty rooms here," I said.

Amoura brushed her hand over her pendant. "We must be close. I feel Mama's energy is nigh."

I cautiously followed Amoura into the white void. The entryway disappeared the moment we were inside. What was the deal with these trick doors? With no way in and no way out, were we trapped?

"What do we do now?" Amoura asked.

I crossed my arms. "How am I supposed to know?"

Suddenly, there was a rumbling noise, and the bottom of the chamber began to pool with water, rising at a rapid pace. It flooded through my socks and made my jeans grow heavy.

I tried to remain calm. "This isn't ideal."

"But we can still breathe underwater, can we not?"

"I don't know if this is like the mermaid kingdom. We're in a magical labyrinth designed to test us. Our powers might not work the same way here. Let's look around and try to find a way out."

Amoura and I searched the room, but everything was white and barren. When the water rose to waist-deep, I held my breath and attempted to squat under it. Just as I suspected, my ring didn't activate.

"It looks like we have a time limit. Keep searching. Feel around the walls."

The walls were smooth and cold as ice. No matter where we felt, there didn't seem to be any hidden button or trigger to deactivate the trap. Soon, the water flooded up to our necks. There wasn't much time left.

"Spero..." Amoura sputtered in an attempt to keep her mouth above the water. "Are we going to drown?"

Fear weighed down the corners of her eyes. I couldn't give up on her. That would mean giving up on seeing Melanie again, too.

"No," I promised. "We're the essences of hope and love, remember? As long as we're together, we can survive anything."

She nodded at me before inhaling the last bit of air in the chamber. Breathing in deeply, I dove under. Water stung my eyes, but the empty chamber was clear as day with its bright, glowing walls. Amoura kept swimming around frantically in a desperate attempt to find a hidden switch or compartment. Dark circles formed in my vision as my oxygen depleted. I fought it with all my strength. There had to be a way out.

As I dove to the bottom and brushed my fingers over the floor, a flicker of glowing blue symbols appeared. I tugged Amoura's skirt and pointed at the floor. She didn't look like she could hold out much longer. With our last ounce of strength, we pushed ourselves to the bottom of the chamber as the pink and blue lights spiraled beneath our touch. The floor gave way beneath us, and the sweet relief of delicious air followed, as we landed with a thud on the hard floor of a new area. We clung to each other, gasping for breath as the dizziness and fear dissipated.

"You all right?" I let go of her so that she could stand up.

"I think so," she replied, wringing out the bottom of her dress. "It's a wonder we survived that."

"I told you. We're Imperium's heroes. It would take a lot more than that to defeat us."

She narrowed her eyes at me. "You must admit that was a close call."

I flashed her a confident grin. "It was probably designed to scare us, but lucky for you, I don't frighten that easily."

I jumped a mile back when a growling sound revealed that we weren't alone in the chamber.

Amoura smirked at me. "I thought you did not frighten easily."

We turned toward the sound. A giant blue squid-like creature loomed over us, blocking out the light from the center of the room. Behind it was a glowing round pedestal, like the ones in Caliga's lair. This one had a broken piece of blue crystal floating over it that gave off an eerie light. It had to be the water shard. I reached for my sword.

Amoura brushed her hand over her crossbow and then stopped. "Spero, I know not if I can do this."

As long as her pacifism didn't get us killed, I wasn't too concerned. Maybe this was my chance to be the hero I'd always dreamed of. I gave her my most reassuring smile.

"It's okay. You have a ranged weapon. You don't need to do anything unless I need backup. Just let me handle this."

"But—" she protested.

"Don't worry. I've beaten hundreds of video game bosses before. I know how this works. Besides, you already stopped another monster earlier today. I'll take care of this one."

I raced toward the squid with my sword drawn and slashed at its tentacles. To my surprise, the sword passed right through without causing any damage. I reached for one of the tentacles to find that it had no physical substance, like a projection. Was this thing just an illusion all along? Maybe we wouldn't have to fight it after all.

I headed toward the pedestal to grab the shard. The next thing I knew, the creature opened its ugly, round mouth, revealing several rows of sharp teeth. Something sharp stabbed me in the leg, knocking me off balance. It seemed like it came from inside the squid. When my vision entered the massive blue illusion, I figured out what was happening. This was an augmented reality field. The image of the squid was appearing over a smaller creature, making it harder to find. I slashed around inside the projection until my blade met resistance. A high-pitched braying alerted me to the location of my enemy.

Forcing my field of vision inside the giant blue mass of tentacles revealed what I was actually fighting. A pale blue unicorn with a glowing horn shaped like a conch shell raced toward me. Aiming its horn directly at my heart, the legendary creature was going straight for the kill without wasting any time. I blocked the horn with my sword, causing the illusion to flicker out. The impact made me slip on the wet ground. My sword flew out of my hand, sliding across the floor. I was defenseless. There was no button I could press to recover my sword.

The angry unicorn loomed over me, ready to take another stab at my heart. A shimmering blue hoof pressed on my stomach, preventing me from rolling out of the way. Amoura was my only hope now. I had no choice but to rely on her to do the one thing that went against everything she stood for. That goody two-shoes would have to come through for me now that it actually counted. My fate was in her hands.

Eleven

Amoura

error gripped my spine. My pulse raced as the unicorn restrained Spero, ready to strike the final blow. Time stood still. Raging voices shouted in my head, for me to help him. My hands shook, trying to find my crossbow, but all sense of feeling had abandoned me. The scent of cinnamon and roses teased my nose, reminding me that this unicorn held a piece of my mother's magic. How could I hurt it when a piece of her was buried within it?

The conch-shaped horn pressed dangerously close to his heart. If I didn't act now, I would lose him for good. Spero had so many chances to abandon me, yet he always came through when it mattered the most. I needed to do the same for him. This couldn't be the end of our journey. Save the unicorn or save him? I had to make a choice. The crossbow rattled in my hands as I took aim at the unicorn's heart. I squeezed my eyes shut as I released the bolt, blinding myself to the moment of impact.

The horrifying whinny that made me think of Jackson back at the farm signified that my aim was true. Gasping for air as though we were still trapped in the water chamber, I opened my eyes to make sure I wasn't too late. Spero was still alive, prone on the ground as the unicorn reared back, clinging to its final moments of life. I made my choice. Now I would need to live with the consequences.

With a piercing shriek, the unicorn bubbled into a transparent blue silhouette and burst into a blast of water that filled the shallow lake forming on the floor of the chamber, soaking the bottom of my dress, which was still damp from the previous area. A beam of light shot through the ceiling, taking the scent of Mama's magic with it, leaving a stale odor of salt in the air. Spero struggled to get up. My crossbow landed in the water with a splash. I lifted my skirt, which had grown heavy from the rising flood, and sloshed my way to his side.

"I knew you'd come through for me." He winced.

I knelt beside him, my heart pounding. I've already taken one life today. I refused to lose another one.

"You're hurt. Pray, let me look upon you."

He relaxed, allowing me to inspect his injuries. "Don't tell me you're a doctor too."

I smirked. Was he being cheeky, or were there actually female doctors whence he came?

"Hardly. My mother's necklace gives me healing powers."

"Of course it does. You're just full of surprises."

I assessed the gash on his ankle. It was deep, but it didn't appear to be broken. It reminded me of a time I helped a sheep whose leg had gotten caught in a fence. I rolled up the cuff of his trousers and brushed my still trembling fingers over the wound.

"Does this ail you?"

"No." The way he tensed told me otherwise.

I pray you, Mama, lend me your strength.

I pressed my pendant against my heart and felt for the warm threads of power it had granted me before. The strength to heal Spero was almost in my grasp, but fleeting. I drew on my fear of losing him when he was attacked and thought about the gentle way he held me when I saw Mama in the tower. A surge of power flowed through my veins. I grasped onto it, refusing to let go, pouring all of my strength into Spero's recovery.

The gash on his ankle receded, leaving a small bloodstain that washed away in the puddles that had formed all over the floor of the chamber. To my surprise, the usual sense of drowsiness that washed over me when I used my pendant wasn't as draining this time. Perhaps the magic was stronger in Imperium, or the piece of Mama's spirit we had freed from the unicorn was aiding me somehow.

Spero sat up and inspected my work. "Amoura, you're incredible."

I shook my head. "It wasn't me. It was Mama's magic. She let me borrow it before she went away."

"Even so, most people wouldn't use it as selflessly as you have."

I helped him back to his feet, and we collected our weapons. Every time I tried to lift my crossbow, it shook, splashing water around my ankles. I wondered if it was possessed until Spero placed his hand on my shoulder, and I realized how much I was still trembling. Taking a few deep breaths, I allowed him to stabilize me as I returned the weapon to its clasp around my waist. I leaned on Spero's shoulder, waiting for the shaking to cease.

"I'm sorry you had to strike the finishing blow. I wasn't expecting to fumble so quickly. I know it was hard for you."

"It was nothing," I lied. "Once I saw you were in trouble, it was an easy choice."

He narrowed his eyes at me, unconvinced. I inhaled and exhaled several times, syncing my breathing with his until the trembling stopped. Then I removed myself from his grasp, embarrassed to need his help with my emotional state yet again. After all, he had no reason to be nice to me. If I had been willing to fight alongside him, he probably wouldn't have gotten injured in the first place.

"I thank you," I mumbled, afraid to look him in the eyes.

"Are you ready to get the shard?"

The crystal shard floated ominously over the pedestal, its blue glow radiating off the puddles on the floor. We stared at it for a few seconds. I wondered what sort of power it contained.

"We just take it?" I asked. "What if it's another trap?"

"I think we've found just about every trap this labyrinth has to offer."

Spero grabbed the shard and winced.

I reached for my pendant. "Are you still injured?"

He made an odd expression. "It's not that. It's the shard. There's some kind of weird energy coming from it."

A loud rumbling noise came from somewhere nearby. We searched the area for the source. The whole room started shaking.

I shook my head. "You were so certain it wasn't another trap."

Before we had even a moment to brace ourselves, a giant whirlpool burst out from under us, pulling us into its spinning center. I clung to Spero.

"I think the labyrinth is destroying itself," he shouted over the sound of rushing water. "It was only here to protect the shard. This must be one of the anomalies Katrina's dad told us about."

"What do we do?" I shouted back.

His arm wrapped around my waist as the spinning increased. "Enjoy the ride?"

The whooshing sounds became unbearable, screaming in my head as we were pushed relentlessly in an endless spiral. Through the spinning waters, I could see the labyrinth collapsing around us. Sea salt burned my eyes until I was forced to shut them. Finally, we fell to the ground with a thud, and the horrible vibrations ceased. When I opened my eyes, Spero and I were back at the spring where we had encountered the mermaid. His blue hooded shirt and my shoes were there waiting for us.

I gripped my stomach, trying not to vomit. "I pray we never have to do anything like that again."

He grinned. "I take it you've never been on a roller coaster before."

I pulled my brown turnshoes back onto my feet. "Should I know what that is?"

"It's an amusement ride that shoots you all over the place really fast. This was tame compared to some of the ones I've been on."

I stared at him incredulously. "And people enjoy these torture devices?"

"Some do."

He opened his hand, revealing the blue crystal shard. Small cuts and scrapes marred his soft palm. He must have been holding onto it tightly to avoid losing it in the whirlpool.

"Do you need me to heal you again?" I asked upon seeing his hand.

"I think we've had enough magic for today."

"Excellent work, my children," my aunt's voice echoed from somewhere nearby. In a flash of purple light, she materialized at the edge of the spring. "I knew I could count on you. I will bring the shard back to its rightful place now."

Spero clutched it in his bruised hand. "Maybe we should be the ones to return it. We did recover it for you, after all."

"I'm flattered. You wish to return to the palace with me? You left so quickly last time, I had the impression it wasn't to your liking."

He clenched his fist around the shard. "What we don't like is being manipulated and spied on. What happened to that little fairy you sent after us, anyway?"

It occurred to me that I hadn't seen Fey since rescuing Sparky from the tree.

"She failed to keep the two of you on task, so she has been reassigned."

Did that mean Fey was a servant of Caliga? I tried to imagine Mama commanding an Imperial fairy as her guardian, but I simply could not picture it. Was she truly happy serving Lord Thomas as the wife of a tenant farmer when she had come from a place where magical beings served her? A sinking feeling entered my chest as I wondered if she only felt bound to our world because of me.

"Reassigned to where, exactly?" asked Spero.

My aunt pursed her lips. "That's of no matter to you. If you wish to return to the palace, I have no objection. You can have a nice meal and sleep in a warm bed before journeying to the next labyrinth."

I glanced at Spero. Knowing his status, both of those things should have been impossible to resist. Instead, he turned to me.

"What do you think, Amoura?"

It was odd to be consulted for my opinion by a noble. I needed to choose what was best for both of us.

"Sleeping on the ground was rough," I admitted. "Neither of us has had anything to eat or drink aside from the water in that spring. We should accept her offer. We thank you, Mistress Caliga."

"Please, we're family. Call me Auntie."

"Er, will Aunt Caliga suffice?"

"As you wish, my dear."

In a flash of light, we were back in my aunt's chamber. Spero placed the crystal shard on the pedestal with the blue waves carved on it. The shard lit up and hovered over its flat surface.

Spero's stomach growled loudly. "What was that you were saying about dinner?"

I stifled a giggle.

"Of course. Follow me. It's been so long since we've had guests here in my sisters' absence."

My heart fluttered as I thought about Mother asleep in the tower. I hoped it wouldn't be much longer before I could speak with her again.

Twelve

Spero

I figured I owed Amoura one after she saved my life, so I put the ball in her court to decide if she trusted Caliga enough to stay in the palace. It didn't hurt that my stomach couldn't resist a good meal, especially after everything we had just been through in the labyrinth and our bout with the sea monster. Since Caliga still needed us to get the rest of the shards, I wasn't too concerned about her trying to poison us yet.

The dining hall was unnecessarily opulent for a palace occupied by one. The long, rectangular table looked like it could seat at least twenty, and the tall chairs had intricate carvings of the Star Tech logo along with some symbols I didn't recognize along the legs and back. A massive crystal chandelier hung over us without any light bulbs, probably powered by magic. Amoura looked like she was in heaven, savoring every bite. It must have been a step up from the vegetables she harvested on her dad's farm.

The food in Imperium reminded me of some sort of avant-garde tea party. Multi-tiered platters held strangely colored bite-sized snacks and hors d'oeuvres. A delicious scent, like freshly baked brownies, filled the room. I helped myself to some flower-shaped cookies, a sandwich containing a juicy yellow fruit between two large spongy blue leaves, and some crunchy seaweed that tasted like french fries. With each mouth-watering bite, the growling in my stomach subsided a bit more. It would have been a great meal if it weren't for Caliga's presence looming over us.

"This food is heavenly!" Amoura exclaimed, patting the corner of her mouth with an embroidered lavender napkin. "I thank you, Aunt Caliga."

"It's the least I can do after what you've done for me, dearie. Just think, one quarter of Imperium's magic has been restored."

"About that," I interjected. "The merfolk said something about anomalies. Whirlpools, sea monsters, that sort of thing. Are we going to encounter more of that when we find the other labyrinths?"

Caliga's warm smile melted into a grimace. "Until the balance is restored, the magic of Imperium is bound to be unstable."

I crossed my arms. "And you just sent us out into the wild with a sword and crossbow, hoping for the best?"

"You would know a thing or two about hope," she mumbled.

"You're so powerful! The least you can do is get us to the labyrinths safely."

"If I recall correctly, you were the one who left immediately after arming yourself. No one was stopping you from asking for directions."

"That didn't stop you from coming to us the moment we recovered the first shard."

She sighed. "If you want my help, all you need to do is ask. I'm not your enemy."

"Aunt Caliga is doing the best she can," Amoura added.

"Besides," said Caliga, "the challenge of finding the labyrinths will help you acquire the skills you need to survive them when I'm not around. Surely you've learned by now that acquiring the shard wasn't as easy as simply walking in and taking it."

I slumped my shoulders. "I guess you have a point. At least we have a place to stay for tonight."

Amoura fidgeted with her long brown hair. "Aunt Caliga, may I ask you something?"

"Of course, dearie."

"Why did I sense my mother's magic within that unicorn we fought? Are the guardians of the crystal shards connected to her?"

Caliga pursed her lips as though she was deciding how to answer. "Solara gave her powers to the guardians to prevent the crystal shards from being discovered by our sister. A foolish decision, if you ask me, considering the consequences it's had on Imperium."

"So, if we destroy the guardians, Mama will wake up?"

"I'll need the power of the crystal to wake her. Bring me all the shards, and you will get your wish."

I pushed my empty dish aside. Its gilt edges glinted under the light of the chandelier.

"Where is this other sorceress, anyway?" I asked. "I keep hearing about the three sorceresses, but we've only seen two of them."

"Estella has not been seen since her betrayal. She is a powerful architect of magic. If she doesn't want to be found, she has ways to make herself all but disappear."

My foot bounced against the sword I had swung over the back of the chair. "Is there a chance we'll have to fight her too?"

"Doubtful. She doesn't like spending much time around other people."

That lined up perfectly with my dad's story about the pink-haired woman who mysteriously disappeared right after giving him my ring. If Estella provided something that got me out of so many scrapes in the past, how could she be our enemy?

I frowned. "Fey told us that Estella created the crystal. Is that true?"

Caliga looked even more irritated by that question. "As a magical architect, creating devices to harness power was her specialty as a guardian. However, she hasn't been much help with that since she disappeared after Solara went into stasis."

"If Estella created the crystal, why would she want to destroy it?" asked Amoura. "Could she not just make another one?"

Caliga frowned. "She used very rare materials that can only be forged once from our world. The crystal is one of a kind. It cannot be reproduced."

"That doesn't explain why she would want to destroy it," I pointed out.

Caliga shook her head. "I do not claim to understand Estella's intentions. I only know that she needed to be stopped, and Solara sacrificed everything she had to do so."

Amoura looked apprehensive. "I do hope to meet my other aunt someday, even if she has done these terrible things."

Caliga gave her a sympathetic smile. "Maybe one day you will. It's getting late. You can choose any rooms you like in the east wing. We can make arrangements for the next labyrinth in the morning."

Amoura and I found rooms near each other in a red corridor with golden accents. I turned the crystal doorknob and pushed open the door, which had a gold filigree pattern painted over it. A large window in the guest room overlooked the silver springs, rainbow-colored flowers, and deep purple night sky of Imperium. A thick blue comforter with silver embroidery draped over the large canopied bed. It wasn't as soft as memory foam, but it sure beat sleeping on the ground. I lay awake for what felt like hours before I heard soft footsteps outside my door. The hinges creaked as I pushed it open. Amoura tiptoed down the hallway. She jumped back a foot when she saw my door open.

"I'm sorry. I didn't mean to wake you," she stammered.

I shook my head. "You didn't. I couldn't sleep."

"Nor I. I keep wondering if this is what Mama intended for me when she left. In her current state, there's no way to ask her. I know Aunt Caliga says Imperium needs our help, but it makes no sense that my other aunt would be so greedy over her own creation."

She slumped onto the ground as though she could barely hold herself up. Bags had formed under her eyes. If she kept worrying about this, we'd never make it through the next labyrinth in one piece. There had to be a way to help get her mind off the crystal and her crazy family for the time being.

"As long as we're both awake, I saw a balcony down this corridor. How would you like to do some stargazing?" I suggested.

Her face lit up. "I love stargazing."

That was one thing we had in common. Amoura followed me down the hall. We slipped through a sheer purple curtain that led us to the edge of a wide balcony surrounded by crystal pillars. The night sky of Imperium spread over us like a giant canopy.

I tried to find the Little Dipper to locate the North Star, but nothing came close. Struggling to connect the dots, I was able to make out a rough heart, a unicorn, and some sort of swirling pattern. "I don't recognize any of these constellations."

She drew her fingers between the stars as if trying to solve a puzzle. "Me neither. I guess we really are in another world."

The twinkling dots glittered brighter than I had ever seen in California. I couldn't help but notice how lovely Amoura looked under their dim pulsating light. "It is beautiful, though."

She leaned on my shoulder. "Indeed."

I wasn't prepared for the way my heart started racing. Amoura's presence was so comforting that I almost wished I could take her back home with me after all this was over, but that wouldn't be right. Not only was she born centuries before me, but she belonged to this crazy world, which had no place for me once the crystal was restored. There was no point in thinking about how she made me feel. Any future between us would be impossible. Besides, I still had to look out for Melanie. Who knew what sort of trouble she could have gotten into since my disappearance?

"Amoura," I whispered.

"Yes?" She gazed up at me with her sparkling green eyes that shone brighter than the stars of Imperium.

I had to fight this. It would be wrong to give her false hope. Holding back the powerful desire to pull her toward me and never let go, I took a step back.

"Are you feeling better now?"

"Aye. Thank you, Spero."

My breath caught at the way she said my name. Maybe if I stopped looking at her, these feelings would go away. I didn't have time for this. We were two pawns in a much larger game. I had to stay in control and see this thing through to the end.

"Good. Let's try to get some sleep. We have a long day ahead of us tomorrow."

"Of course."

I could see that she was disappointed. She followed me back to the red corridor, where I hoped we could finally get a good night's rest.

Thirteen

Amoura

My head sank into the soft, feathery pillow. The flutter of my heart echoed through the large, silent room. Why did I feel heat rushing to my cheeks every time I was near him? Back home, it would have been an honor just to be acknowledged by a noble. Spero not only treated me like a peer, but he was also going out of his way to help me restore the crystal for Mama, even though it was nothing but an inconvenience for him. That had to mean something, didn't it? Helping me wouldn't grant him land or titles. In fact, we'd probably never see each other again once Mama woke up and sent us both back home. Were all boys this confusing, or did courting rituals change after hundreds of years?

The rose-colored comforter made me feel warm and cozy, like a fresh-baked pie. I had to keep reminding myself that my aunt had invited me to her home and that I belonged here. The scent of cherry blossoms danced on my nose, and the thick walls kept out all the cold night air. In any other circumstances, such luxuries would belong only to royalty, not farm girls like me. I never imagined I'd have the opportunity to sleep in such an extravagant room. Even the walls were adorned with shimmering golden embellishments that reflected glints of starlight from the night sky through the lace curtains. What sort of life would I have had if my mother had raised me here?

I woke with the dawn. A disquieting silence filled the halls, and I had no desire to disrupt anyone's slumber. Did Mama still have dreams all the time she slept? Walking up the long spiral staircase helped me burn off the energy I usually used helping Father with morning chores. Bracing myself, I squeezed my eyes shut before entering the small, circular room. I took a deep breath and then opened them. She was still there, floating in her chamber. The scent of cinnamon and roses was stronger than before we defeated the unicorn. It was as though she could wake up at any second.

"I love you, Mama," I whispered. "I shall do everything I can to save you."

"I had a feeling I'd find you here."

My heart skipped a beat. I turned to find Spero standing at the entrance with his arms crossed. He looked tired and groggy. Why did he always know where to find me?

I pointed an accusing finger at him. "You startled me!"

"She's going to be okay, you know. You don't need to keep checking."

I pulled a lock of hair over my shoulder. "I just needed to speak with her. It's been so long."

"You can always talk to me. I'll actually respond, too."

I gasped at the insensitive comment. "Was that a jest? It

wasn't very amusing."

He glanced away, brushing a hand through his yellow hair. "You're right. I'm sorry."

"Besides," I said with a smirk, "even in this state, she's still a better conversationalist than you."

He chuckled. "If anyone else said that, I'd be hurt, but that was pretty good for you."

I took that as a small victory. "How did you know to come here, anyway?"

He shrugged. "You've told me enough times how important she is to you. It only made sense."

How could someone who grew up so differently from me know me so well?

An illusion of Caliga's face materialized over us, floating in a circle of light.

"Good morning," she said.

"Good morrow," I responded.

"Are you ready to enter the next labyrinth?"

I glanced at Spero, who shrugged, leaving the decision in my hands again.

"Yes, I believe so, Aunt Caliga."

"Wonderful! Come meet me in the dining hall for breakfast when you're ready."

The illusion shimmered away like steam escaping from a teapot.

"Bossy as ever," Spero mumbled, following me down the stairs.

"She means well… I think."

He struggled to keep up with my pace. "I don't."

"Why are you even helping her then? We could probably convince her to send you home if we tried."

He paused on a curved step that creaked beneath him. "Do you really think I'm doing this for her?"

I turned to face him. "I have no idea why you're doing this. I've been trying to figure it out ever since I asked her to send you back, and you refused."

His blue eyes gazed at me with such sincerity that my breath caught in my chest. "Amoura, it's clear how much all of this means to you. You've been separated from your family for too long, and if there's anything I can do to help, I'm more than willing."

Heat flooded my cheeks. "You have my gratitude. I know not what else to say."

"Besides, a crybaby like you will never get anything done without me around to keep you in line."

I shoved him, forgetting I was standing on a narrow step, and nearly lost my footing. He caught my waist, saving me from an embarrassing tumble. I turned around and continued to the bottom of the tower without another word.

Caliga was waiting for us in the dining hall behind a spread of biscuits and tarts that emitted a warm scent that reminded me of the market back home.

I curtsied. "Good morrow, Aunt Caliga."

Though I had already greeted her illusion, it only seemed polite to do so again in the flesh.

"Good morning, children."

Spero gave her a standoffish wave of the hand as he crammed a biscuit into his mouth.

Caliga's posture stiffened. "Are you ready to enter the next labyrinth?"

I washed down a sweet tart with a few sips of delicious spring water. "I believe so."

"Good. Follow me."

Caliga led us down the pink carpeted hallway to the palace entrance.

"You'll find the fire labyrinth in an environment that isn't suitable for your mortal dispositions. Thus, I've arranged a ride for you outside. I believe you've already been acquainted."

"We have?" I scrunched my eyebrows, trying to recall who we'd met so far on our journey.

Spero opened the grand marble door to find Sparky and his mother perched in the courtyard. The baby dragon bobbed through the air, trying to reach me, but his special wing held him back. I reached out and grabbed him, smothering him against my pendant. He cooed as his head rubbed against me, bringing a smile of delight to my face.

"It's good to see you, too, Sparky."

"We get to ride a dragon? Cool!" Spero exclaimed.

"It's the only way to navigate the volcanoes of the Glowing Canyon," responded Caliga.

His excitement melted away. "Did you say volcanoes?"

"You can return here once you've recovered the fire shard." She vanished in a flash of purple light.

The dragon's scales were sharp, but their coarse texture created easy hand and footholds to climb onto its massive back, like sitting on a large boulder. Spero climbed up behind me.

"Hang on tight, Amoura. It sounds like this is going to be a rough trip."

Sparky clutched onto the collar of my dress. His mother's scaly hide made for a rough mount, but the scales grasped against my dress, allowing for little fear of falling. I braced myself as the massive dragon spread its green, bat-like wings, revealing their lavender undersides. Sparky began pulling at my necklace, causing the chain to irritate the back of my neck.

"Pray, do not touch tha-AAAAAAAAAAAAAAAH!"

I wasn't prepared for the sudden increase in velocity as we shot up to the fuchsia sky of Imperium. Spero placed his arm around my waist, causing heat to flood my cheeks again.

"Not used to flying, are you?" Spero asked from behind me, stifling a giggle.

I turned around. "Do you mean this is normal whence you come?"

He gave me a sheepish grin. "Not this, exactly, but my parents have a private jet."

I widened my eyes at him. "You have a *what*?!"

Sparky's mother stabilized her wings as we plateaued into a comfortable glide.

Is my mommy a private jet?

A tiny voice came from my lap that sounded like a small child. Could it be Sparky? What had he done to my pendant? Maybe Mama's magic let me understand him.

"Did you hear that?" I asked Spero.

"Hear what?"

"Sparky just said something!"

Mistress Amoura can understand me now! Sparky made a new friend!

"Do not call me that. I'm not a sorceress. Just Amoura will suffice."

Spero chuckled behind me.

I turned back around, narrowing my eyes at him. "Does something amuse you?"

"Even the dragon knows how important you are. Just admit that you're royalty here."

"I am not!" I huffed.

"You're the daughter of one of the three sorceress guardians of Imperium. That basically makes you a princess."

I crossed my arms. "It does not!"

Princess Amoura. Sparky likes the sound of that!

"Look what you've done! Now Sparky thinks I'm a princess too."

"He's not exactly wrong."

In a fit of frustration, I began to wobble, forcing my vision to overlook the ground far below us. A strange sensation overcame me as I gazed down at the brightly colored trees. They looked like little jewels sparkling in a massive treasure chest. Despite their beauty, a terrible fear seized the pit of my chest as though I was falling. I didn't realize how heavily I was breathing until Spero grabbed my shoulders, forcing me to face him. The dizziness went away, replaced by a heat flowing through my cheeks as his blue eyes met mine.

"Don't look down. You'll make yourself sick."

"Is that something you learned on your private jet?"

"Actually, I like looking out the window from high up, but it isn't for everyone."

"Does everyone own some sort of flying transport device in the future?"

"Most people just have cars. They're like carriages that can go as fast as two hundred horses."

I grimaced, thinking about how much work it would be to groom two hundred horses at a time.

"How can they care for so many horses?"

"They don't. Cars run on gasoline or electricity. Technology has come a long way in half a millennium."

I glanced back up at him.

"Will you tell me more about it?"

He adjusted his position so that it was easier for us to face each other.

"Where do I begin? My dad runs a tech company that makes smart devices, which are like magic wands that tell people where to go, what time it is, what the weather is going to be like, and let them talk to each other from all across the world."

"So everyone's life is run by a magic wand in the future?"

Spero chuckled. "Maybe some. My parents' lives are for sure."

"You said your father runs his own company, but you've told me little about your mother."

"My mom's a famous actress. She's always traveling for gigs and press tours, so we don't get to see her very much."

"I love the theater!" I exclaimed. "She must be very talented."

"I guess. In the future, people can watch recordings of the same shows from anywhere at any time. It's kind of like your aunt's crystal ball, but bigger."

"That's amazing! It's no wonder you're not used to being outside as much as I am. You still have farmers, right?"

I wondered if Father would have chosen a different line of work in Spero's time.

"Yeah, but it's not a very popular profession. Most people prefer to stay indoors and work on their smart devices."

"Are the devices as smart as people?"

"No, but they're getting scarily close."

I pursed my lips. "I know not whether that's a good thing."

"Yeah, some people are worried the machines might try to take over the world one day."

"Mayhap they need a magic crystal too."

The dragon circled a mountain with red liquid spewing out

of it. Heat radiated through my body.

Spero grimaced. "Caliga didn't say the volcano was active!"

I fanned myself with my hand as sweat poured down my dress. "How are we supposed to enter the labyrinth now?"

Don't worry. Dragons are fireproof!

"Indeed," I replied, "but what about us?"

Spero leaned toward me. "Who are you talking to?"

"Sparky. He says dragons are fireproof."

"Actually, that could be helpful. If we can find the entrance to the labyrinth, the dragon can climb right up to it without us having to step into molten lava. Remember how everything outside disappeared when we entered the water labyrinth?"

I leaned toward Sparky. "That might work. Sparky, tell your mother to fly low to the ground. We need to find a passageway of some kind."

Sparky gave an adorable screech, and the heat rose even more as we glided over the burning liquid. No matter where we flew, nothing but molten rock surrounded us.

"Tell her to fly over the mouth of the volcano," Spero suggested.

Sparky screeched to his mother, and up we went. A big bubble protruded from the mouth of the volcano, with lava erupting around it. An empty room with a red glass floor shimmered inside the bubble, similar to the entrance of the water labyrinth.

Spero hoisted himself to his feet. "Looks like this is our stop."

I gave him an incredulous glare. "Surely, you intend not to jump."

"Do you have a better idea?"

"I—no, but—"

Before I could finish my thought, we fell toward the bubble at an alarming rate. Familiar pink and blue magic symbols lit up around us as we plummeted into the chamber. The entrance vanished as quickly as it had appeared.

"You okay?" Spero held out his hand to help me up.

I ignored him and pulled myself back to my feet without his help. It all happened so quickly, but I was pretty sure he pulled me down with him.

"*Never* do that again."

"You know the rules. I would have fallen into the volcano if you weren't with me."

Where did Mommy go?

I looked down and realized I had been clutching Sparky the entire time. I guess there was no rule against anyone entering the labyrinth *with* the essences of hope and love.

I held the baby dragon in front of Spero. "Looks like we have a stowaway."

Sparky will help!

I placed my hand on my hip. "We shall see about that."

Fourteen

Spero

L ike the water labyrinth, the entryway to the fire labyrinth had glass floors, only these were red instead of blue and had a smoky pattern trailing across them. The mouth of the volcano above us vanished, eliminating the chance of stray lava dripping through. The adorable dragonling that Amoura had bonded with might come in handy for the trials ahead.

As I took a step forward, a blast of smoke clogged my nasal passages, forcing me to breathe through my mouth. Once I stopped coughing, I examined the walls. Tiny, nearly invisible holes lined each side of the room in a long row, indicating a motion-activated trap. I'd played several video games with these before.

I turned to Amoura. "Okay, here's what we're going to do. On my count, we're going to hold our breath and run to the end of this hallway as fast as possible. Ready?"

She nodded, clutching the baby dragon in her arms.

"One… two… three… Now!"

Amoura shot off ahead of me like a stray bullet, dodging every smoke stream in her path. Struggling to keep up with her, I accidentally inhaled a little smoke, triggering another coughing fit. My lungs burned, and my eyes were watering by the time I caught up with her at the end of the hallway.

"Spero, are you all right?" Her eyes were filled with concern.

"Yeah," I wheezed. "I do this in video games all the time."

"What happens now?"

Without warning, a huge pillar of flame burst out from the floor, blocking the next area. I instinctively pushed Amoura behind me. Heat radiated throughout my body. Waterfalls of sweat poured down my back from the intense heat. Amoura was struggling with the dragonling.

"No, Sparky, you are not going in there!"

I turned around, moving as far from the scorching heat as I could get.

"What's he saying?" This would have been a lot easier if we could both understand him.

"He wants to block the flames so we can get through."

I considered the idea. If dragons were fireproof, Sparky would make a great shield. However, I also understood Amoura's reluctance due to her protectiveness of his deformed wing.

"I hate to say it, but that might be the only way through."

Sparky took that as permission and pummeled himself out of Amoura's grasp. His bad wing made him fly in erratic patterns, forming strange shapes in the huge bonfire blocking our path. Lowering himself to the ground, he was able to form just enough of a gap near the bottom of the flame for us to crawl through. His inconsistent flight pattern didn't do much to calm my nerves.

"You first," I told Amoura.

She darted through the gap, popping out on the other side of the flame like a spring. Grabbing my chance, I bent down and shoved myself through.

"Spero, your shirt!"

I looked down. A small flame was traveling up the string of my hoodie like a fuse. I patted it out, burning the palm of my hand in the process.

"Thanks."

The dragon bobbed and weaved its way back to Amoura.

"Yes, Sparky," she said. "You were very helpful."

I rubbed my eyes until the burning stopped, and squinted as the world around me slowly came into focus. Black molten rock was spread across the floor in lumps and craters. Ash swirled in my face, forcing me to protect my eyes as I struggled to breathe. The bumpy surface was interrupted by a series of circular plates that looked like manhole covers.

Covering my nose and mouth with my arm, I made my way to the center of the room and slid my fingers under one of the covers. It gave way without much effort.

"One of these hatches must lead to the next area."

Sparky slammed into me, pushing me out of the way as an enormous bonfire spewed out of the hole I had just uncovered. My head rolled against the bumpy black floor. I sat up on the uneven surface.

"Okay, so not that one."

Amoura was at my side in an instant. "Are you all right?"

I nodded. "Thanks to Sparky."

The dragonling puffed out its chest with glee. Amoura

turned to him.

"Is that really a good idea?" she asked.

"What's he saying?"

"Sparky wants to check the hatches himself. He'll not be affected by the flames."

I got back on my feet. "That would be a big help. It's a good thing he tagged along."

Taking that as an invitation, Sparky darted from manhole to manhole, digging his claws under the steel plates and tossing them aside. More pillars of flame filled the room. Sweat poured down my shirt. Smoke filled my lungs to the point where it felt like I was choking. A quick glance at Amoura told me she wasn't doing much better.

"He says he found the exit," she wheezed between coughs.

"Great," I rasped. "Where is it?"

"Erm…"

She glanced around, but all we could see were open flames in every direction. I could have sworn all my skin was about to melt off my bones. Finally, the scaly bundle of joy burst through a pillar of fire and led us around the rocky walls to a singular gap between two beams of flame. Eager to be able to breathe again, I jumped down the opening and crashed onto a rocky platform. Dark ash smeared across my hands as I pushed myself back to my feet. Amoura came down after me with a much more graceful landing. Sparky hovered over us.

We were standing at the precipice of a giant pit of bubbling hot magma. In the center was some kind of goopy lava monster guarding a glowing red crystal shard on a pedestal. At least we were close. A series of black rocks floated in the burning acid, the only safe route to the shard. Amoura counted them on her fingers as though calculating the best path. Heat surged through the air like tidal waves running up and down my back.

"This does not appear difficult," she said. "We just need to jump on the rocks, right?"

I took a step back as a giant bubble of magma burst in front of me, its heat radiating through my shirt. "Just don't stumble."

She leaped onto the first rock as if playing a simple game of hopscotch. "I used to skip rocks all the time in the creek as a child. This seems not all that different."

With all the grace of a prima ballerina, Amoura hopped, skipped, and twirled from stone to stone, expertly navigating her way to the center. Her performance entranced me so much that I almost forgot about the monster waiting for us on the other side.

"Spero!" she shrieked.

The giant mass of burning red liquid loomed over her as she reached the central platform.

"Shoot! I'm coming!"

This is no time to hesitate. If she can do it, you can too.

I jumped onto the first rock and paused to test its stability. I felt it begin to sink into the boiling pit, melting the soles of my sneakers. How did she make this look so easy? I launched myself onto the next one, which looked bigger, but my awkward movement caused me to stumble. Heat singed through my socks, reminding me of the consequences of a wrong move. Meanwhile, the monster chased Amoura to the fiery edge of the platform. Adrenaline kicked in as I raced to her aid.

"Shoot it, Amoura! Use your crossbow!"

Amoura fired a shot through the mass of orange goop, sending it far back enough for her to reach safer ground. Just like the water monster, the image of dripping orange sludge blinked out a few times, revealing a fearsome red unicorn with a spiky orange and yellow horn. Why were they always unicorns? I jumped onto three nearby rocks in one sporadic motion, inching closer to the platform. There was no time for mistakes. I had to reach her.

Amoura was doing her best to lure the creature as close to the center of the platform as she could, away from the molten lava surrounding it. Smart girl. Unfortunately, this also put her at the beast's mercy. It slashed toward her face with its horn, but she blocked it with her arm, which tore open in a gruesome-looking gash. As it was about to strike again, my foot made contact with the central platform. I raced at the beast, blocking its horn with my sword. Amoura dodged out of the way, a faint pink glow appearing over her injured arm.

The unicorn brayed ferociously at the intrusion, switching its attention to me. I wouldn't let this be like the battle at the water labyrinth. This time, I'd see it through to the end. Clutching my sword with both hands, I slashed a clean strike across its throat, avenging the injury it gave Amoura. With an ear-piercing shriek, the unicorn exploded into a blast of flames, radiating intense heat over both of us. Then it went out like a birthday candle.

I raced to Amoura's side. A long slash ran down the length of her forearm, which looked unnaturally red in the glow of the surrounding lava. She winced, clutching her elbow. A bright light emitted from her pendant, stitching the wound shut by magic, leaving a trail of dried blood in its wake. The spell must have worn her out because her body started to wobble dangerously close to the edge of the lava. I raced over and wrapped my arm around her shoulders, ignoring the way my heart raced as her delicate, calloused hands clung to my arm.

"Are you okay?"

She brushed her fingers over her pendant and gave me a warm smile. "I heal quickly. I thank you for your help."

"Don't let me take all the credit. You handled yourself pretty well back there."

"That unicorn smelled like Mama's magic, just like the first one."

I wasn't sure what she meant. All I smelled the whole time was ash and smoke. I let her go when she seemed okay to stand on her own and headed for the central pedestal.

The crystal glowed an unnatural red, hovering in the air. I placed my hand near it to gauge the temperature in case it burned like everything else in this place. It was warm, but not scalding. I removed it from the pedestal. A surge of energy pulsed through my body, just like when I had touched the water shard. Amoura's eyes widened in concern, but before I could explain anything, Sparky started flapping his wings all around us with urgency.

The ground began rumbling. Lava bubbled and rippled like a tidal wave. I pulled Amoura toward me just in time for the platform we were standing on to shoot up into the air like a rocket. The next thing I knew, we were blasting out of the volcano, platform and all. Luckily, Sparky's mother was there to catch us.

"Talk about an explosive exit," I joked.

Amoura didn't look amused. She glanced down at the dragonling.

"Sparky wants to know if he can come with us to look for the rest of the crystal shards."

She glanced at me, waiting for my input. "I don't see why not. It wouldn't hurt to have a dragon on our team."

Amoura looked back at the dragonling. "Mayhap you should ask your mother."

The dragons screeched at each other in a conversation we couldn't understand.

"He says she's okay with it as long as we look after him. She doesn't want his special wing to encumber his growth."

I nodded. "I think that's reasonable."

Sparky puffed out his green, scaly chest and beamed at me. His mother flew us directly back to the palace. We landed on the ground with a thud. Our adventure had knocked us both out for at least the rest of the day. I reached for Amoura's hand and helped her up to the front door of the palace, where Caliga was waiting for us.

"I take it you have the crystal shard."

"Right here." No sooner had I revealed it than she snatched it from my hand.

"Very good. I may not be able to provide as much assistance with the final two labyrinths."

I scoffed at her. "What assistance did you provide? The dragon did all the work!"

"And we're deeply grateful for it," Amoura added, elbowing me in the ribs.

Caliga raised an eyebrow. "And I suppose you could have tamed the dragon without my assistance as a sorceress guardian?"

I sighed. "I guess not."

"I take it you're both tired from your journey. Feel free to take advantage of the palace before setting out for the next labyrinth."

I rubbed my arm, which was covered in ash and probably a few burn marks. "I could go for a bath in a giant bucket of ice right now."

"That can be arranged."

Sparky followed Amoura inside. Caliga raised an eyebrow at them. "I see you've decided to take on a familiar."

Amoura cradled the dragon. "Sparky's a friend."

Caliga sighed. "Any friend of yours is a friend of mine. Just don't let him make a mess in my palace."

It looked like this was going to be another long night.

Fifteen

Amoura

I curled up in a deep purple velvet armchair in the luxurious guest room. Sparky's claws poked tiny holes in the arm of the chair before I could stop him. The soft upholstery massaged the minor burns and cuts on my arms from the hazards of the labyrinth. I feared growing so accustomed to it that I might forget my true stature. Did Spero enjoy such a comfortable lifestyle every day? I couldn't blame him for wanting to return home as soon as possible.

Why can't Sparky stay with Spero? Sparky likes Spero!

I pulled him into my lap, forcing his claws to rip out of the chair's arm.

"Because Spero cannot understand you like I can."

Then why can't Spero stay here with us?

Heat flooded my cheeks as I recalled the way he held me in the labyrinth after I had expended too much energy healing my injury.

"It just isn't how things are done."

Why not?

"Because he's...you know..."

Does Amoura want to make dragonlings with Spero?

"Sparky!" I shrieked. "Come help me pick a dress for the morrow."

Tatters marred the hem of my work dress after running through flames, and tears and bloodstains ravaged the sleeve that covered my injured arm. Spero's outfit had not fared much better. To help make us more comfortable in the palace, Aunt Caliga enchanted both of our wardrobes to create new clothes for us. I sifted through one luxurious gown after another. The sheer fabrics with shimmering linings looked more fit for a princess than a girl adventuring through the woods and fending off magical obstacles.

Amoura would look pretty in this one!

Sparky buried his little head under the skirt of an enormous fire-red gown with layers upon layers of orange and yellow tulle. It looked like something a queen would wear to a ball if she were trying to divert everyone's attention.

I couldn't help the smirk that pulled at my lips as Sparky tangled himself in the layers of tulle.

"Nice try, but it isn't quite me."

Digging through the excessive layers of gowns, I pulled out a modest pale pink tea dress with green vines and flowers embroidered across the bodice and skirt. It had only a single petticoat, making it ideal for travel. On a shelf below was a pair of comfortable-looking pink moccasins, a shade darker than the dress.

I held up my selection. "What about this one?"

Sparky crawled out from the mass of fabric.

Amoura would look pretty in that too! Amoura looks pretty in everything!

I gave his little green nose a light tap. "You flatterer."

Stars glittered in the deep violet night sky through the tinted glass window, reminding me that I was in another world. I recalled how much I'd enjoyed stargazing with Spero the night before and how hesitant he had been to get close to me. It might be best not to make a habit of that.

"I think I'll go check in on Mama before bed."

Sparky wants to meet Amoura's mommy! Is she big and powerful like Sparky's?

"I'm afraid she isn't exactly in a state to meet anyone right now."

Sparky darted onto my shoulder. His tiny claws irritated some of my burns.

Is she sick?

"Something like that."

I climbed the familiar spiral staircase to my mother's tower. Defeating the second unicorn should have restored some more of her powers. The scent of cinnamon and roses was stronger than ever. Mama sat upright in the crystalline chamber as though she had been taking a light nap. As I approached the glowing cylinder, her eyes fluttered open. My breath caught in my chest.

"Mama!" I shouted through the force field. "It's me, Amoura!"

Tiny slits appeared below her copper eyelids. She gave me a warm, loving smile. Then, her eyes shot open in alarm. Weakly, she reached toward me. I placed my hand on the other side of the force field, which separated us by a thin layer of translucent pink magic. It vibrated with warmth.

"Can you hear me?" I asked, praying she was ready to return.

She shook her head, gazing at me with sadness and worry. Frantically, she began pointing toward me and then behind her. I clutched my pendant, hoping it would help me interpret the message. The look of alarm on her face filled me with a sense of urgency. My heart was racing. I had to figure out what she was saying.

"You want me to go back?"

She nodded just before drifting back into a deep sleep.

"Back whence? I understand not! Mama, I beg you, wake up!"

Sparky appeared through the pink, translucent filter on the other side of the tube.

Amoura's mommy is very sleepy.

I pounded my fists on the force field until they throbbed, reopening some of the burns from the labyrinth.

"Mama! What do you want me to do? Tell me, I pray you!"

My eyes burned as my vision went blurry. My knees gave out when a familiar embrace surrounded me. Spero's arms wrapped around my shoulders, providing a lifeline to cling to yet again in my moment of grief.

"Amoura, what happened?" His voice was filled with concern.

"'Twas Mama," I sobbed. "She was awake. She wanted to tell me something, but then she fell asleep again. There must be a way to wake her up for good!"

I turned to face him. He wiped some stray tears off my cheek and pulled me close enough to hear his heart thudding in his chest. So much for not being a crybaby.

"There's no reason to be upset. If she's starting to wake up, that's a good thing. It means that what we're doing is working.

We just need to find two more crystal shards, and you'll have her back again. That's what you want, isn't it?"

I leaned into his steadfast presence. "Yes, but I know not if that's what *she* wants. You should have seen her. It was as though she was terrified to see me."

He gave my arm a gentle tug toward the door. "We can figure all this out after the crystal is restored and your mother wakes up. For now, let's get some sleep, okay?"

Amoura should ask Spero to sleep in our room. We can have a slumber party!

"Sparky, no!"

The dragonling clawed Spero's shoulder. Spero patted its little head.

"What did he say?"

"Um, he wanted to stay out all night and try to improve his flying. I told him he needed to rest."

Spero addressed Sparky in a tone that he probably used a lot with his sister. "You be a good dragon and listen to Amoura. We need everyone nice and strong to find the next crystal shard."

That's not what I said!

Spero walked me back to my room. My hand lingered for a moment on the shimmering knob. In truth, I always felt better when he was near. Yet, he deserved someone better than me. Someone closer to his social class who knew what a V-D-O game was and didn't cry all the time.

"I thank you. You always seem to know just what I need."

His hand brushed through his slick, yellow hair. "I know you didn't ask for any of this, so it wouldn't be fair for me to blame you. You're going through a lot right now. Hopefully, what we're doing will restore what you've lost."

"You've been so kind to me when I've done nothing but burden you with my troubles. I wish there were a way I could pay you back for all your help."

He shook his head. "There's no need for that. This whole experience has been a wild ride for me. I never thought I'd get to ride a dragon or fight in a real battle. It's way crazier than virtual reality."

I brushed my hand over his. "I never could have done all of this without you. I hope you know how much I appreciate it."

"Don't sweat it."

Spero lifted my hand and placed a gentle kiss on it as though I were a princess or a noble lady. I blushed.

"Good night, Amoura."

"Pleasant dreams, Spero."

I changed into a shift and nestled under the covers of the bed that still felt too grand for me to sleep in. My heart was heavy as I recalled the disturbing vision I had of my mother in the chamber, but Spero helped make it a bit lighter. Sparky curled up on the chair next to me, blowing tiny sparks in his sleep. I woke up later than usual the next morning, growing dangerously accustomed to the palace lifestyle.

I changed into my new dress, which, although less extravagant than most of the gowns in the magic wardrobe, was still nicer than any dress I had ever owned. The soft fabric floated over my form like a breath of fresh air. Combined with the lightweight shoes, it felt like I could take on any challenge. I was ready to bring Mama back.

Sixteen

Spero

Caliga was nice enough to give us some new clothes after ours got burned to a crisp in the fire labyrinth. I wasn't expecting to find anything similar to what I had on before, but I tried to match it as much as possible with a dark blue tunic, soft gray pants, and black leather shoes with thin soles. The burns from the fire labyrinth made my muscles sore as my fingers wrapped around the crystal doorknob. I forgot all my problems in an instant when Amoura appeared, shining like a beacon in a dress that brought out the pink glow of her cheeks and made my heart skip a beat. She was already beautiful before, but now she looked the spitting image of a fairy-tale princess.

"That dress really suits you," I stammered, trying not to look like a complete idiot.

Her face lit up with a warm smile. "I thank you. You look nice too."

I'm not sure how long we stood there gawking at each other before Sparky zipped around between us, screeching something to Amoura that she didn't appear pleased with, based on the look she gave him. We headed downstairs for a quick breakfast in the dining hall that consisted of some sort of blue porridge that tasted like cotton candy.

"I hope the next labyrinth has air conditioning," I joked.

My ill attempt at humor flew right over Amoura's head.

"I'm willing to take on anything to bring Mama back."

"We're both going to see our families really soon. I'm sure of it."

Caliga waited for us in the lobby. At least we'd had some time to ourselves before we needed to deal with her again.

"Good morrow, Aunt Caliga," said Amoura.

"Good morning, dearie. I see the wardrobe served its purpose well."

Pale pink fabric swirled around Amoura as she twirled in a circle.

"I thank you for the lovely dress. Pray tell us where to find the next shard. We're ready."

"The earth labyrinth is hidden somewhere deep in the woods," Caliga explained.

"How is that supposed to help us?" I groaned. "There's nothing *but* woods out here!"

"No one knows the woods better than the fairies," she continued, ignoring my comment. "I've provided a guide to bring you to their queen. She might know more about the labyrinth's location."

The dark-haired fairy, who had sent us to rescue the dragonling, flew from behind a statue. Her dull glow, combined with the nervous expression on her face, formed a stark contrast to the chipper attitude she had in the woods. What did Caliga do to her since we saw her last?

She hovered in front of me. "Mistress Caliga has entrusted me as your guide. Are you going to listen to me this time?"

It was no wonder she didn't trust me after the way I ran off that first morning. The sting of guilt crept through my veins.

"You're in charge. Lead the way," I replied as cheerfully as I could.

She perked up. "Great! Queen Gemma is expecting you."

She darted out the front door in a beam of light.

"I'll be awaiting you back here once you have the shard," said Caliga with a hint of warning in her voice.

"Of course you will," I mumbled.

"We shall not let you down," promised Amoura.

Amoura and I raced to catch up with the trail of pixie dust leading away from the palace. Once we were out of Caliga's line of vision, I ran to catch up to Fey, which wasn't easy because she could zip through the air like nobody's business.

"Fey, right?"

"You remembered!" she squeaked. "I thought you hated me."

"If anything, I owe you. I would never have gotten to Amoura in time if it wasn't for your help."

She hovered over my head, dripping sparkling dust over my new tunic while I relished the much-needed chance to catch my breath. Between Sparky's special wing and Fey's hyperactive pixie dust, there wasn't going to be much relaxation happening on our journey. The tiny bells on her shoes chimed as her feet kicked back and forth through the air.

"You really mean it? You don't hate me?"

"I don't hate you. It's Caliga I don't trust. I may have taken it out on you that first night here. I'm sorry."

A hint of apprehension filled her sparkling brown eyes, as though Caliga might sneak up on her at any second. "You need to understand that Mistress Caliga cares deeply about Imperium. She may not express it in the same way as Mistress Solara or Mistress Estella did, but unlike them, she remained in the palace to take care of all of us. If we lose her, we won't have anyone left to protect us anymore."

She made a good point. Symbols of the three sorceresses were plastered all over Imperium, but only one of them was still around as far as most people knew. Two-thirds of their governing structure was missing. That would be concerning to anyone.

"I guess I didn't think of it that way," I admitted. "I'll try to be more respectful. I just don't like being bossed around."

Amoura walked up next to me. "Once Mama is awake, I'm sure she'll be able to help protect Imperium, too."

"If she doesn't abandon us to live on Earth again," Fey mumbled.

None of the teasing I'd done to Amoura when we met held a candle to the pure rage that darkened her soft features after Fey's comment. I half expected her to reach for her crossbow.

"Is that truly what you think? She didn't abandon you! She started a family. Families are supposed to stick together. Don't *you* have a family?"

A twinge of nervousness entered the fairy's high-pitched voice. "Of course! All the fairies in the vale are family."

"Yet you presume to judge mine?"

"Mistress Solara went missing for years. What were we meant to think?"

"That she found happiness! Is that not what everyone

wants?"

Amoura's hands clenched into fists. I placed my hand on her shoulder.

"Take it easy."

The fear of angering Amoura restored Fey's previous energy levels. She flew in circles around us, spreading glittering dust all over the ground.

"I didn't mean—that is—you're not—Look! Sparkleberries, my favorite!"

She flew over to a bush with glittering heart-shaped pink fruit on it. I was proud of Amoura for finally showing some backbone, but this probably wasn't the best time to tell her that. We each sampled the berries, pushing aside the topic of the sorceresses for another day. Sweetness overwhelmed my tongue, forcing me to spit it out. The cotton candy porridge at the palace was bland compared to this.

Sparky seemed to enjoy the berries so much that he chewed up half the bush and went after the one I spit out when Amoura grabbed his wing in midair.

"I think that's enough for today," she scolded the dragonling.

As we traversed deeper into the forest, disturbances interrupted the otherworldly ecosystem. Crushed flower petals littered the ground, bright green leaves had faded to brown, and rotten berries peppered several bushes.

"I don't know much about fairies, but don't they usually like places that thrive in nature?"

"Of course we do!" Fey squealed.

"The flora around here doesn't seem to be doing very well."

Fey darted around a bush where half of its white flowers had wilted to a crushed brown texture like fall leaves.

"Everyone in Imperium has been struggling with the effects

of the shattered crystal. Didn't the merfolk tell you about the anomalies?"

I nodded. "Yeah. We had a little surprise encounter with a sea monster on our way to the water labyrinth."

"That's all? Nothing else attacked you in the woods?"

"There was that monster in the cave when we first arrived here," Amoura pointed out.

"That's right," I said. "Caliga took care of it for us."

Fey kicked a dead leaf off a tree, following its trail to the mossy ground below.

"You've been lucky. The rock golem has been a big killjoy! He stomps all over the place, destroying everything in his path. It's been driving Queen Gemma bonkers."

She darted in a zigzag pattern, breaking off small twigs from random branches to emphasize her point.

"The unicorns used to protect the forests, but no one's seen them since Mistress Solara went into stasis," she continued.

The color drained from Amoura's cheeks. "Unicorns?"

Uh-oh.

She hovered too close to Amoura's face for comfort. "That's right. Have you seen any?"

Amoura stopped in her tracks, leaning against a nearby tree. Her shoulders slumped like a deflated balloon. "We…"

I jumped in before she could say something she would regret. "It looks like they were given a new mission to protect the crystal shards. They've been doing a great job."

Fey's eyes widened. "That explains it! It's nice to know they haven't disappeared."

Amoura's voice shook. "Yes, but we…"

I gave her hand a light squeeze. "Come on, Amoura. We don't want to keep the fairy queen waiting."

She stumbled after me, her green eyes misting over. "Spero, the unicorns were protecting the forests… What have we done?"

I shook my head. "They were trapped in the labyrinths since before we got here. This isn't our fault. Maybe the crystal will bring them back after it's restored."

She wouldn't look at me. "If you say so."

The torment radiated from her like heat from a flame. I wished I could reassure her more, but I didn't understand enough of how this world worked. It seemed strange that unicorns guarded the labyrinths instead of the more traditional monsters that they had disguised themselves as.

Fey stopped at a solid wall of trees and vines.

"Here we are! The fairy court. Ta-da!" She waved her arms around dramatically.

I looked around for signs of other fairies. "There's nothing here."

"That's because you have to fly over the barrier, silly! We wouldn't leave our court out in the open where anyone can attack."

I glanced at Amoura. "Do you think Sparky's mother could give us a lift?"

She shook her head. "That isn't necessary. 'Tis not even that high."

She leaped up the wall like an Olympic gymnast, zipping from vine to vine. I gripped the nearest tree and hoisted myself up. The branch supporting me gave way with a sickening snap. Before I fell back to the ground, I grabbed a nearby vine to stabilize myself. From the top of the wall, I could see Amoura waiting for me down below. Using the vines like rope, I lowered myself to the ground. The final vine snapped, and

I landed with a thud in a glittering grove of giant flowers in pink, gold, blue, and lavender. I pulled myself back to my feet.

This looked closer to what I would expect from a fairy court. An unhealthy brown color crept up the edges of some of the fairy homes, just like in the woods. On our approach, several pixies scurried into their flowers, which closed up into large buds around them. Had no one in this crazy place seen a normal person before? Fey tried to stop some of them to no avail.

"It's okay!" she squealed. "Amoura and Spero are friends. They're going to save Imperium!"

"Thank you for bringing them," said a majestic voice.

A brightly glowing golden fairy hovered over us. She wore a gown made of glittering yellow flower petals with tiny pink and silver accents. Nestled in her bright red hair was a crown of small, pointy petals that matched her gown.

"Introducing Her Royal Majesty, Queen Gemma! Da-da-da-da-DA!" Fey sang, impressing no one.

Amoura gave a sweeping curtsy. "Well met, Your Majesty."

I tried my best to give a bow that matched Amoura's graceful curtsy, but I probably looked like an idiot.

"Thank you, my dear," replied the queen. "I've heard a lot about the two of you."

"Good things, I hope," I mumbled.

She smiled at me. "I've heard that you are both very brave and have devoted yourselves to restoring the crystal of Imperium. I would like to offer my assistance."

"That's awfully kind of you," replied Amoura. "We were hoping you could tell us where to find the earth labyrinth, Your Majesty."

She flew onto a tiny chair made of leaves and golden petals.

"I'd be happy to, but I need you to prove yourselves to me first by doing us a favor."

Another test? What was up with this place?

Amoura fidgeted with her long brown hair. "What sort of favor?"

"Rid the woods of the rock golem that has been plaguing us. Then I will show you the way."

Amoura and I exchanged a glance. So far, the only things we had fought head-on were the two cloaked unicorn guardians. The dazed sea serpent didn't count, but it did prove that Amoura was quick on her feet. Hopefully, we had gained enough experience with our weapons to take on a new threat.

I reached toward the sword on my back. "Consider it done. As the heroes of Imperium, we can easily defeat a mere rock golem."

Hopefully, the fairy queen couldn't detect when someone was bluffing.

Seventeen

Amoura

I followed Spero back over the wall protecting the fairy court with a heavy heart. We already needed to slay the unicorns to recover the crystal shards. Now the fairy queen had recruited us to slay another? Did they see us as mercenaries? I still wanted to bring Mama back, but I didn't realize it would require so much destruction on my part.

"Why did you tell her we could defeat the rock golem?" I asked Spero when we returned to the forest. "We know naught about slaying monsters."

He gave me a casual shrug as though he had just agreed to a trip to the market as opposed to a fight to the death.

"You still want to free your mother, don't you? This is the quickest way. If we didn't agree to it, she wouldn't show us where the labyrinth is."

I ran my fingers through a thick chunk of my hair. "But you know how I feel about fighting."

Sparks crackled through the air from the dragonling hovering beside me. *Sparky will help! Sparky is big and strong!*

Spero gave me a reassuring grin. "Don't worry. We can take on anything as long as we're together. Look how much progress we've made already."

I glanced down at my crossbow. It had already been used to destroy two innocent unicorns. Their blood was on my hands. I knew it was for the greater good and that they had to be defeated to restore Mama's magic, but that didn't stop the guilt weighing down every step I'd taken since their demise. Was more destruction really the answer? How was Spero so carefree about all of this? What sort of future did he come from?

It didn't take long to locate the golem's trail. Crushed flowers, broken branches, and a disturbing amount of unidentified pixie dust led us down a narrow path where we were met with the screams of horrified fairies. Peering through the trees, we could make out the silhouette of an enormous monster forged from a series of boulders piled on top of each other like a snowman, forming arms, legs, a torso, and a head with a crude carving of a face. Smaller rocks encompassed something that resembled fingers, allowing it to grasp at the unfortunate fairies that were playing in the area.

It swiped its rocky hand toward a dark-skinned fairy in a lilac dress who flew out of the way just before a male fairy in a suit of red leaves and a pointed mushroom cap darted in front of her.

"You big bully!" he shouted. "Leave Lila alone!"

Lila hovered over a nearby cliffside that was just beyond the golem's reach.

"Arden, no!" she shrieked.

Before anyone could react, the creature grabbed Arden in its bulbous, rocky hand, where he looked no bigger than a fly. Arden's cries were sickening as the stony fingers squeezed him until a stream of glittering dust leaked out like salt from a shaker. A shiver ran through my body. Lila's screams echoed from the top of the cliff. Then she hovered down towards us.

"I thought you two were supposed to be heroes!"

Glittering drops poured from her tiny brown eyes like fresh morning dew.

My eyes misted over at her loss. I was frozen in place. All I could do was stare at her in shock. I glanced toward Spero, who was already running toward the creature with his sword drawn.

"I am deeply sorry…" I sputtered.

"I'm going to report this to Queen Gemma."

The pixie fluttered away. Sparky darted toward the golem, but his wing got caught in a tangle of tree branches.

Sparky will avenge the fairy!

"No, he won't," I scolded. "Sparky will stay right here where it's safe."

But Sparky wants to help Spero!

I bit my lip. Sparky seemed confident enough, but after what I had just witnessed, I worried about his special wing, especially after the agreement we had made with his mother. He couldn't be the rock golem's next victim. I sucked in a breath, holding back my tears for a later time. Forcing my arms to move again, I pushed aside the branches that surrounded Sparky's wing.

My heart was racing in my chest as Spero swung his blade against the golem's massive fist. The enchanted black steel bounced off the hard rock surface with an uncomfortable clang. A few pebbles that made up the creature's fingers got knocked off by the blade, shortening its reach.

The golem ducked down and scooped up the missing pieces of its finger. They reconnected to its hand by magic, eliminating the possibility of a weakness. Still, this seemed like something we could use to our advantage. If we could dismantle it quickly enough, it might not have enough time to put itself back together. Spero appeared to have the same idea, as he began aiming for joints where the rocks in its body met.

With a trembling hand, I lifted my crossbow and shot a bolt between the two rocks making up its left leg. Its foreleg separated from its thigh, causing the creature to falter. Spero used this tactic to his advantage. He slashed between the boulders that made up its right leg, bringing the golem down to its knees, lowering its high stature to Spero's level. Unfortunately, this made Spero an easier target. A fist-shaped rock formation flew toward him as he darted out of the way just in time, forming a small ditch in the soil where the golem had been aiming.

From this distance, I was invulnerable. There had to be some way I could help before Spero got hurt. I glanced up at the cliff Lila had fled to. A large pile of boulders sat precariously on the edge. If I could create enough tension below them, I might be able to trigger a rock slide that was large enough to crush the golem. I just needed to warn Spero to avoid the falling rocks without drawing the golem's attention toward myself.

"Sparky," I whispered. "I have a mission for you."

Sparky can help! Sparky loves helping!

He untangled himself from the rest of the vines.

"I need you to get Spero back here so I can bury the golem in those rocks up there."

Yay! Sparky gets to help Spero! Sparky likes Spero!

We had a brief reprieve while the golem reconnected its knee joints. I had to do this quickly. A brief examination of the rock pile on the cliff revealed a keystone that would create a rock slide with enough impact. I fired a bolt at it and prayed. The rocks on the edge rumbled a bit but otherwise didn't budge. I glanced back at the battle for a moment to observe Sparky tugging on Spero's tunic, trying to get him to retreat. He looked toward me for confirmation. I gave a quick nod before aiming at the cliff a second time.

Our brief exchange attracted the golem's attention, requiring all of us to act faster. Spero and Sparky raced toward me as the golem reached for them with its massive hand. Spero gave a few quick strokes with his sword, breaking off several more of the rocks forming the golem's fingers, but there were still enough to crush him with. I rapid-fired a second, third, and fourth bolt at the keystone.

Finally, the fifth impact caused the rocks to come careening down onto the golem just before it could make contact with Spero. Hundreds of boulders came tumbling off the edge of the cliffside, knocking the golem off-balance. Sparky helped Spero pull himself free, but the rocks wouldn't stop falling, even after the golem was sufficiently buried. They slid toward Spero. A small rock hit the back of his knee, knocking him off his feet at the worst possible time as a huge boulder flew right over his head.

"Spero!" I cried.

I dropped my crossbow and ran toward him. The blue jewel on his ring lit up, creating a transparent blue barrier around him as he rolled to safety. The boulder hit the edge of the barrier and bounced off, giving him enough space to get away. The rest of the rocks crashed down, forming a thick plume that turned the air brown with dirt. Spero got back to his feet, covering his nose and mouth to avoid the pollution in the air. I threw my arms around him and pulled him toward me.

"I thought I had killed you. After we failed to save that fairy, I never would forgive myself if…" I began trembling.

Spero placed his hands on my shoulders, steadying me with his calming presence. "Hey, it's okay. I made it. We won. Everything is fine. You were great. That rock slide idea was brilliant!"

Sparky landed on Spero's shoulder.

Sparky helped!

"Yes, Sparky was very helpful," I replied.

I couldn't hold back my distress any longer. The dam inside me burst. I buried my face in Spero's shoulder. I knew I couldn't save everyone, but I still wanted to. No matter how many times I witnessed death on the farm, I never grew numb to it. Spero wrapped his arms around me until I calmed down. Sparky flew onto my shoulder and patted my face with his wing.

Amoura shouldn't be sad. Sparky saved the day!

I brushed my nose with an unflattering snort and looked back at Spero.

"Your ring lit up when the boulder was about to crush you. I think it saved your life. Did you do something to activate it?"

"Besides wishing really hard not to get crushed? Not really." He crossed his arms in contemplation. "I have no idea how this thing works, but I think it may have gotten me out of more than one sticky situation in the past."

I stabilized my breathing, focusing on our conversation. "You never told me whence you got it. Your parents aren't magical, are they?"

"Not that I know of. I think my dad may have gotten this ring from your aunt."

"Caliga?"

I raised an eyebrow in surprise. If Spero suspected Caliga had done something kind for his family, he certainly hadn't shown it when he was around her.

"The other aunt."

"You mean Estella?"

He lifted his index finger and pointed it at me. "That's the one."

I took a step back, contemplating his words. "But we know not what she even looks like. Aunt Caliga said she was greedy and vengeful. Why would she help you?"

"I have no idea, but now you know why I don't trust everything Caliga has told us."

I fidgeted with my hair. "How could you possibly know it was her?"

He twisted his ring around on his finger. "There were portraits of all three sorceresses when we got separated in the water labyrinth. One of them matched my dad's description of the woman who gave him the ring."

I leaned my head against a tree trunk. "This is all so confusing. If Estella wanted the crystal for herself, why would she give magical protection to the only other person who could enter the labyrinths and take it from her? And why would she want to destroy it if she was the one who created it in the first place?"

Spero nodded. "That's what I'd like to know."

"Then again," I reasoned, "if she was able to create the crystal, it doesn't seem like a stretch for her to have made a magic ring. Or a magic pendant…"

My fingers brushed over my necklace.

Spero nodded. "If we can somehow get Estella to come out of hiding, maybe she could fill in all the blanks that Caliga left behind."

"I wonder why she's hiding in the first place. Her absence and Mama's deep sleep have placed a terrible burden on the people of Imperium."

"If Caliga really thinks she's the problem, maybe she did something to keep Estella in line."

"But they're sisters!" I gasped. "Family would never hurt each other."

Spero glanced away. "You'd be surprised how easy it is for family to forget about each other when it isn't convenient for them."

I reached toward his arm. "I'm sorry. You're still concerned about Melanie, aren't you?"

"I'm sure she's fine. I'll get back to her soon enough." He brushed it off, but his distress tugged at the corners of his eyes.

Sparky began clawing at Spero's shoulder, ripping a small hole in his tunic. I hoisted the dragonling off.

"You speak true. We need only find two more shards, and then we'll both have our families back. Let's go back and tell Queen Gemma we completed the task."

Spero and I made our way back to the fairy court to uncover the entrance to the third labyrinth.

Eighteen

Spero

Amoura looked so distraught after the battle; I knew I had to do something to cheer her up. Her reaction to the fairy's demise made me realize her sensitive nature came from her big heart, something I had grown to admire about her in the time we'd spent together. Caliga had called her the essence of love for a reason, after all. Fighting just wasn't her thing. I had to admit it was a lot less nerve-wracking in video games than it was in real life. We passed more wilted flowers on the way back. Would restoring the earth shard fix all of this? I noticed some pink flowers that resembled the ones on her dress. Maybe that would cheer her up. I plucked one when she wasn't looking and presented it to her with a flourish.

"A flower for the princess?"

The look on her face was priceless. It was a mix of gratitude, embarrassment, and sheer delight.

"I told you I'm not a princess!" She gave me a sheepish grin and accepted the gift. "But I thank you. It was very thoughtful."

I watched her string the stem through her hair until the blossom rested comfortably on the side of her head. She looked as if she had stepped right out of a fairy tale. Why she didn't believe she was a princess was beyond me.

The climb into the fairy court was easier the second time around. Queen Gemma flew over to us the moment we climbed down. A few other fairies darted into their flowers, still distrustful of us.

"Welcome back," said the queen. "I've heard you were successful, save for a single loss."

Amoura's mood darkened again in an instant. "I am deeply sorry. We could not get there in time to save him."

Gemma nodded. "My fairies know the risk of leaving the vale. He wasn't the first casualty of the rock golem. Still, you've kept your word, so now I shall keep mine as well. Come with me."

She left a trail of rainbow-colored sparkles through a grove of bushes covered in peach and lavender flowers. The further we went, the greener and more flourishing the plants and flowers got, as though there was a source of life nearby. It must have been the earth shard. We hit a dead end at a wall made of dirt and moss. Queen Gemma hovered over it.

"Here we are."

I peered through the moss for some sign of a door, but I couldn't find any gaps in the carpet of green that covered it.

"What gives? Where's the labyrinth?"

Her glittering golden eyes rolled back in her tiny head. "Don't you see it? You mortals are so unobservant."

She flew over our heads and brushed her hands over a small

stone disk embedded in the wall, about the size of a quarter. It looked just big enough for a fairy to enter, but nowhere near large enough for two humans.

"'Tis so small," Amoura gasped.

Gemma tilted her head as though she had never considered our drastic difference in size until now. "Is it? It looks like a regular door to me."

I crossed my arms. "Are you kidding? We'd never be able to get in there!"

She shrugged. "Oh well. You're the essences of hope and love, aren't you? You'll figure something out. I've done my part, so Mistress Caliga ought to be satisfied. Good day."

With that useless quip, she floated away back to where we'd come from.

"No, Sparky, you must not go in there for us," Amoura said firmly, restraining the dragonling as he tried to fly up to the tiny door.

I thought back to the labyrinths we'd faced in the past. "We can still touch it, can't we? That's how we activated the other labyrinths. Maybe it'll let us in the same way."

"I know not if I can fit my whole hand over it."

Amoura stood on her tiptoes and reached toward the disk, brushing a few fingers against the foreign symbols. They sparkled with a pink glow.

"It looks like that's good enough," I said.

I reached up and placed my hand on it, brushing the warm skin around her knuckles. I hoped she didn't notice the way my heart started racing. Pink and blue lights sparkled under our touch, and the world around us grew bigger.

"Are we shrinking?" I asked.

"Sparky, no!"

A giant, clawed green hand reached for us as we were absorbed into the small opening that appeared in the wall. Then it vanished, and we were alone in a familiar-looking hallway with green glass on the floor and long vines hanging along the walls.

"I think the shrinking magic doesn't work on Sparky," Amoura observed.

I nodded. "That makes sense. He doesn't have the power to break the seals like we do."

A disturbing rustling sound echoed down the hall. I took a step back to observe our surroundings.

"Spero, behind you!" Amoura shrieked.

Something wrapped around my waist. I reached for my sword. The vines snaked around my arms and legs, crushing me against the wall. Pushing the blade straight back, I managed to free my dominant arm. Distracted by my plight, Amoura didn't notice the vines from the wall on the other side snaking around her torso.

"Amoura, get away from the wall!"

It was too late. She shrieked as she was pulled into a cluster of foliage. Without being able to use her crossbow effectively from such a close distance, she was helpless. There was no time to think. I slashed and hacked at the vines restraining my legs and upper body, feeling them slither around me as I worked. Increasing my speed, I managed to outpace them and cut myself free. Before they could get another grab at me, I raced to the other side of the hall to free Amoura, who was drowning in a sea of green.

Working quickly, I sawed through clumps of vines all around her until I was able to grab hold of her waist and pull her away from the angry plants. She wriggled her wrists out of the trap and wrapped her arms around my neck, leaving only her ankles. I aimed low, but another vine got hold of my sword arm, causing me to drop it. It clattered to the ground, where a low vine snaked its way around the hilt. Before I could reach for it, my wrist was restrained above my head. Thankfully, Amoura had an opening. She bent down and grabbed it, hacking at the vine on my arm. Before we were restrained again, we ran down the hallway. The vines chased after us, gaining momentum as they expanded in size. Flinging ourselves into the next room, a net of green blocked the passage behind us.

Once we were safe, Amoura handed back my sword, which I returned to the sheath on my back.

"A thousand pardons for using your sword without permission, but you were trapped."

"Are you kidding? I think I've lost count of how many times you've saved my life now. Feel free to use it whenever you want."

A sweet scent filled the air. A soft pink dome surrounded us, leading up to a point in the ceiling. A round yellow carpet spread beneath our feet. With every step I took, my ankles got more tangled in the tall fibers. Amoura inspected the walls, which had the texture of a fleece blanket.

"I think we're inside a peony," she said.

"You think we're inside a *what*?"

The corners of her mouth twisted into an adorable grin. "It's a type of flower, silly."

Looking down, I realized I wasn't standing on a carpet at all, but in the middle of the flower's stamen.

"Oh. That makes more sense."

She pushed on the walls, or rather, the giant petals. "If we can just get it to bloom, maybe we'll find the next crystal shard."

I pushed on it with her, but instead of opening, the petal began to stretch like plastic wrap. In our shrunken state, we were no match for it.

"What if you use your pendant?" I suggested.

Her hand brushed over the pink jewel. "My pendant is used for healing, not growth."

"Wouldn't healing a flower help to accelerate its growth?"

She considered my suggestion. "I suppose there's no harm in trying."

With one hand on her pendant and another on the giant petal, she closed her eyes and concentrated. A soft glow spread from her hand to the soft walls around us, bathing the room in a warm light. The flower rumbled for a moment, and then the walls pushed outward. The domed ceiling opened up, unveiling a new chamber.

We climbed down the petal ramp to find a series of moss-covered steps leading up to a platform that probably contained the earth shard. Since there was no burning lava to worry about, this should be a piece of cake. I stepped into the first one. It rumbled under my foot sending panic jolting through my veins. The platform under my foot disintegrated into nothingness, forcing me to grab the next step and avoid plummeting into the chasm below. There just had to be a trick to it.

I glanced over to see how Amoura was doing. She followed a nearby set of steps without any trouble, leaping from platform to platform, making her way to the top with plenty of time to spare. Her movements were so fluid that I wasn't even sure if she noticed the steps disintegrating as she went. Meanwhile,

I was already starting to lose my footing as the next step crumbled underneath me.

I took a deep breath and grabbed onto the next platform, pulling myself up as my footing gave way beneath me. My fingers almost slipped from the weight, but feeling it start to disintegrate motivated me to keep going so I could reach Amoura before she got hurt again. The step crumbled beneath me as I grabbed onto the next one and made a flying leap for the central platform. Finally, I joined Amoura in the middle, where another rock golem was waiting for us. It resembled the one that attacked the fairies. Its stout, rocky casing was covered in brown speckles. There were no rock slides to cheat our way out of this one, if it was even a real golem. Based on our previous experiences, I had a strong suspicion it was another unicorn in disguise.

Amoura fired a test shot through the boulder, holding up its head. The bolt went straight through to the other side of the chamber. Another illusion, then. I guess it was less embarrassing to think you're fighting a monster than a dainty little unicorn. The golem lunged at Amoura, shrouding her in the massive illusion. I darted into the augmented reality covering, where I saw a brown unicorn with a green vine wrapped around its blocky horn, snarling at Amoura. She was scared, but remained unharmed. Good. I poked my sword at its tail, drawing its attention away from her and dissolving the illusion.

"Over here, you coward!"

It turned around and leaped at me, the vine around its horn extending toward my arms to bind them in place. Learning from our adventure in the hallway, I pivoted my sword out of the vine's path and sliced it off in one fluid motion. Then I went for the horn. I gave a hard, confident swing and managed to crack it, causing the unicorn to reel in pain, giving us an opening to plan our next move. The unicorn was in too much agony to fight back.

I wondered if we could just grab the shard and leave at this point. Maybe we didn't have to kill the guardians. That might help calm Amoura's nerves. As the injured unicorn writhed on the ground below, I reached over and grabbed the brown shard, which was surrounded by an eerie green glow. The moment I made contact with it, the unicorn exploded into a net of vines like the ones blocking the entrance to the chamber. The vines branched out in all directions before falling into a lifeless pile on the ground. It looked like taking the shards had the same effect as killing the unicorns. I looked toward Amoura for confirmation.

She nodded. "It worked. I felt Mama's magic leave this place. Mayhap she'll wake up soon."

A surge of energy radiated from the shard. I placed it in my pocket to avoid the draining feeling I got from the other shards we had recovered. Amoura probably felt something similar to this when she used her pendant.

Now that the labyrinth had served its purpose, the entire chamber started rumbling. California earthquakes were a joke compared to this. The ground bounced both of us into the air as if we were on a very painful trampoline. Amoura and I clung to each other, forming new bruises with each tremor. Finally, it was over, and we shot back out through the fairy-sized door in the wall outside. Just when I thought I would get impaled by the massive blades of grass below us, we grew back to normal size, landing on the ground with a thud. Sparky barreled into us, irritating the fresh bruises from the earthquake.

"Yes, we recovered the shard," Amoura explained to him. "I know not why it didn't let you in. Maybe next time."

"I think I need a minute," I groaned, supporting myself against the wall.

I assessed the locations of all the aches and pains covering my body, rubbing them all with my hands. Amoura placed her hand on my shoulder. Her necklace lit up with its healing pink glow. Immediate relief filled my body as her soothing magic flowed through me like a warm drink. I stood back up, ready for a good night's sleep back at the palace.

"You're a lifesaver," I told her. "Thanks."

She scanned the surrounding area. "I'm surprised Aunt Caliga isn't already here waiting for us."

"Maybe the fairy queen's magic blocks her powers somehow."

"Aw, look! 'Tis adorable!" exclaimed Amoura.

I followed her gaze to a snow-white kitten that was purring delicately in a nearby bush. It was weird to see a normal-looking animal in such a magical place. Amoura raced over to it, her face glowing with delight. She kneeled toward it and nuzzled its chin affectionately. The kitten leaned toward her and purred, an unusual behavior for stray cats, which tend to run away from strangers.

"How precious," she cooed.

Sparky blew some small flames, trying to divert her attention. If I didn't know any better, I'd think he was jealous.

Great, just what we need. A new pet.

Nineteen

Amoura

⚜

The aches and nausea from the violent tremors of the earth labyrinth melted away the moment the darling kitten's pink eyes met mine. They glowed with a soft light that reminded me of Mama's pendant. Her snow-white fur stood out like a beacon in the dirt and foliage surrounding it, impossibly clean. Could she belong to the fairies? I would have expected fairies to keep much smaller pets. The kitten purred at us as if waiting for something. I knelt and reached out to her. She leaped into my arms, rubbing her soft head against me. I rubbed her between the ears, and she purred with delight.

"What do you think she wants?" I asked Spero.

He shrugged. "Maybe she's lost?"

Sparky will let you rub him between the ears, too!

My other little friend was getting jealous. The kitten hopped back onto the ground and poked my ankle with its tiny head as though it wanted me to go somewhere.

I stood up. "I think she's trying to tell us something."

"Can you use your necklace to translate like you did with Sparky?" asked Spero.

My fingers brushed over the smooth pink gem hanging from my neck. "I can try. I know not if it will work on an ordinary animal, though."

I bent back down and tapped the pendant gently against the kitten's nose. Curiosity filled my thoughts. Perhaps it knew something about Mama or the crystal. A surge of energy ran through me as a soft, feminine voice emanated from the cat's direction.

How dare you call me ordinary! I'll have you know that I am Nix, the beloved familiar of one of the three sorceress guardians. I am a vital member of the Imperial Court, unlike the two of you, who are merely pawns in Mistress Caliga's game.

"It worked!" I exclaimed.

Spero grinned at me. "What's it saying?"

"She said something about being a sorceress guardian's familiar."

"Which one?"

"Um," I hesitated, looking at the kitten expectantly.

I serve Mistress Estella, the wisest of the sorceress guardians. She wanted me to fetch you.

"She says Mistress Estella sent her to fetch us."

Spero crossed his arms. "That's unexpected. I'd like to meet her, but we might be walking into a trap. She could be after us because we're the only ones who can access the labyrinths. It seems like everyone around here is after the crystal."

I rubbed the kitten's chin. "How can she possibly be leading us into a trap? Just look at her. She's so precious."

How dare you accuse my mistress of foul play! Mistress Estella lives only for knowledge. She would never attack another world.

The kitten hissed and scratched at the cuff of Spero's trousers.

"Hey!"

"I don't think she likes people talking ill against of her mistress."

Spero sighed. "Fine. Let's see what she wants, but don't say I didn't warn you."

I nodded. "Lead the way, Nix."

Nix guided us out of the fairy vale, leaping over the wall in one fluid motion. Following the furry beacon, we wandered deep into the woods. As the sky faded to a deep shade of violet, the flora and fauna around us grew sparse. I walked closer to Spero as darkness fell with an eerie silence. It became clear why my Aunt Estella had gone missing for so long. She lived in the middle of nowhere.

I jumped when Spero placed his hand on my arm to get my attention. "Caliga might come after us if we stray too far from the palace. She's always watching us. She probably knows exactly where we're going."

You may inform the unenlightened one that Mistress Estella has equipped her precious familiar with a cloaking spell that extends to anyone within range. I have a good mind to bite his ear off for thinking she would be so ill-prepared.

"Er, Nix says that Estella is hiding us with magic," I translated, leaving out the more insulting bits.

"Interesting. So she's just been hiding out here in plain sight all this time?"

I hugged myself as an icy chill blew through the abandoned woods. "It would seem so."

Nix gave an assertive "Meow."

We've arrived.

I looked around. There was nothing but trees in every direction. I bent down to ask Nix for further explanation, but she ran ahead, vanishing into thin air.

"Where did she go?" asked Spero.

"She… she says we're here," I stammered.

He reached for his sword. "I knew it was a trap!"

Sparky is brave! Sparky will find the kitty!

Sparky vanished into an empty patch of forest where Nix had disappeared.

I gasped. "Sparky, come back!"

Sparky flew back out unharmed.

There's a funny-looking house in here! Amoura and Spero should come and see.

I pushed my hand over the area where Sparky and Nix had disappeared. I gasped as my hand disappeared as well. A rush of panic burst through my chest as I wondered if my hand had permanently vanished. Relief flooded through me as I pulled my hand back out to find all five fingers fully intact. I wiggled them for confirmation.

I turned to Spero. "Mayhap it isn't a trap after all."

Still pensive, Spero entered the strange void, disappearing before my eyes. I rushed after him, not wanting to be left alone in the unsettling night air. On the other side of the invisible barrier was a bizarre hut made of straw, metal, glass, and other materials that I didn't recognize. Tubes were sticking out from strange places, and purple smoke was emitting from what I could only assume was a chimney. It didn't look much bigger than Father's cottage, but the structure was like nothing I had seen before.

Spero looked amused. "Very steampunk."

I widened my eyes at him. "Very *what*?"

He rubbed his yellow hair sheepishly. "It's, er, when people try to make advanced technology using old-fashioned materials. Basically, this."

A red door with circular windows lifted into the air like the lid of a trunk. A middle-aged woman emerged from the other side. Nix leaped into her arms and licked her face affectionately. The tangles of silvery pink hair knotted around her head reminded me of Mama's. Her pale skin glowed like the moon under the night sky. Two small glass disks covered her narrow violet eyes. A brown coat, smudged with dark stains as though she had been performing heavy labor in it, fell all the way to her ankles like a gown.

"Don't just stand there," she commanded in a gritty voice. "Come on in!"

Nervous that she meant us harm with all her foreign gadgets, my hand grasped Spero's. I glanced at him with a question in my eyes, but he merely shrugged. With no other option, we followed the woman into the strange house.

If the outside of her home made little sense, the inside wracked my mind even more than the labyrinths we'd been journeying through. Glass containers of bright, colorful liquids littered the small room. Books splayed open to various pages around the floor with dark markings smudged across them. Strange contraptions rotated, emitted fumes, and took up copious amounts of space in the most eccentric home I had ever been in. I squeezed Spero's hand for comfort, as his intrigued expression indicated more familiarity with this topsy-turvy atmosphere.

I swallowed thickly. "Are you my Aunt Estella?"

Her narrow eyes squinted at me in confusion. "Aunt? I'm no one's aunt. Wait. If you're Solara's kid, then I suppose the way family units work would place me in a position where I'm related to you, and her being my sister…" Her face lit with realization. "Yes, I guess I am your aunt."

I blinked at her. She didn't seem like someone who was used to being around people. I expected her to be more intimidating somehow after what Aunt Caliga had told us.

"How about getting to the point?" Spero demanded. "What are we doing here?"

Estella clapped a calloused hand on Spero's shoulder. Her proximity emitted a scent like burned metal from a smithy. "Now that's what I like to see! No time wasted on small talk. Just getting straight to the point. If everyone did that, maybe we would have solved this magic crisis already. It's no wonder you're the essence of hope."

"Are you referring to the anomalies? Won't they be resolved when the crystal is restored?" I asked.

"That's Caliga's solution, although I'm surprised you would want to steal energy from Earth, seeing as how you both came from there."

A sinking feeling entered my gut. "I thought restoring Imperium's magic would protect Earth as well. Aunt Caliga said that if Imperium lost its power, Earth would too."

Estella gave an inappropriate chuckle as Nix purred in her arms. "Is that what she told you? She has made a mess of things, hasn't she? But that's why you're here. You might as well make yourselves comfortable."

I shrieked as a chair unfolded itself beneath me, forcing my legs to buckle as I fell into it. A spring released an arm containing a sweet-smelling liquid. Spero had a less dramatic reaction to the strange furniture. Estella pulled down a white screen from above her head that seemed to materialize out of nowhere. Images lit up all over it, containing strange symbols and pictures. She picked up a thin silver wand, gesturing to the images on the screen. I glanced at Spero to see if he was as mystified by all this as I was, but if anything, he looked bored. Maybe he was used to being lectured where he came from.

"Now, as you probably know, Imperium is ruled by the three sorceress guardians: Mistress Solara, Mistress Caliga, and yours truly."

Portraits of Mama, Aunt Caliga, and Aunt Estella lit up on the screen.

"When one of us goes missing, it upsets the balance of power between the worlds. One day, Solara decided to go see what life was like in a world without magic. We didn't think much of it at the time."

She pointed to a blue and green circular icon that I assumed depicted the Earth. Mama's portrait floated over it.

"Problem was she never came back. After some investigating, Caliga and I discovered that she'd fallen in love with a human and decided to have a baby. You probably knew that part already." She gave me an expectant look.

I clutched the arm of the chair. "Aye. That was all I knew until recently."

"Since she was gone for so long, the anomalies began. Natural disasters, monsters, that sort of thing."

She pointed to an illustration of mermaids getting swallowed by a whirlpool and another of fairies being crushed by a rock golem. The sinking feeling in my gut deepened.

"To make up for your mother's absence, I pooled together some of my resources and compiled a conduit made up of the four basic elements of nature that would be able to restore the imbalance of power and keep Imperium safe again."

Sparky flew onto my lap, seeking attention. I rubbed his chin. "You're referring to the crystal, I presume."

"Right." She pointed to a small sketch of a glowing crystal. "As I'm sure my precious little Nix probably explained to you, I'm a genius when it comes to magical doohickies, but not so great at harnessing power. That ability fell to the third sorceress, Caliga. So I let her take on the responsibility of fine-tuning the crystal. Do you know what happened next?"

"Let me guess," Spero asserted. "She tried to attack Earth."

Estella's face lit up for all the wrong reasons. "One point for the tech wizard!"

"But Earth wasn't attacked, was it?" I asked, my gaze darting between them.

"That's all thanks to moi!" Estella bowed like an actor at the end of a play. "You're welcome, by the way. I used the interdimensional telecommunicator, patent pending, to let your mom know what Caliga was planning, and poof! The third sorceress was back in Imperium. But there was a problem."

I swallowed the bile rising in my throat. "Caliga still had the crystal."

"Right-o! To prevent her from using it to harm your world, Solara cast a Guardian Transference spell, lending her powers to the four unicorn guardians of the forest, who would do anything for the three of us. She split the crystal into its four basic components, and formed the labyrinths that could only be entered by the essences of hope and love. I'm pretty sure she knew her daughter was the essence of love, which put you in danger. That's when she added the essence of hope to the spell as a failsafe, knowing that there wasn't anyone who could fill that qualification, at least not at the time."

Spero sipped his drink. "Then you gave my dad the ring, knowing I'd be born for this mission."

A sparkle of joy appeared behind the glass circles covering her eyes. "The Ring of Hope was one of my finest creations! Caliga begged me to find someone who could unlock the other half of the seal. I respected Solara's wishes to protect Earth, but I could never resist a good challenge. The time Solara spent in your world intrinsically linked it to her magic, whether she knew it or not, which meant I had to take a little trip to the world without magic."

She wrinkled her nose. "The time period she chose was so bland. No indoor plumbing, no electricity, no imagination! So I finagled the time stream a bit and found someone in a technologically advanced society who had amazing, forward-thinking ideas for the future, but he was down on his luck. By harnessing the power of fortune and potential through the Ring of Hope, I was able to guarantee his success, leading to the birth of a child who had all the hope in the world resting on his shoulders!" She bowed again, this time in Spero's direction. "You're welcome, Spero."

Spero crossed his arms. "My life isn't as great as you think it is."

Their voices blended together, as an uncomfortable buzzing sound filled my head. I stood up from the strange chair, which collapsed beneath me. The sinking feeling in my gut reached its peak. My heart throbbed, ready to burst out of my chest. My breath grew shallow. My hands shook. Glancing down, Sparky blurred into a green ball bouncing on the ground beneath.

"What you are telling us," I wheezed, "is that everything we've been doing was in direct violation of my mother's plans to protect Earth. We are saving no one. Instead, we have done everything we could to willingly ensure the one thing that she sacrificed everything she had to prevent." My voice cracked, and I could speak no more.

Spero stood up, causing his chair to collapse as well. "Amoura…"

Estella puffed out her shoulders smugly. "Well, now you know the whole story, so you can decide what to do next. I figured I'd better tell you before it was too late. You sure are glad you met me, aren't you?"

Bile rose up my throat as my eyes burned with tears.

"Excuse me," I whimpered. "I need some air."

I leaned against the bizarre door, forgetting that it rotated upwards instead of sideways like a normal door. As it popped out over my head, gravity pushed me onto the lawn, where I collapsed with the horrible realization that Spero was right. We had been working for the enemy all along. No wonder Mama had looked so upset in the chamber. Aunt Caliga had been manipulating me from the start, and I went along with it, which made me no better.

Twenty

$$Spero$$

Everything was a lie, just as I had suspected. Amoura practically collapsed out of the door. I couldn't get to her in time, but I wouldn't leave her. Was this what it meant to be the essence of hope? For everyone to push their problems onto me and expect me to fix them all? If that's what they thought, then these sorceresses had another think coming.

"You really need to work on your people skills," I told the crazy cat lady.

Estella glanced toward Nix as though the cat would enlighten her about how to talk to other humans. "What did I say? I thought they'd be happy to know the truth."

I studied her for a moment to see if she was serious. There was no hint of sarcasm on her face. Nix curled up against the bottom of her lab coat.

I crossed my arms. "You can't just tell people that their sole purpose for existing was to fulfill some sort of crazy scheme you concocted and think they'll be fine with it. Imagine if someone told you your whole life was a lie."

She raised her eyebrows at me. "But I'm one of the three sorceress guardians. My life is very important."

I shook my head. "Just forget it."

I headed outside to check on Amoura, slamming the vertical door in Estella's face like the trunk of a car. Amoura was slumped over the ground, trembling in the middle of a panic attack. I couldn't get to her fast enough. It wasn't fair for her to have to take on the burden of these crazy sorceresses. I kneeled in front of her and wrapped my arms around her. Each shudder hit me like a punch in the gut. What good was being the essence of hope if I couldn't protect the person I…

Wait. Do I love Amoura?

I leaned my head in close enough to feel her tears rub against my cheek, forcing back the moisture that beckoned behind my own eyes. "We'll get through this. Somehow."

She lifted her head toward me, allowing me to see the redness marring her perfect face. It felt like a knife through my heart. Fighting our way through three labyrinths was so much easier than this. At least there we knew what to do. Now, an uncertain future wavered on the horizon. Should I ask Estella to send me back to Melanie? But that would mean abandoning Amoura, and I promised her I would never do that again. I had to see this thing through to the end.

"You don't understand," she sobbed. "All of this is my fault."

I ran my fingers through her soft brown hair. "Neither of us knew the crystal was going to harm our world."

She pulled away from me, exposing herself to the cold night air. "I'm not talking about the crystal."

I studied her face, trying to determine what sort of game she was playing. "You're not?"

"Nay." She stood up. "Dost thou not see? All of this happened because I was born. Mama couldn't return to Imperium because she wanted to take care of *me*. Aunt Estella and Aunt Caliga were forced to work together to make up for her absence. It's *my* fault our world was placed in danger. It's *my* fault Mama had to give up her powers. My existence has brought naught but pain and suffering to both worlds."

Her green eyes misted with tears. I wished I could whisk her far away and let the sorceresses deal with it themselves, but we were in too deep. All I could do was try to make her see her true value. She had no idea how important she was not just to Imperium, but to me.

I got up to face her. "What she did was her own decision. You didn't tell her to sacrifice herself, and frankly, I don't think she should have abandoned you the way she did. You deserve to be loved."

"How can anyone love me after all the destruction I've caused?" she sobbed. "And all the destruction that's yet to come?"

"Amoura," I said firmly. "Even if the whole world turns against you, it won't change the way I feel about you. Nothing ever could."

The flow of tears receded, and a hint of starlight reflected in her pupils. "How… do you feel about me?"

I placed my hands on her shoulders, staring into her beautiful green eyes. "I think you already know."

Her lips trembled, and the tears began to flow again. "I know not, truly. You are so brash with your words, yet there's so much that you keep to yourself. I fear if you do not tell me, I may never know."

Consequences be damned. She needs me.

I leaned toward her, pausing for a moment to give her a chance to pull away, but she didn't. Then, our lips met, blocking out the bitter night air. I could taste the dried tears on her face, but that didn't bother me. Her fingers threaded through my hair, pressing my face against hers with desperate urgency. I wrapped my arms around her as tightly as they could go. I didn't even loosen my grip when the gem on her pendant dug into my chest. At last, her breathing stabilized against my heartbeat, and the painful shudders subsided.

She fit so perfectly in my arms as though she belonged there. I was desperately in love with her. How had I not realized it before? I never wanted to let her go. Even if everyone else forced us to do their bidding, this was the one choice that was ours alone. Maybe we were an impossible pair, but we were together now. We'd deal with the future when we came to it.

"I hope this isn't what you meant by people skills."

Our tender moment was disrupted when I realized Mistress Estella had emerged from her bizarre house and had been watching us for who knew how long. Sparky bobbed up and down behind her, blowing angry sparks at us to get our attention.

I loosened my grip on Amoura but refused to let her go. "What do you want?"

The sorceress raised an eyebrow at our open display of affection. "I just came to warn you that if you exit my cloaking field, you'll be back in range of Caliga's scrying ball. You probably knew that already, though."

I clenched a fist behind Amoura's back. "So you're saying we're stuck here? We're your prisoners?"

Her eyes widened as though the notion shocked her. "Gracious, no! You're free to leave whenever you want. But Caliga is going to expect you to give her the earth shard as soon as you're back in her temporal field."

I turned toward Amoura. "It's not exactly a palace, but how do you feel about hiding out here for a while so we can figure out what to do next?"

Amoura sighed. "Life was so much simpler back home. I wish Mama were here. She'd know what to do."

Estella began petting Nix, who leaped into her arms. "That's easily resolved. Solara will be back to normal as soon as you defeat the last unicorn guardian."

Amoura stared at her. "Aunt Caliga said she couldn't wake up without the power of the restored crystal."

Estella huffed. "She really wants that thing, doesn't she? I should have considered the moral ramifications of harnessing so much power into a single vessel. It may have harmed her mental state."

I rolled my eyes. "No, you think?"

She peered at me through her spectacles. "Yes, I'm rather certain of it."

Some people just don't get sarcasm.

A flicker of hope flashed in Amoura's eyes. "Are you saying that if we enter the final labyrinth, Mama will wake up even if we do not give the last two crystal shards to Aunt Caliga?"

"Of course. The crystal has nothing to do with her powers."

Amoura gazed up at me with big puppy-dog eyes and an unspoken question behind her lips. If this would give her the confidence she needed, it was a no-brainer.

"Yes," I told her. "Of course I'll help you find the last labyrinth."

Her face lit up with delight as she gave me another warm squeeze.

"Why would you need to find it?" Estella interrupted. "Didn't my sister give you a radar?"

"No," I replied, "but that would have been very helpful."

"Come back inside. I can give you one that will pinpoint the exact location of the air labyrinth."

Nix scampered through the door in front of her. I escorted Amoura back into the sad excuse for a house. Estella handed me a small beeping device with a blinking red dot on it. The archaic technology made for a pretty rudimentary GPS, but I guess they wouldn't need something as detailed as Google Maps for a place like this.

"When I realized the number of dots was shrinking, I knew my sister was up to something," she explained. "I figured if I sent Nix to the next labyrinth, she'd eventually run into you. Of course, I couldn't send her into an active volcano, so it took a little longer than I thought. I'm sure you understand."

If we had known what was going on earlier, we never would have given Caliga the other two shards. At least we still had one that she hadn't gotten her grubby mitts on yet. Maybe we could use that to our advantage.

"Can the shards be destroyed?" I asked. "That way, Caliga can't use them to destroy Earth."

Estella stroked Nix's fur pensively. "I don't think you realize the ramifications of tampering with the magical polarity of the core elements when they're already in a state of instability."

"English, please," I groaned.

She rolled her eyes. "Breaking the crystal into its core elemental essences is the maximum amount of damage it can take without causing a natural anomaly so big that it could obliterate all of Imperium. Didn't you notice that removing the shards from the labyrinths caused them to collapse at an accelerated rate?"

I crossed my arms. "Yeah. We noticed."

She rotated her finger through the air like a tornado. "Imagine that happening on a planetary level. Nothing would be left."

Amoura gasped. "Spero, we mustn't let that happen!"

"No, of course not," I assured her.

Amoura regarded her eccentric aunt. "Would you be so kind as to hold on to the earth shard for safekeeping here?"

"I can," responded Estella, "but I can't promise you Caliga won't find it, eventually. She's pretty determined. And I can't harness its power without the risk of getting corrupted like her."

Amoura pulled the shard out of my pocket.

"Hey!" I objected.

A green glow surrounded it, like when we found it in the labyrinth. Amoura winced. "Why does it feel the same way my pendant does when I activate it? All I did was touch it."

Estella took the crystal and held it a few inches away from Amoura's hand. Its glow receded.

"Fascinating. It seems to have bonded with you."

"That energy pulse isn't normal?" I asked. "I felt it too."

"Solara's spell tying the crystal to the essences of hope and love must have had a more powerful effect than she realized. I'd like to try an experiment. What happens if you both touch it at the same time?"

She handed the crystal shard back to Amoura. She held it out toward me. I encircled my fingers around hers with the shard between our palms. An unexpected surge of electricity shot through my body. Was this what it felt like to be struck by lightning? The room spun around me, and the corners of my vision darkened. It felt as though the crystal shard was trying to suck out all my energy. From the look on Amoura's face, she was experiencing something similar. I opened my hand and squeezed the shard out of Amoura's fingers, forcing it to clatter to the floor.

Amoura caught her breath. "By the saints!"

I wrapped my arm around her waist. "What the heck was that? Are you trying to kill us?"

Estella picked up the shard and placed it in some sort of oversized microscope. She peeked into the viewfinder.

She shrugged. "It was merely an experiment. Your bond with the crystal may become beneficial in the future. I'll have to take down this information."

She waved her finger over a journal. A series of handwritten notes appeared on a blank page.

"Will this bond help us stop Aunt Caliga?" asked Amoura.

Estella adjusted some knobs on the viewfinder device and peered inside it again.

"That remains to be seen. We can conduct more experiments tomorrow. It's getting late. I'm guessing you two will be staying the night to avoid Caliga's temporal field. Am I right?"

I glanced at Amoura. "It's up to you. What do you want to do?"

She fidgeted with a lock of long brown hair. "We can stay with Aunt Estella. Once we free Mama tomorrow, we can all figure out a way to protect Earth for good. Then, mayhap, we can go home."

I beamed at her. "Sounds like a plan!"

She glanced away from me as she always did when she was

embarrassed. "But that means we shall be separated back to our own times…"

As much as I wanted to get back to Melanie, the idea of never seeing Amoura again left a bitter taste in my mouth. Would I never be able to kiss her again? I refused to let the unknown hold us back.

"Well, tomorrow's a new day. Maybe we can still find a way to be together. We are in a place of magic after all."

Estella pressed a button, and a section of the floor flipped over to reveal a large mattress and some pillows.

"I don't usually have guests over, but I'm always prepared for anything." A misplaced sense of pride filled her voice. Nix meowed and nuzzled her ankle.

I glanced at Amoura, trying to see if she noticed the obvious problem. When she didn't react, I spoke up.

"There's only one bed…"

"This is lovely," she interrupted me. "I thank you kindly."

Our situation had shaken up in the course of a single day, but as long as Amoura was by my side, I knew we could get through anything. We just needed to find one more crystal shard, and then all this craziness would be over.

Twenty-One

Amoura

unt Estella's words blew me to the edge of a cliff, and only Spero could break my fall. I no longer wondered if he felt the same towards me as I did towards him. Yet, I'd let down so many others with my actions, and they would not all be as forgiving. The unicorns could no longer protect the forests. Though I knew now that Aunt Caliga was in the wrong, an uncomfortable guilt still burrowed within my stomach for choosing to go against her. Would Mama forgive me for going after the last shard to bring her back, despite what I'd learned? No matter what I did, someone would get hurt. The essence of love within me burned like the pit of a volcano.

My head hit the stiff mattress, which reminded me of the one I slept on at the cottage back home. Spero paced back and forth next to it. Exhaustion crept into the corners of his eyes.

"I can sleep on the floor," he offered.

"You will do no such thing," I replied, pulling him down next to me. "We are not going to insult Aunt Estella's hospitality."

In truth, his proximity was the only thing preventing the dam inside me from bursting again, but he didn't need to know that part.

He relaxed on the stiff mattress. "You are way too trusting, Amoura. Look where it's gotten us."

"Perhaps you're right," I admitted, "but I know for certain that my trust in thee isn't misplaced."

He nudged me with his elbow. "You're impossible, you know that?"

I leaned back and snuggled into his chest. He gave up resisting and wrapped his arm around me. Before we could get too comfortable, our scaly friend wedged himself between us, hogging my pillow.

Yay, slumber party! Sparky loves slumber parties!

As I yanked the pillow back, it snagged on his wing with an uncomfortable tearing sound. Considering the state of Aunt Estella's home, I hoped she wouldn't notice.

"Sparky," I warned.

What? Sparky didn't get a bed.

"You can stay here for one night as long as you behave."

A snort echoed from the other side of the bed as I realized Spero was laughing. Reaching over Sparky, I whacked him with my torn pillow.

"That's not funny!" I whined.

He shielded himself with his own pillow. "Yes, it is."

"Perhaps a bit," I admitted. "I pray we steal a few hours' rest. It has been a trying day."

"That's fine with me."

He rolled over and started snoring. I slept uneasily with

thoughts about the fate of both Imperium and Earth rushing through my mind like tidal waves. How did the responsibility of protecting two worlds fall on me? A week ago, I was naught but a farmer's daughter. Now, I was both the cause and the solution to everyone's problems. How could Spero rest so easily despite knowing all this?

* * *

I woke to a bright light shining through the small circular windows. I couldn't remember the last time I'd slept past dawn. Blinking my eyes open, I saw Spero across the room talking to Aunt Estella about the radar. Foreign words rang in my ears, bogging down my thoughts as I regained consciousness. How familiar was Aunt Estella with Spero's timeline? Mama never used such confusing technical jargon around me. Spero operated the strange device as though he had done so a thousand times before. It must have been similar to the magic wands he told me about from the future.

"I get that these numbers are longitude and latitude, but what's this other one, and why is it so high?"

Estella peered at the strange device. "That's the altitude. The air labyrinth is higher up than the ones you've completed so far."

Spero shook his head. "But this high an altitude would be all the way in the clouds. That can't be right."

She looked perplexed. "Why not? It's a more reasonable destination than an active volcano. You have a dragon, don't you?"

I moaned and rolled over.

"Good morning, sleepyhead," Spero greeted me.

"Must we ride the dragon again?" I mumbled into the pillow.

"Amoura's a bit acrophobic," Spero explained to Estella.

"I am not!" I huffed, throwing my pillow at him. "What's that?"

"Fear of heights," Estella responded.

I stood up and ran my fingers through my hair. "Oh. Perhaps a little."

"How can we prevent Caliga from coming after us when we get the last shard?" asked Spero. "We'll need to keep them hidden in a safe place after Solara wakes up."

Estella pointed to the device. "The radar has a cloaking mechanism in it, so you should be fine as long as you hang onto it."

"That sounds good."

I joined them next to the table of oddities. "Aunt Estella, I was wondering something."

A glint appeared behind her eyes. "Ask away. I may not have all the answers, but I've sure got a lot of them!"

"If you created Spero's ring, did you also make my pendant?"

She glanced at the pink gem hanging over my heart. "Oh yes, the Healing Pendant was such a fun project! It was a parting gift for Solara on her trip to Earth. I didn't know what kind of dangers she would face there, so I gave her something to keep her safe from injuries. Of course, we didn't expect her to stay away as long as she did. Maybe it worked a little too well. I should have given her something less useful, like a vase or a magnet."

"Can you tell me how it works? I'm getting better at it, but I understand not whence the magic comes."

She peered at me through the glass circles covering her eyes. "You're able to use it?"

"Yes, I believe so."

"That's great! Congratulations, Amoura. You're a sorceress, just like us!"

"Truly?" I gasped. "That must be a falsehood. I have no powers."

"Sure you do. The pendant enhances your innate healing abilities. It doesn't grant them."

I glanced at Spero to gauge if he sensed some sort of trickery in her words, but he shrugged.

"But the magic always felt like it came from the pendant. I thought Mama was blessing me with her love from afar."

Nix jumped onto the table, and Estella petted her between the ears. "That's sweet, but it doesn't work that way. If you don't know how to channel your powers without the pendant, it's probably because you were living on Earth for so long. There's also that inferior mortal side of your blood."

"My father is *not* inferior!" I huffed.

"Sure, he is. He doesn't have magic. That makes him inferior. I always wondered what Solara saw in him."

"Fie on thee!" My hand clenched into a tight fist. "I would have you know that my father singlehandedly raised me and ran an entire farm in my mother's absence!"

Spero's fingers wrapped around my wrist. "Maybe we can save this for another time. Why don't we head to the labyrinth now?"

I calmed down at his touch, but I was still shocked by Aunt Estella's brash behavior, and to think I once thought Spero had no manners.

"Very well," I sighed. "Let's go."

Spero guided me toward the bizarre-shaped door.

"Hold on!" shouted Estella.

She pressed a button on a strange-looking metallic machine that rattled unnaturally and released dark pink fumes. Two brownish bars with clumps of a wheat-like substance popped out of it.

"You can't leave without breakfast. My patented protein-o-matic machine infuses all the best nutrients in Imperium into an easily digestible bite-sized bar!"

Spero looked at the bar with disgust. He probably had grand banquets every day where he came from. "Uh, thanks."

I graciously accepted the oddly shaped snack. "This was very thoughtful of you, Aunt Estella."

I bit into it. It had a strange texture, but it tasted like fresh bread and berries. By the time I finished, I felt surprisingly full.

"'Tis delicious!" I beamed.

Spero took a reluctant bite.

"Not bad," he admitted.

I grabbed Sparky before he broke one of the colorful-looking glass tubes on Estella's worktable.

"Sparky, do you think you can summon your mother for us when we get outside?"

Mommy always comes when Sparky calls her!

"Then let us be on our way."

Spero and I stepped out of the cloaking bubble, causing Estella's house to disappear into a patch of empty forest. I wasn't sure I would ever get used to that. Hopefully, we'd be able to find our way back to it when we needed to. There weren't many landmarks nearby. Sparky fidgeted out of my arms and squealed so loudly that Spero and I were forced to cover our ears.

"Is there a volume button on that thing?" Spero shouted.

"A *what?*" I shouted back.

"Never mind."

Once the ringing in our ears died down, the massive dragon landed in the clearing. Sparky flew into his mother's claws, and she nuzzled her nose against him. A faint tinge of smoke filled the air. Spero held out the radar in front of the creature's enormous, emerald-green eyes.

"So, we need to go forty miles due east of here at an altitude of thirty-thousand feet. Does all of that make sense?"

The dragon studied the radar and nodded, gesturing for us to get on its back. I wished we could travel on foot, but that didn't seem possible for where we needed to go. I waited for Spero to climb up first and accepted his help to support me in front of him. Sparky rested on the back of his mother's neck.

"Are we clear for takeoff?" Spero asked.

"Give me a min-UUUUUUUUUUUUUUUUUUUTE!"

I screamed as the dragon shot up like a bolt from my crossbow at a perfect vertical angle. My heart caught in my throat as we slid down its back to its tail, which curled out from under us. I squeezed my eyes shut and held my breath, awaiting the inevitable plunge to our deaths. But it never came. Spero gripped me around my waist, his back supported by the dragon's spiky tail. It didn't look very comfortable, but at least we were still alive.

"Sparky!" I shouted. "Can you tell her to slow down?"

Sparky screeched something to his mother. Her response interrupted her flight path as Spero's grip on me tightened. If I lived to see Mama or anyone else after this experience, it would be a miracle.

Mommy says she needs to go this fast to get us high enough!

I sighed.

"I'm guessing that was a no," Spero mumbled from behind me, a hint of amusement in his voice.

"Surely you're not enjoying this!"

"It's a bit rougher than most roller coasters I've been on. Definitely more turbulent than our private jet."

If I hadn't been so worried about plunging to my doom, I would have elbowed him in the ribs. Finally, the dragon straightened out, allowing us to sit up on her back. The protein bar Estella gave us worked its way back up my stomach. I took a deep breath and leaned into Spero's grip. He was the only thing keeping me grounded.

"That was pretty rough," Spero admitted. "Looks like the worst of it is over."

Once the dizziness subsided, I realized the surrounding scenery was actually quite beautiful. We flew through cotton candy-like clouds of pink, lilac, and peach. I reached out and ran my fingers through one of them. It felt soft and light under my fingers.

"This is incredible," I admitted.

Spero grinned. "It wouldn't be safe to be out in the open at this altitude on Earth. This is a new experience for both of us."

Further ahead was an oddly shaped cloud that looked thicker than the rest. It formed the shape of a small castle, no bigger than our cottage. Nestled in the white fluff was a familiar stone disk with foreign symbols on it.

I straightened my posture. "Is that the labyrinth?"

"Let me check the radar."

Spero felt around his pockets and then all over the dragon's rough scales. Finally, he gave up searching.

"Don't tell me you *lost* it!" I shrieked.

He gave me a sheepish grin. "It must have fallen when we were flying up. You have to admit that was a rough ascent. Anyway, I'm pretty sure we're here."

Sparky's mother let us off on the cloud. It was incredibly soft, although I was worried it might not support our weight for long. Spero and I reached out and touched the stone, causing the symbols to glow with pink and blue light. The door opened, and we stumbled across the uneven, vaporous ground.

Wait for Sparky!

Sparky's plea faded into the distance; an empty white room with glowing walls swallowed everything around us. Once we passed this final challenge, I would finally be able to speak to my mother again.

Twenty-Two

Spero

When we entered the final labyrinth, I expected to find traps and danger around every turn, not an empty white void. The space seemed endless. Were we just supposed to stand here and wait for something to happen? I fumbled around the room until my hand hit a smooth surface.

"Invisible walls, huh? Nice gimmick."

"Spero? Where did you go?"

Amoura's voice alerted me that she was gone. So far, only the unicorns we fought had an AR filter over them, but here, it shielded the entire labyrinth. That meant I couldn't believe anything I saw, not that there was much to look at.

"Amoura? Can you hear me?"

"Just barely!" she shouted back. Her voice grew fainter.

"Keep talking. I'm going to find you."

Feeling my way through the blank, bright space, I slipped

through a gap that led to another passageway. My fingers brushed along the cold, smooth walls, searching for more hidden paths. No matter how deep I went, the white void around me never shifted.

"Spero?"

She sounded closer this time.

"Hang on!"

Pivoting around a corner, I came upon a horrifying sight. A giant snake monster had knocked Amoura to the ground. Coils of orange scales wrapped around her. Its upper half resembled a woman with dark hair, sharp teeth, and solid black eyes. The creature matched the features of a lamia. Was it another anomaly or a trick being played by the labyrinth?

"No!"

I drew my sword and raced toward it, but the blade slid right through it, driving straight into an invisible wall. Another illusion, then. I hoped that meant Amoura's lifeless form was an illusion as well. Bending down to brush my fingers through her hair, I felt nothing but air, just like the monsters we fought before revealing their true forms. The dangers here surpassed everything we'd faced so far. Holograms manipulated the air around us.

"Amoura," I shouted, "If you can hear me, don't believe anything you see here. It's all an illusion."

"I think I found the shard!" she shouted back.

I tried to pinpoint the direction her voice had come from. Then I noticed the weight missing from the sheath on my back. My sword was still stuck in the wall. I gave it a quick tug, but it wouldn't budge. Feeling a little like King Arthur, I jiggled it around until it came loose and returned it to its proper place. I was chasing the sound of Amoura's voice when I smashed into another wall. Black spots dotted my field of vision. I felt something drip from my nose. Rubbing my finger under it revealed a trickle of blood because I forgot to feel my way around first. We couldn't get out of this place soon enough, if we tried.

"Spero?" Amoura called. "Are you all right?"

"Fine," I lied.

"I still can't see you."

"Don't move. I'm going to try to make my way around to you."

Feeling along the wall, another pivot brought me back in the opposite direction. I'd played games before where dungeons forced you to take a long winding path to reach a short distance, so I continued running my hand along the wall before it finally swiveled back around to the other side.

Around the corner, the white space was broken by a pedestal with a glowing shard floating over it. As much as I wanted to reach the end of this place, I knew my eyes were deceiving me. No monstrous unicorn guarded it. More importantly, no timeless beauty with long brown hair and intense green eyes awaited me, and I refused to go anywhere without her.

"Amoura, are you still there?" I called.

"Yes!"

I pushed along the wall past the pedestal, following Amoura's voice. When I glanced behind me, a gaping hole punctured the ground where it had been. I shuddered to imagine what would have happened if I had gone after the shard, or worse, if Amoura had. After turning a corner, I finally saw her waiting for me in the distance. I crossed my fingers, hoping the vision of loveliness before me wasn't too good to be true. In front of her was a series of floating stones leading to a platform above our heads, where something glowed brightly. Hoping I wouldn't smash into another wall, I ran to Amoura and scooped her into my arms. Her soft warmth filled me with relief.

Her arms wrapped around my back, and she rested her head on my shoulder. "I'm glad you're not another illusion. We've had some difficult trials in the labyrinths before, but this place is terrifying. I know not what to believe anymore."

"Tell me about it. Back there, I saw…"

She lifted her head to face me. Concern filled her eyes. "What did you see?"

"Nothing. Never mind."

She leaned and placed a light kiss on my lips that made me yearn for her.

"What was that for?" I asked.

"Just making certain it's really you."

I smirked. "You're welcome to double-check if you want. I don't know if that was convincing enough."

She nudged me with her elbow. "There will be plenty of time for that after we leave this place. I think we just need to climb the stones. We've done this before."

I frowned. "Yeah, but there was always some sort of gimmick involved. Jump on the wrong one, and we might be stuck here for good."

I tried to place my foot on the first stone, but there was nowhere for it to land. Stumbling forward, I teetered down toward an invisible pit like the one I saw when I passed the fake crystal shard. Amoura grabbed my shoulders and pulled me back.

I straightened my posture, relieved to be back on solid ground. "That's a no-go on the stones."

Amoura leaned down and studied the stone I had fumbled on. She carefully examined the white space surrounding it with her hands. Then she started to climb up an empty space next to it, looking as though she was floating in thin air.

My heart leaped into my throat as flashbacks of the lamia crept into my head. "Be careful!"

She leaped unscathed onto the next level as though she were standing in midair. She waved her arms back at me. "I've figured it out. The stones are illusions, but the real steps are right next to them. Just follow my lead."

I approached the invisible platform and climbed up after her, keeping my gaze plastered straight ahead to avoid losing my balance from the steep drop below us. Growing accustomed to the distance between the floating stones and the actual steps, we began to gain momentum. Amoura hesitated when we reached the platform, feeling the area next to the stone.

"I think there's no step here."

I felt around the invisible platform with my feet. The ground under my foot gave way if I tried to go straight, but it kept going if I stayed at an angle. Recalling the long passageway that looped backward in the previous area, I determined our next move.

"I think it's a ramp. We need to loop around to get to the top."

Amoura followed me as we ascended the invisible ramp that led us around to our destination. Finally, we reached a stone pedestal with a white crystal shard shimmering on top of it. But we weren't alone. Disbelief flooded my eyes as I took in the sight of the little girl with curly blonde hair staring at me with wide eyes, a girl I hadn't stopped worrying about since I got sucked into this crazy world.

"Melanie?"

Her blue eyes lit up with sheer delight upon hearing me say her name. Her curls bounced up and down, reminding me of home.

"Spero, I missed you!"

I squeezed my eyes shut. "No. You're not really here. This is an illusion."

Amoura's eyes misted over as she took a step toward the dangerous apparition. "This isn't your sister."

"I know that."

"'Tis my father."

"What? Amoura, no."

I grabbed her arm as she inched closer. We just needed to get the crystal shard. Then this would all be over. Yet, the entity before us that looked like my little sister was welcoming Amoura with open arms. As their hands touched, a shimmer of blood trickled down her hand.

"Get back!" I shouted. "This is a trick."

"Take heart, Spero," Amoura replied. "He'd never hurt me."

I drew my sword and pointed it at the illusion.

"Get away from her."

"Are you going to kill me, big brother?"

Every instinct in my body urged me to retreat. Hearing those words come out of Melanie's mouth made it impossible for me to act. It looked so much like her.

It isn't real. It isn't real.

My hands shook over the hilt of my blade, ultimately dropping the sword of their own volition. I couldn't hurt my sister, even just someone who looked like her.

"I knew you couldn't do it," she said as an uncharacteristic smirk formed on her lips.

Then the creature was on top of me. I felt a stabbing pain in my side. The illusion blinked out, revealing a pure white unicorn with a silver spiral drill for a horn that dug its way into my flank. I grabbed its muzzle and pushed back as hard as I could, but my strength abandoned me.

"Father, desist, I pray you!" Amoura squealed. "Spero is my friend!"

"Just grab the shard!" I wheezed. "Then all of this will be over."

Amoura reached toward the glowing pedestal, but the unicorn reared back and knocked her off her feet with its hooves. I took advantage of the opportunity to roll out of the way, pulling myself upright on the pedestal as I reached up toward the crystal. I clenched it in my fist. The familiar surge of energy pulsed through my body, widening the open wound in my flank, as my vision started to blur.

The unicorn whinnied, and I saw a blur of silhouettes flash before my eyes of every other monster we had faced in the labyrinths. First, there was the kraken. Then there was the lava blob. Finally, the rock golem morphed back into my sister, and then a brown-haired man that I assumed was Amoura's father. It blinked out of existence in a blinding burst of light as my legs gave way. I hit the ground, where the white void surrounding me faded to black.

Twenty-Three

Amoura

I prayed it was another illusion, but the pounding in my heart knew otherwise. A dark red spot bloomed across the side of Spero's tunic. If I didn't act quickly, he'd remain trapped here forever, and all hope would be lost. Would the passionate kiss we shared last night be our last? No, I couldn't let that happen.

The labyrinth collapsed all around me. Illusions faded away, revealing the actual layout of the room. The white void shifted to stone walls. Everything around me changed, except the one thing I longed for the most. Spero would not wake up. Why couldn't I harm the unicorn when I had the chance to prevent all of this? My heart kept fighting what my brain tried to tell me, and Spero got hurt as a result.

I knelt beside him, adjusting his prone form to assess the wound. A crystal shard rolled out of his pocket. I ignored it. One less shard for Caliga to manipulate for her nefarious purposes. His wound was quite deep, worse than any I had healed before. I closed my eyes and concentrated on the love that burned through me with every fiber of my being. A bright pink light emitted from my pendant, but it wasn't enough. The floor caved in around us. It wouldn't be much longer before it took us with it. I let the magic pour out of me until I reached the point of exhaustion.

"Leave me not, my love," I whispered as the light from my pendant faded.

Spero's eyes fluttered open, not a moment too soon. The torn flesh finished stitching back together, but he had lost a lot of blood. The floor below us gave way. I clung to his shirt and felt his arms wrap around me as a gust of wind blasted us out of the labyrinth. The soft, spongy surface of the cloud we entered through broke our fall. As the gate puffed out of existence, the crystal shard flew into my hand, with nowhere else to go. Threads of magic surged through my body, tugging at my remaining strength. I should have known I wouldn't be able to rid myself of it that easily.

A surge of panic dropped into my stomach as the cloud gave way, leaving nothing to protect us from the ground far below. Thankfully, our dragon friend anticipated our return. We landed on her back with a thud. A familiar bundle of joy flew into my arms.

You left Sparky behind again!

"Not by choice," I assured him. "Can you tell your mother to be gentle with her flight? Spero is hurt."

Oh, no! What happened?

"It's a long story," I sighed.

Spero sat up on the dragon's scaly hide, wincing in pain. "Looks like we made it out of there."

I couldn't meet his gaze. "I'm sorry I couldn't do more. Thy wound was quite deep."

His fingers nestled under my chin, forcing me to look at him. "No need for apologies. You're probably the only reason I'm still alive."

"Thank goodness for that. I would never have forgiven myself if you had not made it out because of me."

He frowned. "What do you mean?"

"I was so sure I saw my father standing there. My crossbow was right by my side, yet I did nothing, and because of that, you…" I blinked away tears.

Spero crossed his arms. "That wasn't your fault. I couldn't attack that thing either. It looked too much like my little sister."

I showed him the crystal shard that was still clutched in my hand. "I tried to leave this behind, but it wouldn't let me."

"Mistress Estella, or your mother, will know what to do with it. We won't let Caliga get her hands on it. Don't worry."

We glided to the ground. I climbed off the dragon and waited a moment for the dizziness to subside.

"Amoura?"

My breath caught in my throat. I hadn't heard that voice in nine years. There, waiting for me in the empty patch of forest, stood a woman with long blue hair, reaching out to me. The world around me faded away until only the pounding of my heart and her open embrace remained.

"Mama!"

I threw my arms around her, sobbing. She looked the same as she had the day she left us. Soft layers of pink chiffon covered her sun-kissed skin.

"My sweet daughter," she cooed. "You've grown into such a

lovely young woman."

I brushed a stray tear from my cheek. "You're not angry that I recovered the crystal shards you sealed away?"

She ran her fingers through my hair. "Of course not, dear. If you hadn't done that, we never would have had the chance to see each other again. Estella tells me you just retrieved the final one."

I clutched the crystal shard between my fingers when I realized the scent of cinnamon and roses was missing. Even the unicorn that disguised itself as Father had carried her scent. "You're not mad at all? Even after everything you gave up to seal them away?"

The corner of her lips twitched for the briefest moment. "No, dear. We just need to hide them again. Just hand me the shard, and I'll take care of everything just like I did back then. It'll be like nothing changed."

I took a step back. "But everything's changed. I know about Imperium now. I know that the anomalies were caused because you stayed on Earth to care for me. Do you plan on returning to Father and me and abandoning your people again?"

She held out her hand to me. "Give me the shard, Amoura. We can discuss all that later."

The shard cut into my palm as I clenched it. "No."

Her voice grew softer, but it still didn't sound like Mama. "What's wrong, dear? Don't you trust me?"

I took another step backward. "You're not my mother."

Her hand lit up with a faint purple glow. I heard Spero slide out his sword behind me.

Her voice darkened. "Fine. I was trying to be nice, but you clearly want to do things the hard way."

She shot a blast of purple lightning at me. My legs buckled as the crystal shard rolled out of my hand. Spero, still shaking from his injury, caught me under my arms before I hit the ground. An agonizing paralysis set in, rendering me helpless. Was this the hex that Spero had told me about on our first day here?

Mama's image melted away into a familiar face with skin dark as night and hair the color of lilacs. Caliga snatched up the last shard as freedom of movement returned to my body. I let out the breath I hadn't realized I was holding. Once I could stand up on my own, Spero ran at her with his sword.

"You'll pay for this!" he shouted.

Another blast of purple lightning caused him to drop his sword and collapse to the ground. I knelt over him, desperately summoning my magic. It poured out of my pendant in waves until my vision blurred and my breath grew shallow. In the corner of my eye, Caliga pulled out the other three crystal shards.

"It was so nice of you to lead me to my sister's hideout. I've been trying to locate her for years."

"No," I whispered.

Like a series of Chinese rings, the four shards clicked into place one by one in the air as though taking on a life of their own. The crystal glowed over us with a shimmering black light that snuffed out any remaining chance of salvation. Its power crackled under my veins, pinching every nerve in my body until the very act of breathing became agony.

"Foolish girl," Caliga cackled. "You thought you could double-cross me! I'm much wiser and more powerful than you'll ever be."

"Desist, I beg you!" I cried.

I pulled out my crossbow and fired a bolt directly at the newly formed crystal. The bolt shimmered in the dark light and faded into nothingness. Caliga raised her arms. Purple beams mixed with the black glow of the crystal, lifting her into the sky. The sweet temptation of slumber tugged at the corners of my mind, but I refused to give in. The world around me shifted into shapes and colors when a vision appeared before me. Mama—my *real* Mama—materialized in a blue shimmer on white feathered wings. Even teetering on the brink of consciousness, I knew it was her.

"Amoura, what have you done?"

"I'm deeply sorry!" I shrieked. "I thought she was you at first, and the unicorn looked so much like Father. All I've done is make a horrible mess of everything!"

A familiar embrace wrapped around me as my head collapsed onto Spero's chest. I should have heeded his warnings from the start. Why couldn't I have been stronger?

"We'll get through this," he promised. "Somehow."

Then Estella appeared in a cloud of pink smoke. Tears in her coat and scratches on her wrists hinted at signs of a struggle. She stood on a glowing pink disk that levitated in the air, carrying her up to Caliga.

"Caliga, calm down. You don't have to do this," she pleaded. "Solara is awake again. That means the balance of magic in Imperium will be restored. The anomalies will stop now."

Caliga's lips curled into a terrifying grin. "You think I did this to stop the anomalies? No, sister. Do you know what your problem is? You always think too small. You thought harnessing the elements would simply make up for Solara's absence without considering the untapped potential to expand our tiny world. There's a whole other civilization out there with billions of people to rule over. Imperium is so small in comparison. How much power do we really have?"

"You don't understand," replied Estella. "Power leads to corruption. Imperium is better off this way."

"No, *you* don't understand. You prefer to live in hiding, conducting your little experiments day in and day out, never considering your importance as a guardian. You're no better than Solara, abandoning everyone for your own selfish desires. Who was here to watch over them in your absence? I know what is best for our people. Thanks to your creation, Imperium can evolve into a world with limitless potential."

"I pray you, Aunt Caliga," I cried. "Surely, there's a way to expand this world without involving mine!"

She spat on the ground. "What do you know? You're just a mortal."

Mama's wings carried her up to the other sorceresses, shedding white feathers around us. Spero and I watched helplessly from the ground. I clutched my pendant, trying to summon my remaining power, but I had nothing left to give.

"Caliga, please don't do this," Mama begged. "You must have spent time with my daughter before I awoke. You must have learned how wonderful her world is. People there work so hard to look after each other, and they do it without magic."

"And that's why it will be so easy to rule over all of them. Join me, sisters, and together we can have unlimited power!"

I fired more bolts at the crystal to no avail. Caliga raised her arms over it, and the pulsating energy blasted through my veins. From the way Spero's arms shook around me, I knew he felt it too. A blast of energy rippled far and wide throughout the surrounding area, knocking us off our feet. Tremors radiated through the ground below us like the labyrinths did when they were torn from existence. Was Caliga going to destroy Imperium?

Instead of collapsing, the land around us expanded. Buildings sprouted out of patches of dirt on the ground. Brick and stone structures from my time loomed over us, alongside towers so tall that they rose into the sky. Time and space had collapsed. Spero stared at the new architecture that formed around us with as much shock and wonder as I felt. There was no returning home for us now. Caliga had pulled Earth's essence into her world, making the two one and the same.

Dazed and confused people sprouted up out of nowhere, trying to grasp their surroundings. A woman in a simple dress clutched her children to protect them from the mysterious force that had brought them here. A man in a gray suit spilled a brown drink on the ground and began yelling at someone. Teenagers chased each other through the woods, weaving between structures as though playing some sort of archaic game.

Caliga's face glowed with satisfaction. "Now, who will help me lead these people? My sisters have proven more than useless. Amoura, my dear, I believe there was someone from your time who earned the respect of everyone in the land. Maybe she will prove useful in showing me how to earn their respect as well."

The agonizing surge of the crystal's energy signature pulsated through me once more as Spero tightened his comforting embrace around me.

In a flash of black light, a woman I had only seen from a distance once before materialized in front of us. She wore a grand white gown. A golden crown adorned her red hair, fastened on top of her head.

"What am I doing here?" she demanded. "What happened to my castle?"

I gave a shaky curtsy. "Your Majesty, Queen Elizabeth?"

Twenty-Four

Spero

Of all the ways I expected Caliga to double-cross us, she found a way to elude me. Caliga didn't destroy the Earth. She absorbed it. And not just one point in time. Somehow, people and places from all different eras were scattered throughout Imperium. Steel skyscrapers, wooden shacks, teepees, and everything in between littered the once peaceful forests. Pollution choked the sparkling mists that once filled the air.

I pulled Amoura out of the way as a BMW from the '60s whizzed past in the middle of her conversation with Queen Elizabeth—the one from her time—who looked like an illustration right out of one of my school history books.

"So you see, Your Majesty," Amoura explained, "despite our best efforts, we weren't powerful enough to stop my aunt from bringing you and all these people to Imperium."

The queen pursed her lips, her gaze looming over Amoura

like an insect that needed to be squashed. I disliked her instantly.

"Intriguing. Well, no matter where I am, I am still a queen by providence, so I expect to be escorted to the castle immediately while I decide thy punishment."

Amoura gulped. "My punishment?"

She tapped a slender finger on her chin. "I'm considering having ye both beheaded, but it may benefit me to keep you alive a little longer since you seem to possess valuable information about the situation."

I tightened my grip on Amoura, wincing from the added pressure on my wound from the labyrinth. "No one's beheading anyone!"

The queen sneered at me. "Such insolence! Thou wilt bow to thy queen and show the proper respect."

"Look, lady, I'm an American citizen, and we don't bow to anyone."

A jolt of magical energy pulsed through my legs, forcing me to kneel.

Caliga descended from the air like a drone with a low battery charge. "That one has been a thorn in my side ever since I brought him here," she explained. "In fact, now that they have served their purpose, I have little use for either of them. Perhaps I should dispose of them right now."

Her hand lit up with a sinister purple glow. I reached for my sword.

"You will do no such thing!" Solara shouted.

White feathers drifted around us from her wings. Her hand lit up with a shimmering glow, forming a transparent silvery wall between us and Caliga.

"We must not tarry," replied Elizabeth. "These things must

follow the proper procedure so that the people accuse us not of tyranny. I believe a trial might be in order to determine if a public execution is necessary."

Caliga extended a hand to the queen. "Why don't you come back to the palace with me, Your Majesty? I'm in charge around here, but I could use some advice on ruling so many new subjects. I think a public execution would be an excellent idea. Why don't we discuss it over tea?"

The queen nodded. "That would be lovely."

Caliga waved her hand. They disappeared in a blinding flash of white light accompanied by a deafening sound like a transformer exploding. I covered my ears and waited for the ringing to subside.

"That wasn't normal, was it?"

"What was that?" Amoura shouted, holding her hands over her ears as well.

Estella floated over on a weird-looking hoverboard. "It looks like her powers weren't compatible with the crystal's magic signature."

I uncovered my ears. "Is that something we need to be concerned about?"

"At the moment, I'm more concerned about the spontaneous degradation of two worlds and its ramifications on society, the environment, and our overall well-being."

"Good point."

Amoura's mother floated down like an angel descending from the heavens. Her feathered wings collapsed in a silver shimmer along with the wall she had formed, which had probably just saved our lives from Caliga's massive energy blast. She looked directly at me. I glanced at Amoura, hoping she would cut in before I made an idiot of myself in front of her mom.

"I don't believe we've met. You seem to be acquainted with my daughter."

This is awkward.

I gave her a polite nod. "I'm Spero, the essence of hope. I helped Amoura gather the crystal shards, which unfortunately led to this whole mess. It wasn't her fault, though. She just wanted to see you again."

She raised an eyebrow at our proximity. "You two seem awfully close."

I placed a hand behind my neck. "Yeah, I'm also kind of her boyfriend."

"He's my suitor," Amoura said at the same time.

She tilted her head with a curious glint in her green eyes that reminded me of Amoura. "Did you two meet on Earth?"

I rubbed my chin, trying to come up with an explanation. "No. I'm actually from the future. I think. Time is kind of messy right now."

"I recruited him," Estella piped in. "There was no chance of getting our third guardian back and stopping the anomalies if we didn't have hope. You should have been more specific with your spellcasting. The required components to unlock the seals were incomplete."

Solara sucked in a sharp breath. "They were meant to be incomplete."

Amoura stepped forward. "Mama, I cannot begin to express how sorry I am for all of this. I should never have trusted her. Spero tried to warn me."

I squeezed her hand. "It's not your fault, Amoura. None of this would have happened if she had just told you the truth when you were a kid."

Amoura reached up and pinched my arm.

"Ow!"

"He's right," Solara admitted. "I should have been more upfront instead of brazenly sacrificing myself without considering the consequences. You're not the only one with regrets."

Amoura let go of my hand and went to hug her mother.

"I missed you so much," she sobbed.

Solara stroked her hair. "You've grown into such a lovely young woman. I wish I had been there to see it."

Mother and daughter reunited at last. This would have been my time to peace out and let her return to her own life if the world hadn't just gotten destroyed. Despite everything that happened, the sparkle of joy in Amoura's eyes gave me some solace.

Estella glanced at me. "Would this be a bad time to discuss corrective actions? I'm not sure if you've noticed, but the worlds are in crisis right now."

I crossed my arms. "We've noticed."

"It's probably not a good idea to go back to the castle with the two queens planning your execution, so the three of you should stay with me for a bit."

"But doesn't Caliga know where your house is now?"

She chuckled. "That's no problem. I'll just press the auto-transport button and send it to a secluded part of the world. I do it all the time. Uninvited guests can be so irritating, present company excluded, of course."

I was about to quip a sarcastic response when an impossibly familiar cry for help interrupted my thoughts, accompanied by an urgent tug of magical force from my ring, burning through my finger.

"AAH!"

No, it can't be. Not here.

After everything we had just witnessed, I couldn't write off Melanie's voice as another illusion this time. I raced through the woods, following the sound of my sister's scream. My ring sensed my desperation and lit up a path for me. Our mansion was slumped at a slight angle in the middle of a clearing as though someone had ripped it out of the ground and plopped it in the middle of nowhere. On our front porch was a ferocious-looking creature with brown feathered wings, sharp talons, and beastly features.

"I thought the anomalies were supposed to stop when Solara woke up!" I shouted.

Estella zipped over to me on her round hoverboard.

"The balance of magic is way out of alignment right now. Did you not notice the entire other planet we just engulfed?"

I pulled out my sword, racing at the harpy, which was gripping Melanie in its talons by her shoulders and was about to make an afternoon snack out of her. It flapped its wings in a desperate attempt to dodge my blade. A crossbow bolt flew into its left wing, cutting off its flight pattern and forcing it to drop Melanie.

Nice going, Amoura!

"Spero?" Melanie gasped. "Is that you?"

The harpy switched targets, staring me down with a horrible screech that revealed several rows of sharp teeth. It clawed at my shoulder, ripping open the small hole in Sparky's favorite spot on my tunic. I waited for an opening when it was prepared to lunge toward me. Ducking at the last second, I thrust my sword and stabbed it in the chest. It went down with one last terrifying scream.

I put my sword away and pulled Melanie into a stranglehold.

"I missed you, Mels."

She pushed her way up for air. "You look just like a hero from a video game!"

"It's not all it's cracked up to be."

I put my hands on her shoulders and studied her for injuries. A gash marred her cheek from where the harpy had clawed her, as well as a few bruises on her arms, but nothing too terrible. Amoura spotted the injuries and placed a gentle hand over Melanie's face. The gash closed up with a soft glow from her pendant before all the color drained from Amoura's face. She'd expended way too much power saving my life, yet she healed Melanie without hesitation.

I put my arm around her, letting her lean her weight against me. "Thanks, Amoura. I owe you one."

Melanie's eyes widened at Amoura. "Wow, you're pretty."

Amoura put on a good show, but I could tell she was barely hanging on. "Thank you. You're a lovely girl too."

Melanie tilted her head. Blond curls spilled around her face. "Spero, is she your girlfriend?"

"That's...not important," I stammered.

Her face lit up at my embarrassment. "She is! Spero has a girlfriend! Spero has a girlfriend!"

Somehow, Sparky had found his way over to us, bobbing and weaving around Melanie to the same rhythm as her chant.

"And you have a *dragon*? I can't believe you were keeping all of this to yourself!"

"I didn't exactly have a choice."

Estella regarded our admittedly large house. "Is this your place of residence? It's huge!"

I shrugged. "It's no palace or anything."

Amoura counted the windows on her fingers. Her eyes

misted over in a daze. "It certainly looks like one!"

Estella jumped on her floating disk. "Since there are five of us now, this would probably be a better place to stay than my hideout. I just need to grab a cloaking device for it. Be right back." She zipped away in a flash of pink smoke.

Amoura regarded her mother, who watched us in silence. "How come you never told me I had two magical aunts?"

Solara brushed a strand of blue hair out of her eyes. "I thought you'd never have an opportunity to meet them. Plus, I wanted you all to myself. Can you forgive me for being a little selfish?"

A spark of realization lit up Amoura's face. "If Spero's sister is here, does that mean Father is too?"

Solara sighed. "I put a protection charm on him a long time ago. A cataclysmic event like this shouldn't have affected him. It seems the crystal selected random people from different time periods. I don't really understand how it works. Estella can probably explain it better than I can."

As if right on cue, Estella whizzed back on her hoverboard with a blinking blue button in her hand. Nix snuggled up on her other arm. She set the button on the ground by my front door and gave it a dramatic push. A translucent bubble formed around the house.

"There we go! Nice and safe."

Amoura shook her head. "No one is safe now. If Spero's sister was attacked, there are probably countless others out there. We need to help them. All of them."

My hand balled into a fist. "What we need to do is get the crystal back from Caliga. There has to be a way to undo what she's done."

Her weight pressed down on my shoulder. Her consciousness was slipping away. She needed a place to rest fast.

Estella stood impatiently at my door. "These are great theories, but can we discuss them inside? I'm dying to see the house of the future!"

I pushed open the door with my shoulder, careful not to lose my grip on Amoura. Her breathing grew shallow. Hopefully, a good night's sleep would restore her strength.

"Welcome home, I guess."

How could we have failed so spectacularly? I thought we could prevent Caliga from getting the last shards, but I should have known better. Two normal people stood no chance against a powerful sorceress. Placing Amoura's happiness first had cost us everything, and that was on me for letting my heart rule my head. I could have stopped her from entering the final labyrinth, but I didn't. The least I could do was provide her with a roof over her head until we figured out how to handle this world-bending catastrophe.

Twenty-Five

Amoura

I knew I shouldn't have used that final burst of magic to help Spero's sister, but I could never bear to see a child hurt. Every muscle in my body ached as Spero carried me up the stairs of his massive home. The pain subsided a bit as my back landed on a soft mattress, and my throbbing head melted into a deep pillow. My eyes fluttered shut with the warmth of a gentle kiss on my forehead.

"You've overdone it. Get some rest. We can figure all this out in the morning."

Soft footsteps faded into the distance. Uneasy thoughts filled my mind as I gave in to my exhaustion. Not only had we failed in our mission to protect both worlds, but we'd made everything so much worse than before we arrived in Imperium. If it hadn't been for Spero's steadfast faith in me, I would have already given up. Aunt Caliga had played me for a fool. I longed to believe her, the only connection I had to Mama since we arrived. Why hadn't I just accepted that she was gone? If I had just minded my own business, maybe I could have lived out our peaceful life on the farm. But then I never would have met Spero. Was it worth all of this? I drifted into a dreamless sleep.

* * *

A bright light streamed through the large window. Based on my surroundings, I surmised that I was in Spero's mother's room, which was richly furnished with silk magenta sheets and black and white portraits of people I assumed she had worked with in the theater. I pulled myself out of the comfortable bed and peered outside. The sun from our world was blinding, turning Imperium's fuchsia sky into a bluish-violet color. I could never return home now. Caliga had taken everything.

A soft knock on the door interrupted my thoughts. I twisted the crystal knob. On the other side, Mama gazed at me with all the tenderness I had missed for the last nine years of my life. My arms tightened around her, the embrace filling me with the familiar scent of cinnamon and roses.

She ran her fingers through my hair. "I'm glad you're feeling better. You used a lot of magic yesterday."

"I missed you so much," I sobbed.

Her eyes roamed across my form, reading my features like a book as a melancholy smile tugged at the corners of her lips.

"I wish I could have been there to watch you grow up. It's my deepest regret."

She followed me into the room and sat in a tall, padded chair in front of a wooden desk. I took a seat across from her at the foot of the bed. I'd dreamed of this moment so many times before, but I never expected it to come with a lifetime's worth of regret.

"Mama, I need to ask you something."

"Of course, dear. Anything you wish to know."

"Why did you leave Imperium? Did you not know of the danger?"

Mama grew quiet and took a deep breath.

"My sisters and I are immortal. We've always protected this world with our powers, and we always will. I didn't know my separation would cause such a calamity, nor did I intend to stay away for as long as I did. I just wanted to see what life was like for those who didn't have magic. I wondered if I could help them somehow. But then I met your father and fell in love, and, well, you know the rest."

"Indeed," I sobbed. "I'm the cause of all this. If I had never been born, you would have returned to Imperium, and Aunt Caliga never would have been corrupted by the crystal."

She ruffled my hair. "Is that really what you think? Amoura, you should know better than that. You were the best thing that ever happened to me. If I could go back and do it all again, I wouldn't change a thing. Well, perhaps I'd change one thing. I would have made sure you never got involved."

I shook my head. "You left a hole in my heart that would have kept growing until it consumed me had I not learned the truth."

Her hand massaged my back. "You were born with a special gift, but being the essence of love can be a burden as well. I wish I could take all of it away from you."

I pulled away. "I wouldn't want to place my burden on anyone else. 'Tis my duty to fix all of this."

Mama placed her hands on my shoulders and gazed into my eyes. "Amoura, you are not the one who implemented the Earth's destruction."

"But I'm the one who agreed to give Caliga the crystal!" I cried.

Mama repositioned herself next to me. "Sweetheart, I should have told you and your father everything. I was just afraid that if you knew the whole story, you wouldn't be able to see me the same way again."

"How could you think that? We love you! We always will."

"I know, dear, but being a guardian is my burden to bear, just as being the essence of love is yours."

I brushed aside some strands of blue hair that spilled over her shoulder. "I was hoping once we brought you back, you would know what to do."

She caressed my cheek. "It isn't always that simple. We're going to need all the help we can get to resolve this."

"If we restore the worlds, will you come back and live with Father and me again?"

Her expression wavered. "It's lovely to reminisce about simpler times, but I'm not sure we can ever return to the way things were. Besides, is that truly what you want? You're practically all grown up now, and Spero seems quite fond of you."

I blushed. "You speak true, Mama. Mayhap I no longer know what I want. I thought it was to bring you back, but I never expected all of this to happen."

She wrapped her arm around my shoulder. "I'm sorry I wasn't more straightforward with you. You were so young at the time."

"I understand," I sighed. "I am happy to have you back,

despite everything."

She stood up. "Why don't we break our fast downstairs? Spero has an incredible kitchen."

"Very well."

I followed her into the expansive hallway that was covered in black and white tiled floors. It may not have been a palace, but the light and comfort that flooded Spero's home mirrored the impression he had made on my heart. It provided some peace of mind in the ongoing crisis.

* * *

Later that day, Mama, Aunt Estella, Spero, and I gathered in a sitting room after Melanie had gone off to play with Sparky in another room. I was glad they had formed such a strong bond with each other. No wonder Spero barely knew the meaning of labor when surrounded by the temptation of such comfortable furniture. I snuggled up next to him on the softest and largest chair I had ever sat on, with four large cushions extending between each arm. My troubles melted away into a soft cloud surrounded by Spero's warmth.

"Nice scrying mirror!" exclaimed Estella, gesturing to a reflective black wall. "Huge interface, high definition, and brimming with power. I bet you could count every hair on a troll's head with that. Can you activate it?"

It took a moment, but Spero appeared to understand her request. He pulled out a small device and pressed a button. I shrieked as the entire wall morphed into a giant woman with a heavily painted face, sleek dark hair, and a scandalously short skirt. Had we brought giants into this world as well?

"Who is she?" I gasped. "And why is she so big?"

Spero chuckled, though I couldn't fathom why. "It's just an illusion, like in the labyrinth, remember?"

I widened my eyes at him. "You have a device that creates illusions in your home?"

"Everyone does. It's how they get their entertainment."

A twinge of jealousy flared up in my gut. "You still haven't told me who she is."

He shrugged. "Looks like a reporter. I guess Caliga zapped into a news station from somewhere."

The important-looking woman spoke into a black stick in an even tone.

"Many are saying it's the end of the world. A strange phenomenon has taken place that has caused the whole planet to merge with what some witnesses are calling a 'magical fairyland.' Historical figures have been popping up from all over space and time, and no one knows what to make of it. Believe it or not, I have with me Albert Einstein, who claims the phenomenon can be explained through science."

Estella scoffed as an elderly man with a wild hairdo appeared on the wall. "Good luck with that."

The man spoke into the black stick with a thick accent. "According to my theory, everyone has moved from the natural time-space continuum to an estranged frequency that has caused anomalies to pop up all over the known world."

Suddenly, the image became distorted. An enormous projection of Caliga's face filled the screen, allowing me to see every pore on her face.

I squeezed Spero's arm. "If we see her, does that mean she can see us?"

Spero pulled me closer. "Normally, no, but there's nothing normal about this situation, so I couldn't say for certain."

"Don't hurt them, sister," Mama said from where she was sitting with Aunt Estella in the back of the room. "I was the one who shattered the crystal. This is my fault."

Caliga gazed over us without reacting, confirming Spero's theory that she couldn't actually see us.

"Citizens of Earth, you are now all under my control. I am Mistress Caliga, ruler of Imperium and New Earth. As long as you do what I say, no harm will come to you."

An image of myself and Spero appeared on the screen. I gripped his arm so hard that I cut off his circulation.

"These two are the cause of all your suffering. They are the reason the worlds have collapsed, and they must be made to face justice. Bring them to me unharmed, and we will have a public trial to decide their punishment. "

Queen Elizabeth's face popped up next to Caliga's. "The girl is a subject of mine, so please be gentle with her. Remember that those of you from England are still loyal to me, your sovereign!"

"That's enough," Caliga groaned at her.

The image faded back into the earlier scene, but this time, the woman was talking to a scruffy fisherman holding a net that contained a mermaid with long blonde hair and a pearlescent tail. Her seafoam-colored eyes widened in terror. I longed to reach out and pull her to safety, but I knew it was only an illusion.

"—never would have expected to catch a mermaid," he said. "Do you know what this means?"

"That we really have entered a world of magic?" asked the reporter.

"No! That I'm going to be rich! If you're interested in seeing the mermaid, call the number on your screen and tell me how much you're willing to pay for such a rare opportunity."

He held up a sheet with a series of numbers on it.

The irritated reporter turned back to face us. "Now back to the station."

A room appeared with a well-dressed man and a woman sitting behind a table. The woman looked directly at us with a serious expression on her face. "In other news, monster attacks have ravaged—"

The image shifted back into a blank wall, cutting off the rest of the dialogue. I turned to Spero and realized he had deactivated it with his device.

"That's enough TV for now."

I stood up. "We need to do something! That poor mermaid!"

Spero stood next to me. "Did you not hear the part about how we're wanted criminals?"

"There shouldn't be any reason for Caliga to call a manhunt," observed Estella. "She could have captured you as soon as she activated the crystal."

My heart fluttered as Spero's fingers entwined with mine. "I think she wants us to suffer. She's angry that we didn't bring her the rest of the shards ourselves. Plus, there was that weird explosion when she teleported back to the palace last time. I wonder if her powers are on the fritz."

Estella seemed intrigued. "Interesting theory. The crystal is powerful, but she would have needed to use an incredible amount of magic for such a strong spell. She may need a few centuries to stabilize her magic."

"That's a good thing, isn't it?" I asked. "It means she can't hurt anyone else."

Spero squeezed my hand. "She's already hurt two worlds. I don't know how much more harm she could possibly do at this point."

I turned to him. "So, what do we do now?"

Mama approached me and placed a gentle hand on my shoulder. "Perhaps Estella and I can reason with her. She must see the error of her ways, especially if it resulted in her losing her powers."

"Great," I said. "You and Aunt Estella can head to the palace to talk to Caliga, and Spero and I will find that fisherman and rescue the mermaid."

Spero crossed his arms. "Amoura, are you sure? When we started on this journey, everyone saw us as heroes. Now, they're all going to turn against us."

I walked toward the door. "She needs my help. I'm doing this with or without you, but I would prefer your support."

He matched my pace. "Then I'm coming with you. I promised I'd never abandon you again, and I meant it."

We exited the room to find Spero's sister playing with Sparky in the foyer. Her face lit up with delight.

"Want to come play with us?"

"Later, Mels," said Spero. "We're heading out."

"Where are you going?"

I gave Melanie a warm smile. "We're going to rescue a mer—"

"We have to meet with some of Dad's clients and explain the situation to them," Spero interrupted. "They're going to want to know why half his merchandise disappeared when the worlds collided."

Melanie frowned. "Oh. Sounds boring."

"Yeah. By the way, have you seen my cell phone?"

She pointed to a small, black rectangle on a nearby table. When he grabbed it, it lit up like the wall in the sitting room, only the illusions on it were smaller. He glanced at it and then looked back at me.

"Amoura, can you keep Melanie company for a few minutes? I need to take care of something before we leave."

I peered at his expression, trying to read his thoughts. First, he lied to his sister, and now he was sneaking off somewhere? I didn't want to pry, especially with Melanie and Sparky listening in, but I couldn't deny the sinking suspicion I felt in the pit of my stomach.

"Is something amiss?"

"No, it's fine. I just need to find out where we're going. You know, boring tech stuff. I'm sure Estella can help me figure it out."

"Come back soon," I sighed.

He turned toward the hallway. "I'll be back in a flash!"

I observed Melanie as she was chasing Sparky around the room and couldn't help the warm grin that formed on my lips.

"Tag! You're it!" Melanie shouted, tapping Sparky's wing.

Bet you can't catch me!

Sparky darted away, bobbing low through the air, to Melanie's sheer delight. His special wing made it easy for a girl of her stature to keep up with him. Without looking where they were going, the two of them crashed into me, causing us to topple onto the floor. I gave a hearty laugh.

"Oops, sorry," said Melanie.

"Take heart. It was all in good fun."

Sparky likes Melanie!

"Of course you do, Sparky. She's Spero's sister."

Melanie gasped. "Can you really understand him?"

"Aye."

"Can you teach me how to talk to him?"

I shook my head. "I'm afraid not. My powers come from my mother."

"Your mother's a pretty angel, like you."

A smile tickled the corners of my mouth. "You are too kind."

"Pretty girls don't usually hang out with my brother."

"He does take some getting used to, doesn't he?"

"Are you going to live here now with us?"

Heat flooded my cheeks. "I'm afraid the world needs to be mended. When everything goes back to normal, I'll return to my own time."

Her eyes misted over with disappointment. "Well, maybe you can still visit."

I bit my tongue. These matters were far too complex for someone of her age to understand. Maybe that's why Spero didn't tell her about the captured mermaid. I glanced back down the hallway for a sign of his return.

Twenty-Six

Spero

I banged on the door of the guest room, hoping Estella hadn't already teleported somewhere with her magic. The combination of magic and antisocial tendencies made her a difficult person to keep tabs on. I breathed a sigh of relief when the door popped open in a puff of pink smoke. She sat on the bed watching the news on our small guest TV mounted to the wall. A rising number across the bottom of the screen indicated the increasing casualties from monster attacks. It was in the thousands and still growing. I needed clarity before I decided what to do next, and I couldn't do that with Amoura's selflessness distracting me at every turn.

I closed the door behind me. "It isn't going to stop, is it?"

The reclusive sorceress slumped over a Star Tech tablet with several browser tabs open. "I'm working on a theory. I might need some help."

Was she even listening? I tried again. "Even if we return

everyone to where they came from, it won't fix things now. Half of them will probably never even be born. Amoura and I won't be able to go back to the same worlds we came from. History as we know it has been erased."

Estella looked up. "Not if we can reverse the crystal's effects. Earth doesn't run on magic the way Imperium does. If we counteract the spell's parallax, it will be as though none of this ever happened over on your world. It's already unstable, judging by how Caliga's powers reacted to it."

I scanned some news articles on my phone. The victim list sprawled through names of people I had read about in history books, associates of my parents, and others I'd never heard of, all recent victims of attacks from basilisks, griffons, and other legendary beasts. My phone shook in my hand.

"It'll bring all these people back from the dead? I know I'm supposed to be the essence of hope and all, but that's crazy. No one should have that sort of power."

She put the tablet down. "No one does. It's the power of the crystal. Reversing its effects will bring your world back to normal, but Imperium will still have to deal with the consequences."

I closed the news app and took a deep breath. "Got it. So it's more important that we help the citizens of Imperium now because the citizens of Earth will be okay after you come up with a way to reverse the crystal's effects."

"Bingo. Just give me a few hours to go over my theory with another inventor. It looks like there are quite a few around here."

Pink smoke erupted from her hand, wrapping around her long coat.

I held up my hand. "Just one more thing."

Her body turned translucent as she flickered in and out of the room. "What's that?"

"Don't tell Amoura about the casualties. It'll destroy her."

"Talking to people has never been my strong suit."

She disappeared in a cloud of pink smoke that dissipated out the window. I opened my call app and entered the number from the news station from a photo I snapped of the TV.

"Hello?" The voice sounded like the same man.

"I got your number from the news. We're interested in seeing the mermaid."

"Now hold on there, sonny, I'm not going to share her with just anyone. Do you know how much people would pay to see a real, live mermaid?"

"I'm the son of Star Tech's CEO. I can make you a great offer, but I don't want to discuss it over the phone. Where can we meet in person?"

"My GPS isn't working right now, but I found a nice little spring with crystal-clear water under a great big waterfall in the middle of the woods. If you can find it, I'll consider making a deal with you."

"I know just the place. See you soon."

I went back to the foyer. Amoura seemed tense, but she relaxed when she saw me.

"I was worried."

I gave her a reassuring grin. "Nothing to worry about. Let's head out."

Melanie's expression soured. "Do you really need to go to a boring business meeting? Amoura was helping me talk to Sparky."

"Sorry, Mels. We'll be back soon."

"Fine," she sighed.

* * *

Imperium had become a completely different place since merging with Earth. A frenzy of people, vehicles, and buildings crowded the once familiar path through the woods. Modern vehicles ran horse-drawn carriages off the road, and people held up signs signifying the apocalypse. I tried to ignore them. The rocky terrain shifted to sand as we crossed over a beach with waves crashing along the shore, muddying the ground beneath us. Imperium had doubled or tripled in size since absorbing our world.

Amoura followed me down a cobblestone street full of merchants bartering everything from ancient Egyptian carvings to wireless earbuds. Even after the entire world had come to an end, people were still working to make a living. A stout Middle Eastern man standing behind a table of pottery, jars, and sculptures waved me over.

"Nice sword. How much do you want for it?"

I kept walking. "It's not for sale."

"I wouldn't be too sure about that. I just caught something incredibly rare, something you can't find anywhere else."

"We're not interested."

"Not interested in a lucky fairy? She's real pretty too. I bet she'll grant you a wish if you ask her nicely."

That got Amoura's attention. She tugged on my sleeve.

"Spero," she whispered urgently.

I followed her over to the table. "I know."

I kept a safe distance to make sure he wasn't scamming us. Sure enough, he held up a jar containing a fairy with fiery red hair and a yellow flower-petal gown. I recognized her right away. The corruption of our world had seeped through the vulnerable fibers of Imperium like poison in a water main. If the fairy queen could get captured this easily, who knew how much danger the rest of Imperium was in?

"How dare you!" Amoura shrieked. "Do you have any idea who this is?"

The man snarled at her. "Your woman needs to learn when to keep her mouth shut. She's quite a looker, though. Maybe I'll take her instead."

I pushed Amoura behind me before he could lay a finger on her and clanked my sword onto the table against a pile of pottery.

"Just take it."

I snatched the glass jar containing the fairy queen before he could change his mind.

"Hey!" someone shouted from somewhere nearby. "Those are the criminals Mistress Caliga is looking for! Get them!"

Just when I thought things couldn't get worse.

I grabbed Amoura's hand, and we started running. A band of tough-looking brutes chased after us, led by an elderly Asian woman.

"Spero," Amoura panted, "you should not have given up your sword. How will you defend yourself?"

"We can figure that out later. I had to get the fairy queen away from that sleazebag, and I wasn't going to let him near you."

The small mob was gaining traction on us, but we had the advantage. I ducked behind a tree.

I pointed to a spot near the crowd. "Can you fire a bolt in that direction? It'll confuse them."

She took aim. "Of course."

The bolt sailed through a tree in the distance, causing a

rustle of branches. Leaves fluttered over the mob.

"They went this way!" shouted the elderly woman.

I held my breath as they dispersed. Once we were in the clear, I unsealed the jar, freeing the fairy queen.

"Are you well, Your Majesty?"

The glittering pixie brushed clouds of dust off her dress and hair. "Certainly not! The fairy vale has been invaded by violent brutes. Why Caliga thought this would benefit Imperium is beyond me."

"We believe my aunt has been corrupted by the power of the crystal," Amoura explained. "Mama and Aunt Estella are going to try to patch things up with her."

Gemma floated over us and sat on a high tree branch, crossing her arms. "Considering how much raw power she's used, it might not matter if she sees the error of her ways. This spell is irreversible."

I shook my head. "I'm sure that's not true. Estella's researching a way to fix it. All of this will be over soon."

"That's only assuming she doesn't go into hiding again."

"She won't," I insisted. "The situation is too dire."

"Let's hope you're right." Gemma hovered over our heads. "Since you helped me, I will do my best to ward off your attackers. Mistress Caliga has done everything in her power to place the blame on you, but I know the two of you would never have brought this sort of catastrophe upon us willingly."

Amoura curtsied. "I thank you, Your Majesty."

"Still, there's only so much I can do," she warned. "I suggest you lie low for a while."

"That's the plan," I agreed.

She flew off in the direction Amoura had fired the bolt. We continued in the direction of the clearing where I met Katrina.

"How can people be so cruel?" asked Amoura.

I entwined my fingers through hers. "It's the way of the world. That's what I've been trying to explain to you all this time. But kind-hearted souls like you make up for it tenfold."

She squeezed my hand. "I just can't bear seeing anyone in trouble."

"I know. You make me want to be a better person. Most people don't care what happens to anyone else as long as they get what they want, like your aunt."

Amoura frowned. "She couldn't have always been that way. Mayhap she'll become a better leader after she realizes the damage she's caused."

"We can only hope."

She glanced toward the clearing in the trees. "I think I hear the waterfall nearby."

"Me too."

We turned a corner. The crystal spring sparkled like a sanctuary in the midst of the chaos surrounding it. The fisherman we had seen on the news stood under the waterfall, scrolling through a Star Tech phone. He had scraggly gray hair, and his face was covered in wrinkles and warts. His ragged clothes looked waterlogged and loose over his short stature. Over by the spring, the wide-eyed mermaid struggled to break free from a net tied to a protruding stone.

"Are you the one interested in the mermaid?" he asked in a crackly voice.

I marched up. "That's me."

His bloodshot eyes lit up with glee. "I heard Star Tech is a billion-dollar industry."

"Multi-billion, actually."

He nodded. "I'll take a billion dollars for the mermaid, and you can do whatever you want with her. She says she's a princess, so it's an even better bargain if she's telling the truth."

"Spero!" Amoura shouted.

I turned around. Amoura freed the mermaid, but unnatural tremors vibrated across the spring. Bubbles and ripples formed along its surface. The mermaid sat on the edge, yanking her tail out of the violent water.

The fisherman glared at me. "Is this some kind of trick? I made a perfectly fair and legal deal, and you're doing some kind of shady business with your partner. Everyone knows you're supposed to pay for goods before inspecting them. I thought Star Tech was a reputable company."

An enormous squid-like creature emerged out of the spring, breaking through its stone casing. The fisherman doubled back in terror and ran back into the woods.

"Forget the transaction! You can keep her!"

One of the beast's orange tentacles wrapped around the waist of the mermaid that Amoura had rescued. Her long blonde hair spilled around the sides of the tentacle encasing her. Amoura took a step back and fired several bolts from her crossbow. The kraken reeled back as they hit their mark. Its grip on the mermaid gave way, and she wriggled out, falling to the ground. However, the kraken plugged the entrance to the spring, granting her no leeway to swim to safety. She landed on the ground with a thud. I reached for my sword, but the empty space reminded me I had just given it away. It was time to get creative.

I picked up the mermaid and carried her to the waterfall so we could deal with the kraken. She stared at me through wide turquoise eyes that were as bright as the ocean, as though she was assessing what to make of me.

"You don't look like criminals," she said.

"Let me guess. Caliga sent the merfolk after us, too."

"She left an order for my father, King Neptune of Aquacia, but he said land business had nothing to do with us. It looks like he was wrong about that. Who knew the great Princess Marina would be the first to fall into a trap?"

Amoura screeched as the kraken's tentacles crept toward her. She raced for cover, firing bolts all around it. Each impact left a red mark resembling a mosquito bite, but the monster remained unfazed. I raced over with no plan except to keep her safe. Reaching out toward the tentacle that swooped down toward her, I held out my arms and imagined I was holding my sword. A surge of energy blasted through me. Before I knew what was happening, the tentacle had been sliced clean off.

"How did you do that?" Amoura's gasped.

Checking the point of impact, I realized my ring had formed a glowing blue laser that reminded me of a lightsaber. Judging from the fresh calamari on the ground, it worked like the real thing. The creature shrieked and came at me with its remaining tentacles. I slashed them off one by one until it finally ran out of strength and retreated into the water. The bubbling surface of the spring fizzled out, leaving a mess of severed limbs and broken rocks.

Amoura and I approached the princess. She gazed at us with a curious glint in her eyes as she pulled some light blue tendrils of hair out of her face. Her regal manner contrasted with Katrina's shallow attitude.

"Are you all right, Your Highness?" asked Amoura.

Her opalescent tail swayed under the waterfall, reflecting rainbow-colored shimmers along her scales. "I am now, thanks to the two of you. I'll put in a good word for you with Father. Mistress Caliga must have been mistaken."

I carried her back to the spring. "I'm afraid there was no mistake. She tricked us into giving her the power to bring all these awful people here."

Marina dove into the water with a splash and gazed back at me. "Interesting. What do Mistress Solara and Mistress Estella have to say about this?"

Amoura brushed aside some rubble from the battle. "They're trying to convince her to undo the spell, but we're not sure if that's even possible."

Marina considered this. "That does pose a problem. If you do happen to find a solution, know that the merfolk are on your side. Good luck!"

She dove back into the water, her glittering fins disappearing below the broken spring.

The pleasant warmth of Amoura's arms surrounded me. "I'm glad you're all right. I didn't know your ring could do that."

"Me neither. I guess I don't need Caliga's toy sword after all. Remind me to thank Estella when we get back."

As though reading our minds, a flash of pink smoke appeared, revealing Estella.

"There you are! Did I hear something about thanking me?"

I held up my ring finger. "Don't let it get to your head, but I think we owe our lives to this thing."

She beamed. "Of course you do! The Ring of Hope contains enough power to get you out of any dire straits. It's some of my finest work. I did need to tweak the levels of orichalcum to make sure it wouldn't damage the user, but I think its crystalline core more than makes up for it. Don't you?"

I changed the subject before she could go on another rant. "Uh, sure. How did it go with Caliga?"

"We'll tell you all about it back at our headquarters. My new friend Ben and I have a theory we wanted to discuss with you."

I narrowed my eyes at her. "When you say 'our headquarters,' you're talking about my house, right?"

Without answering me, she placed her hands on our shoulders. The next thing I knew, Amoura and I were standing on my front porch, coughing up pink smoke. As soon as I opened the door, Melanie and Sparky, pummeled me to the ground.

"Welcome home, Spero! We missed you."

I pushed myself back to my feet. "Can you welcome with a little less energy next time?"

I headed toward the sitting room and wondered if I had hit my head a little harder than I thought. Estella's new friend appeared to be none other than Ben Franklin.

Twenty-Seven

Amoura

unt Caliga's spell had transformed my life into a runaway carriage that I could never keep up with, no matter how fast I ran. The world kept changing around me at a dizzying speed, faster than the vehicles from Spero's time that surpassed hundreds of horses. Aunt Estella's magic returned us to Spero's home faster than I could blink. Part of me longed for the tedious tasks I performed with Father on the farm. At least there, I knew what to expect. Pink smoke curled up my nose, adding to the dizzying sensation of everything that had happened in the past day.

Aunt Estella ushered us into the sitting room with her new friend, a stout man with wavy hair. My racing thoughts calmed at the sight of Mama's face, which lit up with joy when her eyes met mine. She embraced me as though I were still a child in need of her protection, but I could no longer play that part.

"I'm so glad you're all right. It seemed like Caliga had sent half of Imperium after you. I went to the palace today and gave her a piece of my mind."

I placed a hand over my throbbing forehead. "I hope she realizes what she's done. The people she brought here from Earth have captured two royal citizens of Imperium today alone. If we fail to restore the world to the way it was before, who knows what they might do next?"

Mama nodded. "She received messages from the fairy queen and the king of the merfolk with similar reports. They said you freed them."

My heart warmed at the thought of Queen Gemma and Princess Marina returning home safe, grateful that they kept their word to us. "We had to. I could never forgive myself if anything happened to them."

She caressed my hair. "You've become so brave. I'm proud of you."

I'd waited so long to hear those words, yet they rang hollow in the shadows of the huge responsibility that lay before me. What I needed was not her pride, but an impossible solution to fix two worlds. If I had only been strong enough to accept Mama's loss, no one else would have needed to suffer. The burden of this disaster fell squarely on my shoulders now, and I would put my life on the line to fix it if I needed to.

Aunt Estella cleared her throat. "Are you done yet? I want to share this new theory with you. I think you'll find our discoveries are quite fascinating."

"Has she always been like this?" I whispered to Mama.

She gave me a silent nod, and we took a seat on an oversized plush chair. Estella pressed a button that activated a screen near the back of the room. It was smaller than the one in

Spero's theater, but still took up a good portion of the wall. An image of the crystal appeared. Its dark purple aura sent chills down my spine.

"As you may know, I formed the crystal through raw elemental energy infused within the natural resources of Imperium."

Her words eluded me again, but I kept quiet.

"Energy is like lightning, which can be deadly when it isn't controlled," added her friend, Ben.

He pressed a button, which made a crude image of a lightning bolt appear.

Estella continued. "I thought the crystalline core, combined with the essence of a sorceress guardian, would stabilize the energy enough that it wouldn't pose a threat to Imperium. However, I didn't consider the effects it would have on the sorceress's mental state, in this case, the sorceress being Caliga."

An image of an irate Aunt Caliga appeared on the screen.

"When Solara cast the transference spell, it divided the crystal back into its original elements."

She pressed another button. An image appeared of the four shards we had recovered from the labyrinths. The familiar sinking feeling entered my gut as I recalled our battles with the unicorns to fulfill my own selfish desire.

"She tied the essences of two outsiders to its core components so only they could restore the shards." Her eyes darted across the room to Spero, who was sitting on a larger chair that now had scratch marks from Sparky's claws, and back to me. "That's you two."

Spero rolled his eyes. "We know."

Estella nodded. "What you may not know is that this

connection gives you the power to absorb the crystal's energy and reverse its effects, rendering it null and void."

A spark of hope pulsed through my heart. Maybe I could fix everything after all.

Ben held up a small silver box with two slits on top. "It's like how electricity can be harnessed into a single appliance. If it's powered to a high enough level, the appliance will short out. Allow me to demonstrate."

He connected a series of wires to the device, adjusted a dial to the maximum setting, and pressed a button. Plumes of smoke rose from the device as it crackled with sparks and then shorted out with a horrifying sound that made me jump in my chair. The device popped upwards into the air and then crashed back onto the floor. The shiny metal surface turned dull and brown, like unpolished silver. The unpleasant scent of burning wormed its way into my nose, causing me to gasp for air.

Spero crossed his arms. "Did you need to destroy a perfectly good toaster to show us that?"

"The demonstration segment of our findings was necessary," explained Estella. "We wanted to make sure you were aware of the danger of reversing the crystal's effects."

I gasped. "You mean if we do this, we'll explode like that… that… toaster thing?"

Estella nodded. "It's very likely. After all, you're both mortal—well, half mortal in your case, Amoura. Your bodies would be unlikely to handle such an excessive amount of raw power. But it'll get the job done."

Mama stood up, practically knocking me off the chair. "You should be ashamed of yourself, Estella! I went through all this trouble to protect my daughter, and now you want her to destroy herself?"

Estella shook her head. "It was merely a theory. I'm not saying they need to agree to it. But Spero was asking me about how to reverse the casualties, and this is one possibility."

An unsettling heat pulsed through me. "What casualties?"

Spero shot Estella a glare.

"Oh right, I wasn't supposed to mention that part. Forget I said anything."

I glanced toward Spero. "What is she talking about?"

Spero sighed. "There were monster attacks like the one that tried to hurt Melanie all over the world. There's no way we could have stopped them all."

The heat flooding through me burned my eyes, blurring the surrounding room. "And thou thoughtest not to tell me?"

He frowned. "You weren't supposed to find out this way. We can't save everyone, Amoura. There are too many of them."

"You're supposed to be the essence of hope!"

"I know, and I want to fix this. That's why Estella was working with Ben Franklin on this crazy theory, but I didn't know we'd have to put our necks on the line again."

I blinked away tears, redirecting my attention to Aunt Estella. "So if we don't do what you're suggesting, more people from our world are going to die and never come back?"

Estella's eyes darted around the room. "Is it getting warm in here, or is it just me?"

Mama shook her head. "You will take back this ridiculous theory and come up with a better one."

"If I may make a suggestion," said Ben, "perhaps if you used a strong enough conductor, it would be able to redirect the energy from the crystal without destroying you. I once used a key to harness electricity from a storm so I wouldn't get electrocuted."

The storm raging inside me subsided as I realized we already had something like that.

"Like my pendant and Spero's ring! They've been protecting us this entire time."

Estella looked intrigued. "An interesting theory. After all, the Ring of Hope and the Healing Pendant run on the same crystalline core as the elemental crystal."

"Are you absolutely certain that will work?" asked Mama.

She avoided Mama's gaze. "No. It could overload the internal flow of magical energy, causing them to explode on impact. The only way to find out would be to test it on the crystal and see what happens."

"That's still too risky," Mama huffed.

I stood up and sat next to Spero, pleading with my eyes. "We need to fix this."

He took my hand in his. "And we will. But I can't put your life at risk to do that. We'll find another way."

"How many more casualties will there be by then? How many are there now? Hundreds?"

He looked at the floor.

"Thousands?"

His eyes flicked back; I saw the answer to my question within them. "Amoura, I'm not risking your life to do this, and that's final!"

Mama nodded from across the room. "Thank you, Spero. I appreciate that you care so much about my daughter."

I shook my head. "But there might not be another way! As the ones who are responsible for restoring the crystal, 'tis our duty to save both worlds."

"She's right," said Estella. "Not so much about the duty part.

That's subjective. But as the ones who unlocked the labyrinths, you are both intrinsically linked to the crystal. No one else has that level of control, not even Caliga."

"No one asked for your opinion," Spero groaned.

Estella looked confused. "Yes, you did. You both wanted to know how to reverse the casualties."

He rolled his eyes. "Never mind."

"This has been a lot to take in for one day," said Mama. "Why don't we regroup for the night and discuss it further in the morning?"

"Works for me," replied Aunt Estella. "Spero, do you have a spare guest room for Ben?"

"This isn't a hotel," he murmured. "We have a cot I can pull into the study later."

Ben gave Spero a grateful nod. "Thank you for your hospitality."

The group cleared out, leaving Spero and me alone. I leaned my head onto his chest, attempting to memorize the calming rhythm of his heartbeat.

"Spero, I want you to know that no matter what happens, I'm grateful I had the chance to get to know you."

He lifted my face toward his, his blue eyes staring at me with concern. "Amoura, you're scaring me. We already agreed this was too risky, didn't we?"

I nodded. "Yes, but everything is so topsy-turvy right now. We could wake up tomorrow, and everything we know might vanish. So I want to make sure thou knowest that I regret nothing that's happened because it brought me to thee."

His hand caressed my chin. "You don't need to be so formal with me, you know?"

I tilted my head closer to him. "What meanest thou?"

"All these *thous* and *thees*. I noticed you've been using it more with me lately."

I stifled a laugh. "*Thou* is not formal. It's reserved for one's closest and most intimate friends."

The corners of his lips twitched into a grin. "How intimate are we talking?"

I closed the distance between our faces. Our lips met, filling me with warmth and renewed determination. Pressing my weight against him, we reclined into the plush chair until nothing else existed but the two of us. Absorbing his musky scent and the soft tug of his hands in my hair, I pulled him toward me, embracing every sensation of our final moments together.

I waited for him to pull away, but he lingered for what felt like ages until he murmured something about needing to set up the cot in the study. We forced ourselves back up. His arms lingered around me, leaving a pleasant tingle that remained even after he let go. A dizzy, lightheaded sensation flowed from my head to my toes as we parted for the night.

"Good night, Amoura," he whispered.

Heat flooded my cheeks from the gentle, alluring sound of his voice. He'd changed so much from when I first met him. The thought of never seeing him again cut through my heart like a knife.

"Pleasant dreams."

* * *

I wished I could melt into the soft, oversized bed that had brought so much comfort the night before, but I knew I needed to act swiftly. I found a hooded cloak in the wardrobe and pulled it over my head to hide my identity in the night.

Lingering for a moment, I decided to leave Spero a message so he wouldn't think someone had abducted me in the night. The desk contained some featherless quills and parchment. I had never written anything before, but I remembered enough letters to sound them out. The quill made a dark mark on the parchment when I removed the cap, despite the lack of ink nearby. I scrawled a quick note on a sheet of parchment and left it on the desk.

Spiro,

I'm sori.

~Amoura

I gave the door a soft push and peeked into the hallway for signs of movement. A tear leaked from my eye as I gazed over the empty chairs in the sitting room that all the people I cared about had occupied only hours earlier. The eerie darkness gave me an unsettling fear of someone watching me, but everyone had already retired for the night. I tiptoed out the door into the cold night, where the violet sky had turned black as ink. Constellations from Imperium sparkled over me, intermingling with the ones I knew from Earth. The worlds had become a huge mess, and someone needed to fix it. Mama once sacrificed herself to save all of Imperium. Now I needed to do the same for everyone's sake.

Vagabonds and urchins littered the streets, fast asleep in the soft moss, reminding me of my first night in the woods with Spero. Soon, they would all return home safe to their beds without a care in the world. The once familiar path to the glittering palace led me past many oddities, including a glass tower that rose into the clouds, a straw hut, and blinking red, yellow, and green lights. Finally, I arrived at the gate that had been our salvation that very first day. I took a deep breath, attempting to silence the thrashing within my heart that pulsed through my body. Aunt Caliga waited for me at the door as though she had been expecting me. She held it open and let me into the grand entryway, where I gave her a silent nod.

"It's about time you showed up." She peered over my shoulder into the empty courtyard. "Where's the boy?"

I let out a shaky breath as my chest tightened.

"He's not coming. Aunt Caliga, I wish to make a deal with you."

Spero

I woke up in the middle of the night in a cold sweat. My ring finger burned as it did the day the portal opened. The sapphire bathed the room in a dim blue light as though trying to tell me something.

Amoura.

I should have known something was up. She acted so weird last night, but I let her distract me with that kiss. Don't get me wrong; it was a great kiss, but something lurked behind it that I refused to see. I usually found her sulking over her mom at times like this, but the situation had changed. Why couldn't Estella have kept her mouth shut? Amoura never hesitated to put herself in danger when it came to helping others.

Trying not to wake anyone else since my house had become some kind of wacky hotel, I tiptoed to Mom's room, which she seldom used, and tapped on the door.

"Amoura? Are you awake?"

An uncomfortable silence lingered through the dark hallway.

"If you can hear me, I'm coming in."

The door made an eerie creak as I slid it open. The soft blue glow of my ring formed apparitions on the walls of the empty room like a haunted house. I approached the bed and then took a step back.

What am I doing? If she's in here sleeping, I'm going to look like a total creep.

"Amoura?" I whispered.

A deafening silence amplified the pounding in my chest. The comforter lay flat over the memory foam mattress in the dim blue light. Maybe I was being paranoid. She could have had trouble sleeping and gone to the kitchen to grab a snack or something. As I headed toward the door, I noticed a sheet of stationery paper out of place on Mom's desk. I placed my ring over it to find a message written in sloppy, uneven handwriting.

Spiro,

I'm sori.

~Amoura

The pounding in my chest grew louder. Heat pulsed through my veins. She couldn't have gone off on her own, could she? Not after all the things I said about how we could do anything as long as we were together. How could she do this to me? But I already knew the answer. She didn't want anyone else to get hurt, so she decided to take matters into her own hands. I crumpled the note in my hand and punched the desk. A splinter dug into my knuckle from a crack that formed in the wood grain. It stung, but not as much as the note itself.

Dammit. Dammit. Dammit.

The door creaked open. I raced toward the dim light of the hallway. "Amoura?"

No such luck. Melanie rubbed her eyes as Sparky hovered over her shoulder in one of his erratic flight patterns.

"Spero? What happened?"

I clenched the note tighter. "Go back to bed, Melanie."

She peeked into the room. "Where's your girlfriend?"

"Bed. Now."

"But I heard a loud noise."

My tone darkened. "Don't make me ask you again."

Melanie took a step back. "Spero, you're acting weird."

"I said, go back to bed! This doesn't concern you."

Sparky flew over me, and I batted him away. He stuck out his lizard-like tongue and blew some sparks in my face, burning my cheek, but all I could think about was Amoura. What if the crystal had already destroyed her?

No, I can't think like that.

Solara materialized in the middle of the room in a silvery blue shimmer and glanced toward the empty bed.

"*What* is going on in here?"

I met her eyes with a silent plea. "What's going on is that Melanie is heading back to bed."

"Spero's being mean to me!" Melanie whined.

With the grace of a loving mother, Solara kneeled to Melanie's level and placed a gentle hand on her shoulder.

"I'm sure he's just tired and wants to go back to sleep. Why don't you be a good girl and listen to your big brother?"

"But he won't tell me why he's still awake!" she huffed.

"I'm sure he'll tell you when he's ready. Wouldn't you rather talk to him in the morning when you're nice and awake?"

Melanie clutched Sparky in her arms and turned around.

"Fine."

They disappeared down the hallway.

"Thanks."

Amoura's mother gave me a stern look. "I hope you have a reasonable explanation for waking the entire household in the middle of the night."

I threw the crumpled note in her face. "This is all your fault, you know?"

She held out her hand under the note. In a silvery glow, it opened itself up in front of her.

"I don't understand. What is this?"

I raised my voice. "What does it look like? She's turned herself in. She could be absorbing the crystal's power as we speak."

Solara's hand flew to her mouth. "No. Why would she do something like that?"

I pointed an accusing finger at her. "Because that's how you taught her to solve all her problems! By sacrificing yourself!"

"I never told her that was the way to solve problems."

"No. You showed her, and that was far worse."

"I cast that spell to protect everyone on Earth. It was what they needed."

"What she needed was her mother."

My words cut through Solara like daggers. Her mouth opened, but no words came out.

"Take me to her," I demanded.

The glow on the letter dissipated. She snatched it out of the air. "I beg your pardon?"

"You're a sorceress, aren't you? We need to reach Amoura as quickly as possible. I'm not going to waste time when every second counts. Take me. Now."

She hesitated. "I…"

"Now!" I shouted.

Her eyes widened at the intensity in my voice. I expected her to scold me for my attitude problem, like one of my teachers back home. Instead, she closed her eyes and took a deep breath.

"All right."

She placed her hand on my shoulder. A pair of white feathered wings materialized on her back. In a flash of silver light, we stood in the familiar lobby of Caliga's palace. I raced frantically around the room, peering down every hallway and up every staircase.

"Where is she?"

Solara's wings faded away, leaving traces of white feathers on the ground. "I didn't have time to cast a scrying spell. I assume she's here somewhere."

"Amoura!" I shouted. "Where are you?"

Caliga marched down the main stairway in an angry rage. "It's about time you got here."

I unleashed the glowing sword from my ring. "I don't have time for games, Caliga. Where is Amoura?"

She lifted her hand. Black and purple sparks danced across it. The painful energy surge I felt when I touched the crystal prickled under my skin. Agony filled every minuscule movement I made.

"I believe I told you not to test me, boy."

I lowered my ring. "Just take me to her."

The sparks vanished from her hand, and relief washed over me. "Your devotion is admirable, I admit, but she made me promise not to hurt you."

I crossed my arms. "You're not hurting me. You're just

following my request."

Solara stepped forward. "Caliga, is she safe?"

Caliga nodded. "Yes. She can do no harm to anyone where she is, including herself."

"Take me to her already!" I shouted.

Caliga lifted her hand, releasing more sparks. The prickling sensation returned as the sparks exploded and fizzled out like fireworks. I leaped back when she reached toward me, refusing to fall victim to her tainted magic.

"I don't think it's a good idea to use the shortcut right now. Let's walk."

She gave an exasperated sigh. "As you wish."

I followed her through a series of passageways leading to the top of an old, creaky staircase. We began our uneasy descent. Caliga took her time heading down, and I stumbled along behind her, resisting the urge to push her down the rest of the way to get to Amoura faster and calm my racing heart. At the bottom of the stairs, steel bars covered a row of empty cells. A rank smell filled the air.

She unlocked one of the iron gates, pushing me inside.

"Maybe if I had brought you here on your first night, you would have learned some manners."

She locked the door, and a twinge of worry flared in my gut that it might have been a trick. Then I turned around. I saw the outline of a familiar form huddled in the corner. Amoura's face poked out from behind one of my mom's old jackets. I had her in my arms in an instant, smothering her against my chest. Her eyes widened at me, then toward Caliga at the entrance to the cell.

"Spero? You promised you wouldn't harm him!" she shouted.

"Don't blame me. He insisted, Caliga huffed. "You'll have to settle this yourselves. I want no part of your little lover's spat. Just be ready by morning."

Her footsteps echoed as she left the dungeon. Amoura clung to me with all her strength as tremors vibrated through her slight form.

"What's in the morning?" I asked.

"Queen Elizabeth convinced my aunt to hold a trial for my crimes, where they will decide my punishment. I didn't want you involved."

Anger surged through me. After everything we had gone through together, she still intended to take all of this on her own? Fighting the desire to hold her in my arms and never let go, I pushed her away. Serves her right for abandoning me.

"How could you do this to me? I'm so angry at you right now."

She sat on a bale of hay. Her eyes were red and puffy. "Spero, I'm deeply sorry. I thought I was doing the right thing."

There was no point in trying to resist. Amoura was my greatest weakness and my greatest strength. I sat up next to her as bits of hay poked through my clothes, and pressed my lips against hers. Her face was wet with tears. I broke away.

"You're such an idiot, Amoura. I told you I would never abandon you again. I thought that applied to both of us."

She turned away from me. "It did, but I knew if I told you, you would try to stop me."

I grabbed her chin, turning her face toward mine.

"Do you have any idea how worried I was that I'd be too late?" My voice cracked as my eyes flooded with tears.

The circles under her eyes grew darker. "Weep not, Spero. If thou weepest, I shall weep too."

She sat up straighter and pulled me against her, holding me the way I had the first time she saw her mother in the cryogenic chamber.

Who knew I was a crybaby, too?

I could hear her gentle heartbeat as she held me. "I just don't know what I'd do without you. I love you so much, Amoura. Even if we restored the worlds, I could never be happy in my own time without you there with me."

She rested her head on top of mine. "I wasn't trying to hurt you. I hope you know that."

I rubbed the tears out of my eyes until the stinging subsided. "Well, you did. Promise me that we're in this together from now on."

She kneeled down and placed a soft kiss on my lips. "I vow upon my honor, I will never abandon thee again."

The sound of footsteps made us both jump. We pulled apart at the approach of Amoura's mother

"I presumed you would want a moment to speak with my daughter alone. I hope I'm not interrupting anything."

. Solara waved her hand over the bars. They melted away in a shimmer of silver light.

"Come with me. Caliga permitted me to take you to your rooms. I can't believe she locked you in the dungeon. Her own niece!"

Amoura and I helped each other to our feet, brushing off stray bits of hay that had stuck to our clothes. I squeezed her hand tightly, uncertain whether the shaking I felt came from her hand or mine.

"Mama, I pray you're not angry with me, too."

Solara shook her head. "Your suitor has helped me realize that perhaps I was not as good a mother to you as I could have been."

Amoura's grip on my hand loosened. "You're a great mother! Father and I love you so much."

Solara raised a hand to stop her. "Save it. You'll need that energy for tomorrow. I'll be staying here tonight, and Estella will join us in the morning. If you ask me, the whole trial is a farce, but I don't think you have anything to worry about. You have two sorceresses and at least half of Imperium on your side. If there's one thing I can do as a sorceress guardian, it's to ensure that you are tried fairly."

Amoura and I parted ways again as we entered our usual guest rooms so we could get some much-needed rest before the trial tomorrow. I refused to go down without a fight.

Twenty-Nine

Amoura

The morning of the trial arrived before the reprieve of sleep could overtake me. My fatigue dulled the heaviness in my heart as my determination to test my aunt's theory remained steadfast. Guilty or innocent, I knew what needed to be done, and no judgment could change that. Spero's presence would give me solace, though I hoped to protect him from this after all he'd done for me already.

Since I would be tried before royalty, I might as well look my best. I changed into a formal purple satin gown I found in my wardrobe. Nerves fluttered in my chest as I imagined how many people would judge me for my supposed crimes. I knew I bore a portion of the guilt, but none of that mattered if we couldn't reset the world to its natural state.

Aunt Caliga came to fetch me shortly after dawn.

"Are you ready?" she asked. "It's time."

I gulped. "I hope so."

She led me to a large audience chamber where a crowd had gathered. In a marble pool of clear water at the front of the crowd, a merman with turquoise hair and a silvery tail held a golden trident in his outstretched hand. Queen Gemma was perched on a small pedestal next to him in a floral throne. At the front of the room was a long, ornate marble table with golden accents.. Mama, Aunt Estella, and Aunt Caliga took a seat behind it. Queen Elizabeth sat at the end, leading the proceedings.

Spero sat at a smaller table near the wall in a formal suit from my era. I released the breath I had been holding when I took my place next to him. Dark circles nestled under his eyes, but the sight of him still made my heart flutter. Our hands met under the table as my breathing relaxed. We promised to never abandon each other again.

"Citizens of Imperium and Earth," Queen Elizabeth announced. "We are gathered here over a matter of international importance. Our worlds have merged, causing mass casualties and disruption of ordinary life for all who remain. I am no longer able to rule my court because most of its citizens have gone missing, and complaints have been logged from Imperium royals about attacks and kidnappings. This matter of state cannot be ignored for one second longer."

She turned towards us. My fingers wrapped around Spero's, and he gave me a reassuring squeeze back.

"We hereby formally accuse Amoura of England and Spero of America of unleashing this disaster on account of information willingly volunteered by Amoura and Mistress Caliga, one of the three sorceress guardians of Imperium. How do you both plead?"

I took a deep breath. "Guilty."

Spero spoke over me. "Not guilty."

He stood to address the court.

"Your Majesty," he began, "we were both manipulated by Mistress Caliga from the very beginning. She told us that the crystal shards would save both worlds. Then she tricked us into gathering them for her so she could use them to create the world of chaos we are living in now."

Elizabeth turned toward Aunt Caliga. "Is this true?"

Caliga crossed her arms. "I did ask them to bring me the crystal shards so they could restore Mistress Solara and the balance of power in Imperium. However, they deliberately disobeyed me and tried to keep half the crystal for themselves, consumed with greed over the power it possessed."

"That's a falsehood!" I shouted.

Elizabeth glared at me. "Amoura, thou art speaking out of turn."

I cast my gaze toward the table. "My apologies, Your Majesty."

Spero squeezed my hand. "She should be the one apologizing," he whispered.

The queen's regal demeanor returned. "Mistress Caliga, please continue."

Aunt Caliga held up her hand. Purple sparks fizzled and popped in the air like boiling water. "As you can see, their actions have rendered me powerless. Had they been willing to cooperate, I may have been able to maintain my position as a sorceress guardian. Having to take back the crystal by force has taken a massive toll on my ability to lead Imperium."

I caught a glint of satisfaction in Spero's eyes. Although I didn't want to see harm come to my aunt, I had to admit this turn of events was probably for the best.

Elizabeth pursed her lips. "Then by your own admission, you are no longer able to effectively lead Imperium."

Caliga slammed her fist on the table. "I am the only one who led Imperium for years after my two foolish sisters abandoned everyone."

Elizabeth turned toward Mama. "Mistress Solara, what have you to say about all of this?"

Mama addressed the court, but her gaze bore straight toward me. "I've indeed made many mistakes in my attempts to protect both worlds. Say what you will about me, but I believe my daughter is a pure and loving soul who only wishes to make the world around her a better place. Amoura came here in a place of ignorance, leaving her vulnerable to my sister's manipulative tactics because I failed to explain where she came from before I disappeared from her life."

She gave me an apologetic frown before continuing.

"From what I've seen of her suitor, he has demonstrated numerous times that his only intent is to protect my daughter above all else. I believe the two of them have had a positive impact on the well-being of Imperium. They have restored my power when no one else could, even if it wasn't deserved."

Elizabeth pursed her lips. "So you think they are not responsible for the destruction of our worlds?"

Mama turned to her. "I think the blame is shared among many."

"A prudent answer, but not one that can be easily held in a court of law. And what say you, Mistress Estella? I am told that you are responsible for creating the magical device that has caused all of this."

Estella's eyes lit up with glee. "Oh yes, I'd be happy to tell everyone how I did it. First, I forged a tool that detects each of the four elements in their purest form. Then I mined them one by one and refined them using a crystalline base. I charged the magical energy by—"

"We are not here for a scientific lecture," Elizabeth interrupted.

Estella scoffed. "Magic is far more complex than science. I'll have you know I was just talking to my friend Ben the other day about—"

The queen's tone hardened. "Do you think the accused are guilty or not?"

"If you're asking me if they're responsible for restoring the crystal after Solara sealed it away, the answer is yes, of course. They were the only ones who could unlock the labyrinths."

Mama gasped audibly. She shot Estella a sharp glare.

"What? It's true."

"I thank you," said Elizabeth. "And what of abandoning your people in their time of need? Do you have anything to say to that?"

Estella shrugged. "So I don't like making public appearances. That doesn't mean I abandoned anyone. I was the one who helped Caliga find the essence of hope, which ultimately resulted in Solara returning to us. That would have stopped the anomalies affecting Imperium if Caliga hadn't activated the crystal and thrown off the balance of energy between the two worlds."

Elizabeth looked thoughtful. "It seems to me that Mistress Caliga bears the brunt of the responsibility for this situation. Mayhap she is the one who should be beheaded."

Spero failed to hide his grin. I elbowed him in the ribs.

Caliga huffed, pointing an accusing finger toward us. "I wouldn't have been able to do anything if those two hadn't helped me! The crystal shards were sealed by magic. They were the only ones who could access them."

Elizabeth nodded. "Their participation has been duly noted. Now we will hear from the other royal courts of Imperium. Queen Gemma of the fairy court, please step, er, fly forward."

Gemma hovered over the stand to face the crowd. "We of the fairy court believe that Amoura and Spero of Earth would never intentionally bring harm upon Imperium. They have proven themselves on more than one occasion by saving fairy citizens from a rock golem that was terrorizing our land and rescuing me from one of the human miscreants who was transported here when the crystal was activated against their will because of Mistress Caliga's actions."

"Acknowledged." Elizabeth turned to the merman. "And you, King Neptune?"

The merman stretched himself as tall as he could from the shallow pool of water. "My daughter, Princess Marina, had only the highest praise for these two heroes. She said they rescued her from both a human captor and a kraken attack, which, as you may know, has been a problem for us ever since the balance of magic was thrown off by Solara's disappearance."

"Those two are guilty!" shouted a man from the crowd. "They tricked me out of a billion dollars by scaring me with a sea monster so they wouldn't have to pay the mermaid's ransom."

We turned around to find that the fisherman who had kidnapped Marina stood at the back of the assembly. The king glared at him and raised his trident.

"It was you? You dare entrap the princess of Aquacia?"

I shrieked as a blast of lightning shot out from Neptune's

trident, frying the fisherman's wrinkly face. I clung to Spero's shoulder and felt his arm curl around my back.

Elizabeth appeared unfazed. "A swift yet effective display of justice. Now, we are willing to hear out the accused."

All eyes in the room turned to me. Heat flooded my cheeks when I realized Spero's arm was still around me. I leaned over and whispered into Spero's ear so only he could hear me.

"Are you willing to do whatever it takes to save Imperium and Earth?"

He pulled his arm from around my back and clasped my hand. "As long as we do it together," he whispered. "I'm with you no matter what."

I nodded and addressed the court. "Citizens of Imperium and Earth, we stand before you as two ordinary people who were placed in extraordinary circumstances due to our birthright as the essences of hope and love. We've made mistakes, but so have the sorceresses who preside over you today. In the end, I believe no one has all the answers. At one time, I thought my mother could solve all our problems, but I don't think that anymore. We're all just ordinary people doing our best to survive in an imperfect world."

I paused, gauging the people's reaction. Their eyes bored into my soul, deepening the impact of every word I said.

"I think what all this is about isn't who to blame, but how to resolve what's happened. In the merging of the two worlds, both Earth and Imperium as we knew them are no more, creating life-altering consequences for everyone involved. No one in this room feels safe going about their former lives due to the dangers that have emerged upon us all. Therefore, I would like to test my Aunt Estella's theory that Spero and I can reverse the effects of the crystal and restore the worlds by absorbing its energy with our essences. Even if it destroys us in the process, it is a sacrifice we are willing to make for the good of everyone here as well as future generations to come."

Elizabeth looked thoughtful. "This goes for both of you?"

Spero stood. "I support Amoura's decision."

He sat back down. I leaned on his shoulder.

"Thank you," I whispered.

Our hands reunited under the table.

Elizabeth turned back to the guardians. "As a sovereign representative of Earth, I approve of this decision. What do Imperium's leaders have to say?"

Aunt Caliga nodded. "It does seem like the best solution for everyone. I was expecting to extend my reach with the power of the crystal, not taint our world with more of these anomalies, rendering me powerless."

Aunt Estella's face lit up. "I'm always happy to test one of my theories. This might just go down in history as the greatest magical experiment ever conducted."

"I don't approve of this decision," said Mama.

All eyes turned to her.

Queen Elizabeth pursed her lips. "Then it seems we are at an impasse."

Mama raised her hand. "But for the sake of all parties involved, I am willing to support it."

The assembly calmed.

A hint of a smile tugged at the corners of Elizabeth's lips. "Then the only thing that remains to be seen is the punishment of Mistress Caliga."

Caliga crossed her arms. "Why should I be punished? Everything I've done was in the best interest of the citizens of Imperium! I was there for them when my sisters were not."

Elizabeth shook her head. "Based on everything we've heard, your actions not only harmed your people, but mine as well, and resulted in your inability to continue as a guardian. Who among you believes Mistress Caliga to be guilty of treason?"

My eyes widened as the entire assembly, both human and magical, cheered. I glanced at Spero, who was having a difficult time keeping a straight face.

"How dare you!" Caliga shrieked. "I summoned you here to help me be a better leader, not to strip me of my rights! You wouldn't like what happens if you cross me."

Elizabeth raised an eyebrow. "Oh? If you still have powers, then go ahead and use them."

Purple and black sparks erupted from Caliga's hand, fizzling away before reaching the queen.

Elizabeth gave a satisfied smile. "That's what I thought. So, what shall be your punishment? Shall we have you beheaded? It's been a while since I've attended a good beheading."

Some members of the assembly cheered, including the merman king.

Mama raised her hand, emitting a bright silver light that drew everyone's focus. "Cease this at once! Caliga's actions were not in the best interest of Imperium, certainly, but she is still my sister, and I will exercise my rights as a guardian not to see her executed."

Elizabeth pursed her lips. "Reasonable enough. Does anyone else share Mistress Solara's views?"

I stood, ignoring the light tug on my hand from next to me. "Aye. I've done some terrible things at my aunt's behest, but I cannot bear the thought of another life being snuffed out as a consequence of my own actions. I've only just gotten to know her, and I believe that with time, she can find a better way to be of service to the people of Imperium."

Caliga gave me a strange look, and I wondered if the seeds of regret had been planted in her soul.

Elizabeth turned to the other sorceresses. "Mistress Estella, would you and Mistress Solara be willing to perform your duties as guardians in Caliga's stead?"

Estella sighed. "Until she recovers from the mental and physical damage of manipulating the crystal, it looks like I don't have a choice. What do you say, Solara? Should we go back to the good old days?"

Mama gave me a warm smile. "My daughter is an inspiration to us all. Even though she has agreed to sacrifice herself, she still stood up for my sister after she had manipulated her to her will. I would be remiss not to draw inspiration from her actions and resume my responsibilities to Imperium."

"It has been decided," said the queen. "Mistress Caliga shall be stripped of her rights as a guardian. At sunset, all of you will bear witness to the sacrifice of the accused as they attempt to restore the damage that has been caused to our worlds."

Thirty

Spero

The strain of the trial burned out whatever bit of energy we had left after a long, sleepless night. Amoura and I got free rein until our supposed "sacrifice" at sunset, but we were both too exhausted to leave the palace. I walked her back to her room in a half-asleep stupor. She clung to my arm so tightly I couldn't tell if it was still attached. She stopped in front of the door to her room as though waiting for something to happen.

I slumped against the wall, focusing on her face to avoid the temptation to close my eyes and fall asleep on the spot. "I think this is your stop."

Desperation flickered in her eyes. "Leave me not."

I couldn't blame her for not wanting to sacrifice what little time we had left. These might be our final moments together, especially if the conduits failed. I entered the room behind her and closed the door. Taking off my jacket and shoes, I collapsed onto the bed. The world around me began to drift away, but I forced myself to stay awake a little longer for her sake.

Amoura disappeared behind an ornately decorated privacy screen. The purple gown she wore to the trial was beautiful, but probably not the most comfortable. She emerged in a simple white dress with soft frills that made her look like an angel. She climbed onto the bed and snuggled on my chest. My heartbeat echoed against her ear as I wrapped my arms around her, drinking in the scent of hay and wildflowers. She fit in my arms like a missing puzzle piece. Not even the end of the world could stop me from enjoying my final moments with her.

"Are you still angry with me?" she murmured into my shirt as I started to doze off.

"No. You were probably right all along. I just didn't want to admit it. This is the only way to restore hope for humanity's future. You're much braver than me, you know that?"

She curled up against me, wrinkling my shirt as she rotated her head. "I simply wish to do what's right."

I leaned my head down and kissed the crown of her hair. "That's one of the many things I love about you."

She mumbled something about loving me back as I drifted off into a deep sleep. Even with my eyes closed, her face haunted my dreams. She'd live there forever, no matter what happened after today.

I don't know how long I slept, but I woke to the comfort of Amoura's soft warmth still on top of me. I nudged her shoulder.

"You awake?"

She moaned and then crawled up and planted a kiss on my

mouth that almost convinced me I was still asleep.

I started to pull her closer when her eyes shot open in surprise. "Oh my goodness, I thought I was still dreaming! I'm so sorry."

I grinned. "No complaints here. If this really is our last day, I'm glad I got to spend it with you."

Amoura climbed off the bed, leaving an uncomfortable chill in the spot she had occupied on my chest. "What about your sister? Shouldn't you say goodbye to her as well?"

I groaned. "Do I have to? How am I supposed to explain all of this to her? She's just a kid."

"Aye." Amoura got up and smoothed out her dress. "I'll help you."

"How are *you* going to explain all of this to her?"

She fidgeted with her hair. "I know not. We'll figure it out when we get there. Come along."

She reached for my hand. I forced myself out of bed and put my shoes back on. We headed outside. I missed having Amoura in my arms already. The reality of our situation came crashing down on me when we encountered the crowd gathering outside the palace.

Several people from the trial pointed at us and started whispering to each other as we walked past. Somehow, even in an alternate post-apocalyptic world, I still couldn't escape the paparazzi. The pitiful look in their eyes made me wish I could block them all like an unwanted phone number. I didn't need them reminding me of what lay ahead. At least we weren't wanted criminals anymore.

I almost walked right past the empty patch of forest when I remembered my house was still hidden under Estella's cloaking bubble. I pushed open the front door, and Amoura followed me in. Instead of the usual energetic welcome, I found Melanie slumped over on the couch with a sour expression on her face. Sparky's wings were draped over her lap like a blanket.

"Mels? What's wrong?"

She glanced up. "Oh, hi Spero."

"You're not still upset about last night, are you?"

She shrugged. "No."

"Then why are you acting so glum?"

Amoura's fingers brushed over her pendant while Sparky hovered in front of her.

"No, Sparky, you didn't do anything wrong."

"What did he say?" I asked.

Melanie beat Amoura to the punch. "He's upset because you're both leaving us forever."

So much for breaking the news gently.

A sinking feeling entered my gut. "You already know?"

"The whole world knows. Mistress Estella came back and told me all about how you and your girlfriend agreed to test her theory, which will save the world and destroy both of you. She said everyone on the planet is going to be there to watch."

How am I supposed to explain my way out of this one?

I sat down next to her. "Mels, I never meant for any of this to happen. There are just certain things you have to deal with when you grow up that you don't expect."

She crossed her arms. "It isn't fair! Mom and Dad are never around, and now you won't be either."

Ouch.

I gave Amoura a pleading look. She sat on the arm of the couch next to Melanie.

"You're right. It isn't fair. If the world were a just and fair place, everyone would be happy and well, and we wouldn't need to do this. But no matter what happens, know that your brother loves you very much. Even if you never see him again, he won't stop loving you. The same goes for me."

I raised my eyebrows at her. She hadn't spent much time around Melanie, as far as I knew.

Amoura grasped Melanie's tiny hand. "I've never had a sister, but if I did, I would want her to be just like you."

A spark of light returned to her eyes. "Really?"

She rubbed her thumb over Melanie's knuckles. "Really. We're the lucky ones because we got to know you."

Melanie jumped up and hugged her. "Thanks, Amoura."

Then she came over and hugged me. "Thanks, Spero."

I patted her head. "I didn't do anything."

She pulled away. "Okay, then I take it back."

"You're not allowed to take it back!" I grabbed her and started tickling her.

"Stop it!" she squealed. "Fine, I don't take it back. I am really going to miss you, though."

I sighed. "I know. But just think. You'll have the theater all to yourself. You can watch princess movies all day long with no interruptions."

"Yeah, I guess. Thanks for trying."

That was probably the best response we were going to get from her. Estella and Ben came down the hallway. I'd never get used to seeing the two of them in my house.

A puff of smoke emitted from Estella's hand. "Are you two ready? It's almost time."

Amoura glanced at me.

I nodded. "Let's go save the world."

Estella used her magic to send us back to the palace in a puff of pink smoke. A massive crowd had gathered in the courtyard, much larger than the one in the assembly room. Expressions of pity and gratitude filled their eyes with the hope that they could return to their normal lives again. The sun began to set, turning the sky a brilliant shade of purple. The crystal hovered ominously over a carved stone pedestal, emitting an eerie glow. The three sorceresses and Queen Elizabeth waited for us on the palace side of the crystal. Solara ran over to embrace Amoura when we approached.

"My darling, you've become such a strong young lady. I wish it didn't have to come to this, but I won't question you after what I did all those years ago."

Amoura's arms wrapped tightly around her mother. "I love you, Mama. All of this was worth it just to see you again."

Solara turned to me. I stiffened, remembering how I had yelled at her just the other night.

"Spero, I couldn't have asked for a better suitor for my daughter. You've stood by her through every hardship, giving her the gift of hope. Thank you."

She surrounded me with the scent of cinnamon and roses as her arms wrapped around my shoulders. I patted her back awkwardly.

"I'm sorry for accusing you of making Amoura run off. I know you weren't the one who made her do that."

She shook her head. "It's all in the past now."

Caliga stood off to the side, her eyes downcast. If I didn't know any better, I might have felt sorry for her. Amoura approached her.

"Aunt Caliga," she began.

Caliga held up her hand. "I don't want to hear it."

I stepped forward. "That's too bad. Amoura has proven

herself a much better person than you at every turn and offered you mercy that you probably don't deserve, so you're going to listen to anything she has to say because this is her last chance to say it."

I waited for her to raise her hand to shoot some purple sparks at me, but she just nodded.

"You're right."

That was unexpected.

"I am?"

"I see now I may have been shortsighted in my attempt to evolve Imperium, and I should not have taken advantage of both of you. Is that what you were going to say, Amoura?"

Amoura shook her head. "I was going to say that if I survive this, I'd like to start over again. Since you're no longer a guardian, I'd like you to be my aunt in truth."

It may have been the glow of the crystal, but I thought I saw a tear appear in Caliga's eye. I cringed a bit as she wrapped her arms around Amoura.

"I'd like that."

Estella's voice boomed over the crowd like a loudspeaker. "Citizens of Imperium and Earth, this is an important day for the study of magic on a level that has never been breached before. Are you ready to witness the restoration of two worlds?"

The crowd cheered so loudly that the ground rumbled beneath my feet. Instead of the fear and nervousness I should have felt, an odd sense of calm washed over me that I hadn't felt since before arriving in Imperium. My fingers brushed over Amoura's. She was too good for this world. They didn't deserve her. I didn't deserve her.

Solara spoke next. "As the essences of hope and love,

Amoura and Spero have provided an irreplaceable gift to all of Imperium. They will be remembered as heroes for all time for their noble sacrifice."

Amoura and I took our places on opposite sides of the crystal.

"Are you ready?" I asked her.

She gave me a resolute nod. "For hope."

She placed her hand over the crystal. It sparkled with a brilliant pink light.

I placed my hand on the other side. "For love."

Our fingers entwined. Threads of blue light intermingled with the pink. The crystal's rays flooded over the crowd as people gasped and covered their eyes. Then, it started shaking like a broken carburetor. Sparkles exploded from it like fireworks that radiated through my chest.

A powerful force surged through my body until I lost all sense of feeling. I closed my eyes and focused on redirecting the magic backwards to before the worlds had merged. The tendrils of magic shifted course, burning through every blood vessel in my body. My mind teetered on the edge of consciousness when I felt the pure light of Amoura's healing flow through me. She shouldn't be concerned about me right now. We had to save the world.

Squinting through the bright rays of light, I witnessed Amoura wincing in horrible pain. Accessing the power of my ring, I forced her healing magic to return to her, softening the jolts of energy that radiated through us. Grasping onto my last thread of consciousness, I watched in relief as the people in the crowd fizzled away in a white light along with cars, skyscrapers, and other unnatural phenomena all over Imperium. It was working.

A sharp burning sensation irritated my ring finger. The sapphire on my ring shattered. Shards from the crystal cut into my hand as it expended the last of its power. It was sucked dry, its onyx surface now clear as glass. I gasped for one final breath as Amoura fell limp into my arms. Then everything faded away.

Thirty-One

Amoura

The sharp pull of reality tugged me out of the darkness. Light struck my eyes as I felt the hard floor beneath me. Blurry faces surrounded me, accompanied by a sharp pain in my head. I groaned, instinctively reaching for my pendant. My finger scraped on a jagged shard. I was not usually injured so easily. Looking down, I realized the stone had been smashed and had faded to an empty, clear color, like the crystal had turned before I'd lost consciousness. Spero was right after all. If my necklace had worked as a conductor, I prayed Spero had the same good fortune.

"I think she's waking up."

I knew that voice. As my vision cleared, I recognized Anne, the child I had rescued from the stray carriage. I gripped the floor for balance and stumbled back into a bookshelf. As my vision cleared, I realized the crystal had returned me to the library where I had first entered the portal. Familiar faces from my village surrounded me, flooding my heart with joy at the success of our mission. A stray tear rolled down my cheek.

"You gave us a mighty fright," said Anne's mother. "You've been missing for days."

I tried to respond, but a rough dryness blocked my throat. Embarrassed by having so many people looking over me, I attempted to pull myself to my feet. Pins and needles flowed down my legs. I leaned onto a nearby table for support. The room swayed around me like when I rode Sparky's mother to the air labyrinth.

"Where is Father?" I wheezed.

A tall, elderly gentleman with a gray beard and a gentle demeanor made his way to the front of the crowd. Abe, the village doctor, held out his hand to me.

"Bill has been worried about you. Let me take you back."

I leaned on his shoulder. "I thank you."

My eyes misted over with nostalgia as we traversed the rocky path through the only place I had known until recently. My world had grown so much vaster since that time. The scent of wheat danced on the breeze, indicating a successful harvest. The blue sky overhead soothed the prickling sensation through my nerves as the crystal's power ran its course through my body. A deer scampered into a dull green meadow as my eyes adjusted to the ordinary life I returned to.

The sight of my father tilling the fields released a flood of tears from my eyes. I feared I'd never see him again, and the look in his eyes revealed he shared that fear. His expression shifted between disbelief, shock, and relief to pure joy. His shovel clanked onto the dirt, releasing a cloud of particles into the air as he raced towards me.

"Amoura! Thank the saints you're all right."

He threw his arms around me. Abe let me go, and I leaned my weight upon my father as another surge of vertigo coursed through me.

"So much has happened. I know not where to begin. But I've missed you."

I leaned up and left a gentle kiss on his cheek.

Father nodded to Abe. "I thank you for your help. I'll take it from here."

He took my hand and led me into our humble cottage. He had never abandoned his work in the middle of the day before. I took in the rustic wood scent that brought back memories of simpler days. Stray clothes littered the floor, and soiled dishes filled the wash basin. I wanted to help tidy up, but I could barely stand upright as feeling had yet to fully return to my limbs. Instead, I embraced the comforts of home. Even after sleeping in a palace, nothing compared to the warm impression my surroundings left on my heart.

Father pulled a rickety wooden chair out from our small round table.

"You must be starving. Let me get you something to eat."

He prepared a warm stew for me as I sat down, pressing my hand to my throbbing head. The aches that flowed through me gave me a sense of relief that sensation was returning to my body. I took a few deep breaths, embracing the dim light of the cottage after the crystal had nearly blinded me.

"I missed this place."

He turned to me while he stirred the pot. "I was so worried I might never see you again. Your disappearance caused quite a commotion among the villagers. First, your mother, then you. What happened to you, Amoura? Where did you go?"

"The book in the library opened a portal to Imperium."

A thousand explanations of Imperium, Spero, the labyrinths, and my aunts swirled through my mind in a dizzying blur. I couldn't decide where to begin. Fortunately, Father decided for me.

"Did you find your mother?"

"Aye." I coughed, realizing the dryness in my throat still had not subsided.

A glass of water was placed in front of me. "Here, drink. You're beet red, sweet dove."

I took a few sips and coughed some more. The refreshing liquid did but little aid after my harrowing experience restoring the worlds. I feared I might spend hours trying to describe all the strange things I'd encountered, so I spat out a condensed summary as best I could, even if it made no sense to Father.

"Mama went into a magic sleep to prevent Aunt Caliga from getting the crystal, but she tricked Spero and me into entering the four labyrinths to get it back. Then she almost destroyed both worlds. We were the only ones who could stop her."

He placed a bowl of stew in front of me. The savory aroma revitalized my senses. I scooped a full spoon into my mouth, allowing the delicious morsel to dance on my tongue. The juicy flavor washed away the remaining jolts of pain, returning sensation to my body.

Father shook his head. "Slow down. This is a lot to take in."

I swallowed as a comforting warmth flowed through me.

"I feel as though a lifetime has passed since I was away. It would take ages to tell you all I've been through."

He sat next to me. "We have all the time in the world now. We'll get it sorted just like we do with the harvests every season.

You mentioned someone named Spero?"

I gnawed upon my lip as a tear flowed down my cheek.

Father's posture grew tense. "We can speak of something else if you prefer."

I shook my head. "No. I want to talk about him. I love him, Father. I love him so much. But I fear I may never see him again."

"Is he from Imperium?"

"No, he's from our world, but he…" I choked on my words. "He hasn't been born yet."

Father frowned. "Amoura, that makes no sense. How hard did you hit your head?"

I took another gulp of water. "I think… I think he went back to his own time. And now that the crystal is destroyed along with my pendant and his ring, there's no more magic."

Sobs wracked through my body. Father knelt and patted my back, but it only made the tears flow harder.

"Weep not, Amoura. All will be well. Think of what I always said about your mother. Even if I never see her again, I wouldn't wish away the time we had for anything in the world."

I wiped a tear from my cheek. "We had to give each other up for the sake of the world. Everything went back to the way it's supposed to be, except it isn't because we're not together. I broke my promise."

I tore my pendant off my neck. Father stood, keeping a close watch on me.

"I may not understand everything, but it looks like you are suffering from a broken heart. Take a few days off from your usual duties on the farm to rest up."

That made me sob even harder. How could I go from

fighting unicorns and rescuing mermaids one day to tilling the fields the next? I'd only just learned my heritage as a sorceress, but I couldn't explore that if I stayed here. Mama hid her powers away from everyone in our village when she lived here. Would I never see her, Spero, or my aunts again?

Father put my plate away. "I was only trying to help. I meant not to make you more upset."

"You didn't," I assured him. "I've just been through so much in such a short time."

He sighed. "I'm at a loss for words. I wish your mother were here."

As though in answer to a prayer, a silvery blue light appeared. Mama shimmered into the room. White feathers floated around her as her wings faded away. Father stared at her as though she were a ghost.

"By the stars above… Solara, is it truly you?"

Then she was in his arms. I blushed and turned away as their lips met.

"Hello, Bill. I see our daughter made it back home safely."

"Mama," I gasped. "I can't believe you're really here."

She glanced at my crushed pendant on the table. Picking it up, she rubbed her finger along the broken glass.

"After the crystal was destroyed, you and Spero disappeared. I had to make sure you survived."

My heart skipped a beat. "Where is Spero? Did he make it back home too?"

Mama brushed a strand of hair out of my face. "I'm afraid I do not know, dear. Estella said something about Earth's parallax needing to be fine-tuned to his… er… Forgive me, I can not quite remember."

I stood up. "Can Aunt Estella take me to him?"

Father held out his hand. "Who's Aunt Estella?"

Mama chuckled. "I'm afraid you've missed a lot, dear."

He placed another pile of dirty dishes in the wash basin. "No one in this house goes anywhere until they get some rest. You should have seen the state she arrived in."

Mama gave me a warm smile. "I can imagine. Saving two worlds is no easy feat."

Father dropped a pot. "She truly saved two worlds?"

I picked it up and handed it back to him. "I had to. Spero and I were the only ones who could do it."

He turned to Mama. "Is this Spero a good boy? Will he take care of our daughter?"

Mama waved her hand over the dishes, bathing them in a silver light that faded away with every bit of dirt and grime, leaving them sparkling clean.

"Amoura means the world to him. Two worlds, actually."

"Then I suppose I must give him my blessing. It looks like you've outgrown our little farm life, sweet dove. It would be selfish to make you stay here after all you've been through. I am going to miss you, though."

I hugged him. "I'll come back and visit as often as I am able."

I glanced at Mama.

She gave me a warm smile. "If you come back to Imperium with me, maybe your aunts and I can help you tap into your sorceress powers. Then you will be able to travel freely at will."

"Do you really think I have powers?" I asked.

She gave me a warm grin. "You are my daughter, aren't you?"

I turned to Father. "Did you hear that? I may possess magical powers just like Mama!"

He pulled a white envelope out of a drawer. "There's no rush. Let's enjoy our time together for a little while longer before we figure out this otherworldly mess. Lord Thomas's friends at the theatre got me these tickets to the latest Shakespeare play. What say you to a family outing?"

I beamed and gave him a tight hug. "That sounds wonder-ful!"

A warm meal and a fun night out brought pleasant memories of my childhood—experiences I never thought I'd have again. The stiffness of my old bed did little to alleviate my soreness, yet its familiar warmth remained a comfort. For the first time in nine years, I could sleep in it without the shadow of Mama's disappearance looming over me. Though unexpected hardships marred our perfect reunion, I could finally stop dwelling on the past and move towards a bright future. I drifted into a cozy sleep, dreaming of an outspoken boy with yellow hair.

Thirty-Two

Spero

I woke up to a bright light shining in my face. I shielded my eyes and squinted. A uniformed cop stood over me. I tried to stand, but numbness surged through my limbs from when we activated the crystal.

"What's going on?" I groaned.

The dark-skinned cop had a young face that strained to maintain an intimidating expression. "That's what I'd like you to tell me. Your father put half the country on alert only for us to find you in your own house."

My eyes adjusted as the blurry shapes around the room sharpened. Familiar furniture surrounded me, but I had a feeling I wasn't in Imperium anymore. I released a sigh of relief. If I survived, that meant she had too. Her sorceress blood made her stronger than me. Maybe I could look up some historical archives to find out what had happened to her. An emptiness filled my chest. If I closed my eyes, I could still feel her in my arms.

"Do you remember anything from the past few days?"

Not if I don't want to be institutionalized.

"Um, nope," I lied. "Not a thing."

"Have you been drinking or experimenting with any drugs?"

I shook my head, "No, officer. You can have me tested if you need to."

He entered some information into a Star Tech tablet. "I'm going to need you to come back to the station with us. We're going to need you to answer a few questions."

The door creaked open, flooding the room with light. "That won't be necessary, officer."

Overwhelming the room with his presence, Dad stood at the top of the stairs, holding a bill with a picture of the man who slept in our study just one night ago. How long had I been gone?? A month? It felt a lot longer after the time I had spent in Imperium.

Dad spoke in his authoritative business voice. "Thank you for your service. Your work here is done."

The officer shook his head, sighing. "I could write you up for this, but it's not worth dealing with the paperwork. We're dealing with a missing person who's been found, not a serious crime. Call me if you need anything else. Have a pleasant evening, Mr. Dusk."

His footsteps echoed down the hallway.

I tried to get up, but the throbbing in my head weighed me down. My finger slid over something sharp, and I realized it was my broken ring. I slipped it into my pocket to avoid further injury.

"Is he okay?" asked another distantly familiar voice.

Mom's here, too? Is it my birthday or something?

My superstar mother came downstairs and leaned over me in a low-cut dress and heavy makeup, her long blonde hair tied back in a stylish bun as though she had just gotten off a shoot. Her bloodshot eyes indicated she probably hadn't slept in a while.

"Spero, your father got Melanie's text. It didn't make a lot of sense, but we filed a missing person report just in case, after we couldn't get a hold of Fran. Your disappearance was broadcast all over the news. I hope this wasn't a joke."

"No joke," I groaned, pushing myself upright.

"Is he really back?"

Three feet of little sister flew at me, pummeling me back to the ground.

I pushed her away so I could breathe. "Take it easy, Mels."

She bounced back and forth on the balls of her feet. "Where were you? What happened?"

"What do you mean?" I asked. "Don't you remember?"

"I remember you getting sucked into the video game."

Dad shook his head. "Melanie, remember what we said about lying."

I studied her face to make sure she wasn't putting on a show for Mom and Dad. With her big mouth, I expected her to have shouted the whole thing from the rooftops by now. "What about Amoura and Sparky? Don't you remember them?"

She tilted her head. "Who?"

"Did you two sneak off to some kind of party?" asked Mom. "Don't tell me this was just an excuse to avoid the staff for a little brother-sister outing."

Dad held up his phone. "Melanie was here the whole time. We've been video chatting until I could get home. As far as I'm aware, Spero was missing until the cops found him here."

"How long have I been missing?" I coughed. The dryness in my throat could put the Sahara Desert to shame.

Mom glanced at her own phone and opened a calendar app. "About five days."

I did the math in my head. If I was in Imperium for a week, that would account for everything except the two days the worlds merged. Did we actually erase two days from everyone's life? But I still remember every moment we shared.

Dad crossed his arms. "Are you going to tell us where you were or not?"

"I know it sounds crazy, but I really don't remember anything," I insisted.

He started dialing. "Then I'm going to have to get the police back here to conduct a full investigation."

I sighed. "Wait."

He grinned like he just successfully intercepted a bad business transaction. "Something you want to tell me?"

Might as well get as close to the truth as possible.

"I was… with a girl. She's from really far away. There were people from her country looking for her, trying to take her back, so we needed to lie low for a while. I was helping her stay under wraps."

"What country is she from?" asked Dad.

"England," I blurted out.

Mom chuckled. "Is that all? I just got back from shooting in Ireland. We would have been practically neighbors. If you need to borrow the private jet, we can easily arrange a visit."

I shook my head. "She's, um, in the witness protection program. She has ties to the royal family, but they're trying to keep it hidden to avoid getting caught by the tabloids."

This story sounds more ridiculous by the second.

Melanie's face lit up. "Is she a princess?"

I rolled my eyes. "No, Mels. Princesses don't need to hide. They have bodyguards and stuff for that."

"That's a shame," said Mom. "Maybe you can keep in touch over the internet. Did you exchange numbers?"

"Afraid not."

She was born a few centuries too early for that.

Dad sighed. "You had us really worried, you know?"

I tried to stand up again. "I can imagine. I'm sorry for causing trouble. People were chasing after us, so I couldn't give away our location to anyone until I knew she was safe."

Mom helped me get up. "We'll have Luigi cook you a nice dinner. I'm sure you'll feel better after that."

"I hope so."

Less than an hour later, I was seated in our dining room in front of a delicious plate of penne a la vodka. The warm pasta and creamy pink sauce revitalized sensation in my muscles and helped wake me from my stupor. Yet, the more aware I became of my surroundings, the more I also noticed the emptiness in my chest. Would I ever see her again?

Dad took a sip of wine. "So, have you picked which college you want to start in the fall?"

What difference does it make?

"Yale will be fine, I guess."

He nodded his approval. "That's my boy."

* * *

Three Months Later

"Spero, are you going with anyone to the Sigma Tau Omega formal?" asked Lana, a pretty Japanese girl who talked to me often in the Shakespearean studies elective I had signed up for.

A sparkle of anticipation lit up her brown eyes. No matter how much I tried to drown my sorrows in my studies, everyone on campus expected me to engage in endless social activities. Maybe I had more in common with Estella than I thought.

I gave her an apologetic look. "I'm sorry, but I don't date."

"Yeah, I noticed that. And I think I know the reason."

Because I'm in love with a ghost?

She adjusted her book bag. "Everyone's after your dad's company, aren't they?"

Huh?

"I mean, I get it. Who wouldn't want to have the perks of dating the poster child of Star Tech? But I'm not interested in that. I just think you're a really cool guy."

I sighed. "Look, I believe you. I do. It's just that I'm kind of in a long-distance relationship right now."

"Really? Then you should invite her to the dance."

If only I could.

"She can't make it. She lives really far away and has a hard time traveling."

She pursed her lips. "That's no fun. You should go with me anyway, then, just for fun. I'm sure she'll understand."

"I'm sorry. I just can't right now. I'm flattered, really. But when you meet someone like her, there's no going back."

The sparkle in her eyes melted away as she slumped her

shoulders. I almost wanted to take it back. Almost.

She shuffled through some textbooks for her next class. "At least I tried. She's a lucky girl."

As Lana trudged off, my cell phone buzzed in my pocket. I pulled it out. Mom's headshot lit up the screen. She was home on hiatus while her agent was booking new auditions, but she rarely ever called.

"What's up, Mom?"

"Spero, a girl came here looking for you. A girl from *England*."

My heart skipped a beat. "Amoura?"

"Can he hear me?"

That's her voice!

"Spero, is that you?"

"Amoura, I can't believe it! How are you here? You know what? Don't answer that. I'll jump on the next flight and be there in a few hours. Don't go anywhere!"

"I wasn't planning on it. Not without you, anyway."

I ordered a cab to take me straight to the airport. Six hours later, I ran inside the house, hoping it wasn't all some kind of post-traumatic hallucination from the absorbing crystal's energy. My hand shook as I turned the doorknob. It still felt empty without Estella's ring on it. I pushed open the door, and the most beautiful girl who ever lived gazed at me with three months' worth of longing in her eyes. She wore an elegant modern dress. Mom must have taken her shopping. Before she had a chance to say anything, I lifted her into the air and pulled her into a deep kiss.

"Shall I leave you two alone?" Mom cocked an eyebrow at us from the couch.

I wasn't even fazed. "Yes, please."

She headed out the door. "I have an audition in an hour, anyway. My agent told me to show up early. You two kids play nice."

I rolled my eyes.

Amoura rested her head on my shoulder, right where it belonged. "That was certainly a friendly greeting."

"Sorry about the wait. I had to fly across the country. I would have flown all the way to Imperium to see you if I could."

"All is well. I got to know your mother a bit. Melanie was here for a moment, but she got bored and went back upstairs to play."

She fidgeted with a chunk of brown hair and averted her gaze. "She doesn't remember me."

I placed a hand on her shoulder. "I know. We erased everything that happened after Caliga merged the worlds. It's probably for the best. Can you imagine what it would be like if a bunch of people throughout history started ranting about sorceresses and time travel?"

"I suppose you're right." She stopped fidgeting with her hair and gave me a piercing stare. "I missed you so much."

"I did too. I haven't even been able to look at another girl since I met you. You're all I can think about."

She sat down on the couch. "I've been obsessed with finding you again ever since I woke up in my old village. Mama and my aunts are training me to become a sorceress like them. Watch this."

She held out her hand. A transparent pink bubble appeared over it, glittering like diamonds.

"That's really cool, Amoura."

I sat down next to her and pulled her towards me. "So,

what's next? Do you want to stay here for a while, or are we going back to Imperium for another adventure?"

She snuggled up against me. "'Tis of no consequence as long as we're together."

The emptiness in my heart since returning home subsided at last. We kept our promise after all.

My life has never been the same since I fell through a portal into a magical world. I finally know where I came from and was granted the opportunity to meet the rest of my family. Although Aunt Caliga and I have had our differences in the past, she proved to be a valuable mentor when it came to practicing magic. Since she can't use her powers anymore or be a guardian, she seems to enjoy living vicariously through me. In time, I learned to heal on my own, without the aid of my pendant.

I still have trouble understanding Aunt Estella, but she proved invaluable for navigating relative dimensions on Earth to pinpoint the parallax of Spero's timeline. Perhaps I'm beginning to understand her better than I thought. She also crafted a special interdimensional bracelet for me that makes travel easier between the realms. It isn't easy having loved ones scattered throughout space and time.

Mama moved back into the palace and resumed her role as a sorceress guardian and began training me to take her place one day. She believes I may be more suited to the role than she was, but I can't say I agree. Despite everything that's happened, I'm glad I was able to free her from her magical stasis. She deserves to experience all the joys and sorrows of the world just like anyone else, mortal or immortal. Shortly after she resumed her duties, the unicorns returned to the forest, relieving the heaviness in my heart after fighting them in the labyrinths.

After much debate, I managed to convince Spero to stay on Earth to finish his schooling and train to take over his father's business. He made me promise to visit him frequently, but I told him he needn't even ask. I have every intention of spending as much time with him as I am capable of. Not a moment goes by that I don't think of him. Is there a way for us to remain together when we live worlds apart? For now, we shall take it one day at a time.

Mama and I also visit Father often to check up on the farm. He's been doing well for himself, although I don't think he expected to get caught up in all this magic business when he decided to marry Mama and start a family. One day, I'd like to bring him to Imperium. The nature and wildlife there are so different from what he's used to that I'm sure he'd have a lot to say about it. Mayhap we can convince him to move into the palace and continue his work on the grounds there, but I'm getting ahead of myself.

All in all, I feel very fortunate to have been born into a life that's blessed with magic and love from many different places. Mayhap I will choose a place to settle down in time, whether it's with Spero in his timeline, the Imperium palace, or back with Father on the farm. For now, I will continue to absorb all the knowledge I can about my sorceress heritage so I can use my powers to improve the lives of everyone in Imperium and Earth for the better.

***

Acknowledgments

This is it. My lifelong dream of seeing *Hope and Love's Legacy* available to the world has finally come to fruition. This project has been a lifelong labor of love, for which I have many people to thank. I came up with the concept for Legacy as an animated series in 2002. That led me on an arduous 10-year-long journey to Hollywood, during which I rewrote my pilot episode multiple times, including a cringeworthy live-action remake from when those were trending. In time, I accepted that the story in my heart could not come to fruition in the format I imagined it, so I converted it into my 11th book.

Drawing upon my previous years of writing experience, I did extensive research on the current state of the publishing industry, how to perfect my query letter, and how to make this book as marketable as possible. I made many mistakes along the way and realized that I could only stay true to the heart of Amoura and Spero's story by self-publishing. With that in mind, I'd like to thank everyone who contributed their thoughts to this book and helped to fashion it into what it is today.

First and foremost, I would like to thank my alpha reader, Kae-Leah, who had the patience of a saint as I struggled through numerous rewrites and setbacks. A special thanks to Amy for helping me conceive my original character designs back in 2002 and sharing your thoughts on the new path this story has taken. Another big thanks goes to Shannon for your brutally honest developmental edit that revealed exactly what I needed to do to bring this story up to snuff. This book would not sparkle so brightly without the final polish from my line editor, Joanne Armitage at Enchanted Quill Press. Thank you to all my beta readers who contributed valuable feedback to this book, including Tara, Ami, Leah, Abi, Ronél, Vanessa, Joshua, Margaret, Gina, Julieta, Neal, Deanna, and Ciera, and to my critique partners from Team Write Right: Suzette, Jessica, Kara, Sasha, Bethan, Julia, Rhea, and Irene. Finally, thank you to my husband, Derrick, for providing just the advice I needed to take risks and grow as a writer.

If you enjoyed this book, please let me know by reaching out to me on social media or sharing a review on Goodreads or Amazon. It would mean the world to me to know that the story I conceived as a teenager that inspired me to become a writer has made a difference in other people's lives. This is the book of my heart and encompasses every story that impacted who I am today.

About the Author

Lisa Dawn was brought up in New Jersey, where she fell in love with fairy tales and animated movies. She studied screenwriting at Ramapo College with the hope that she could one day write the next great animated princess movie. After attending the DAVE School in Florida to learn computer animation, she moved to Los Angeles to work on 3D movies as a rotoscope artist. Today, she lives in Texas with her husband, Derrick, where she plays piano and reviews all forms of princess media in The Princess Blog.

You can connect with me on:

- http://www.theprincessblog.com
- https://x.com/PrincessOfBlogs
- https://www.facebook.com/theprincessblogger
- https://www.instagram.com/theprincessblogger
- http://www.youtube.com/@theprincessblogger
- http://www.threads.com/theprincessblogger

Subscribe to my newsletter:

- https://www.lisadawnbooks.com

Also by Lisa Dawn

I write clean romance stories inspired by fairy tales.

Titania's Reflection: A Retelling of Fairer-than-a-Fairy and A Midsummer Night's Dream

In a misguided act of pride, a newborn princess is named after the vengeful Queen Titania and spirited away to the fae realm, where she is brought up under the false name, Hermia. Tasked with maintaining an enchanted flame, Hermia falls in love with a prince named Lysander, whose spirit is trapped inside a rainbow. When the flame is extinguished along with her ability to communicate with the prince, she must travel to the dangerous Unseelie Court with two fae protectors, Helena and Demetrius, to restore peace and free her true love.

This story combines an obscure fairy tale from Andrew Lang's Yellow Fairy Book called "Fairer-than-a-Fairy" with William Shakespeare's classic comedy, A Midsummer Night's Dream.

The Stolen Jewel

Ever since her parents died in the Magic War, Princess Charlotte was determined to become the perfect queen for Klingland. However, when her aunt forces her into an alliance with the greedy kingdom of Dorraine, Charlotte takes a huge risk that she pays for with her crown and title. Now she must find a way to save her home and restore magic to the kingdom as a peasant with no idea what the future has in store for her.

*This is the first book in The Stolen Trilogy.

The Stolen Queen

Lily never asked to be queen of Klingland. She loves King Henry with all her heart, but she often feels like a fish out of water. When she discovers a kingdom of merpeople beneath the waves, she encounters someone she never expected to see again. Tensions rise as she struggles to uncover a dangerous mystery and return to her home on land before it's too late.

*This is the second book in The Stolen Trilogy. Though it can be enjoyed on its own, it is recommended that you read The Stolen Jewel first.

The Stolen Slipper

After so many years of chasing down men for power, Krystal has decided to become a better person by setting up Lily's brother with the perfect girl. When she learns that girl is being controlled by an evil stepmother using illegal magic, Krystal realizes she has finally met her match in this original retelling of "Cinderella."

*This is the third book in The Stolen Trilogy. Though it can be enjoyed on its own, it is recommended that you read The Stolen Queen first.

Elf Princess Roweena

When it comes to protecting her kingdom, Princess Roweena has a mind of her own. When the elves of Karn are threatened by a band of wicked gremlins who chop down their trees, Roweena takes matters into her own hands, teaming up with a feisty pixie to protect her land. She winds up with a bit more than she bargained for when she finds herself falling for the enemy…

Of Land and Sea: The Untold Story of The Little Mermaid

What happens when two princesses fall in love with the same prince?

Helena of Kamdren has always believed in mermaids, but she had no idea about the sacrifices that the mysterious maiden Coralie made to be with her betrothed. Learn the untold story of the little mermaid who lost her chance at love and the woman who gained it in her place in this retelling of Hans Christian Andersen's classic fairy tale.

Most Wanted Knight

In the prosperous kingdom of Sederia, Sir Kaladrin's parents are murdered for treason. He escapes with his life and becomes Sir Kane, the outlaw knight who rescues peasants while constantly on the run from bounty hunters. Though still trapped within the confines of the castle, his best friend, Lady Gwendolyn, can never forget him. Together, Sir Kane and Lady Gwendolyn must try to find shelter in an uncaring world.

Rebirth: A Faery's Tale

"Faeries know nothing of happiness, sadness, or love."

Aurelia knows she isn't like the other fire faeries. From the moment she saw the blacksmith, she had feelings for him that no other faery could explain. The Great Phoenix took pity on her and transformed her into a human woman. Now, she must choose between the man she loves and the world of flames that she was born into.

Blood Red

A famous Hollywood icon is haunted by a dark secret from her past. The alleged murder of a loved one pushes her to pursue the hidden truth about her family. Now she must figure out who she can and cannot trust before it's too late. With the help of Granny's physician, Dr. Kurt Hunter, Rebecca Red must piece together the clues of her mother's past before more lives are put in danger in this modern-day retelling of "Little Red Riding Hood."

Castle (and other poems about growing up in a fairy tale world)

There comes a time in everyone's life when they wake up and realize that the fairy tales they cherished so much in childhood are nothing more than make-believe. The real world can be cold and uncaring, but there is still beauty to be found within it. Love does not happen overnight, but when it does, it is the most precious thing in the world. Castle [and other poems about growing up in a fairy tale world] is an anthology of poetry about fantasy, love, and reality. It consists of nearly one hundred poems for children and adults alike who are struggling to make the transition between their perfect world of magic and dreams and the world they are physically living in.